PRAISE FOR
PRIZE MONEY

"Readers are in for a riveting ride… Castro clearly knows her stuff, capturing rodeo culture and the thrill of competition in action packed scenes."

—*Publishers Weekly*

"A rodeo queen and a Hollywood stuntwoman—what could be more delightful? You will fall for Eva and Toma as they fall for each other."

—JENNY HOLIDAY, *USA Today* bestselling author

"From the first page, Eva and Toma grab you and drag you into the saddle with them. It's a wild ride and you'll want to hang on long after it's over."

—TAGAN SHEPARD, Goldie Award winning author

"A slow burn romance masterly woven into the colorful, fast-charging life of barrel racers and bullfighters. The plot is refreshingly unique, the writing is vivid, and the characters are fearless yet tender. Castro definitely wins the rodeo belt buckle with this one."

—CADE HADDOCK STRONG, author with Bella Books.

"From start to finish, this was a delight for this yeehaw loving queer. The tension between Toma and Eva that built up the slow burn between them was everything I could have hoped for and more. Lesbians on horses. What more could you want?"

—M.B. GUEL, author of *Queerleaders: A Love Story*

PRIZE MONEY

CELESTE CASTRO

interlude press • new york

ISBN 13: 978-1-951954-03-1 (trade)
ISBN 13: 978-1-951954-04-8 (ebook)
Library of Congress Control Number: 2020946212
Published by Interlude Press
http://interludepress.com
BOOK AND COVER DESIGN BY CB Messer
BASE PHOTOGRAPHY FOR COVER ©Depositphotos.com/
jacksonstockphotography
10 9 8 7 6 5 4 3 2 1

interlude press • new york

CHAPTER ONE

Staring into the mirror never helped. It always made things worse. Looking for extended periods highlighted every ailment, problem, and blemish in stunning 3D, especially in the harsh lighting of the cramped airplane lavatory with nowhere to run when it got real. Nevertheless, Toma Rozene kept staring: seeing herself clearly for the first time since the dawn of her human existence, everything illustrated. Her short black hair was slicked with gel as if she'd walked off the set of *Grease*. Her dark skin seemed washed out from the harsh lighting when, in reality, it was perpetually French-kissed by the sun. She had the darkest skin color of all the members of her family, and her five older brothers would tease her to the point of tears. *Hey, chocolate, where's the vanilla?* She'd find refuge in the great outdoors, climbing trees, jumping off rooftops, riding horses, coming indoors only because she was forced to and long after the sun had set.

Despite the abuse to her skin, she appeared younger than her thirty-four years. However, if one looked closely, if they met her dead on and searched beyond her chestnut-colored irises with rings of copper and gray directly into her soul, one would see a broken-down, old spirit hiding in plain sight.

The lavatory's paper towels felt like eighty-grit sandpaper and left her face blotchier than before. On the plus side, they hid most of the evidence of her extended exploration of her life and of her pathetic tears of loss and longing. She was the coyote. Life was the roadrunner. The anvil hit midflight between SeaTac International and Boise Regional on a Bombardier Q400 prop plane.

An impatient-sounding cadence of knocking signaled it was time to free up the aircraft's only lavatory. A long inhale, followed by a exhale, and it was showtime. Expecting a scolding, she unlocked the door.

"Sorry," she murmured and kept her eyes fixed on the floor.

"That's so cool," a soft voice said.

"Pardon?"

The woman pointed to Toma's waist. "Your belt buckle."

Toma ran her hand over the shiny metal of her Wonder Woman belt buckle, a relic from a favorite job as equestrian stuntwoman number seventeen on the set of *Wonder Woman*. All the stuntwomen got one—a gift from Robin Wright.

Toma cleared her throat. "Sorry for, you know, taking so long." She tried to edge herself past the woman, but the woman didn't move.

"What was your favorite part?"

"Pardon?" Toma ran her hand through her hair.

"The movie. Your favorite part?"

"Never seen it." Toma shook her head. She'd only seen those dailies that were specific to her stunt work.

"I saw it like fifty times." The woman's oval-shaped brown eyes were wide and expressive and communicated pure joy. Her wildly gesturing hands helped punctuate her every statement. "My favorite part is when Wonder Woman shouts, 'I want love' while she blows everything up." The woman mimicked the sounds of destruction and used her hands to demonstrate a great blast. Her delight and soft laughter warmed Toma, calmed her. "You should totally check it out."

"Thanks." Toma turned her attention toward the back of the small aircraft, hoping that would send a signal that she didn't want to talk anymore. The woman held her ground and stared at her as if she wanted to accept the challenge of searching Toma's soul through her eyes. It had to be the belt buckle. The belt buckle had been a better babe magnet than any puppy or baby. Toma scratched her nose with her left hand. The ring on her third finger usually did the trick, sent the beacon; she wasn't available. Not this time. The woman kept talking with that soft voice and inquisitive gaze as if she saw through the façade and knew the ring wasn't a symbol of someone's love, but a prop used to get out of certain prickly situations.

It was a prop. It had belonged to Toma's mother, was one of the few physical things of her mother's that she owned. She'd never really known her mom. She had only early childhood memories of playing with her, singing songs together, riding horses—all of which ended due to complications suffered from a stroke when Toma was a little girl.

Hoping to quell the crushing ache that threatened to overtake her again, Toma looked at the ceiling of the aircraft. "I should get back to my seat."

The woman nodded and let her pass, but Toma didn't move.

"You look like you might need a friend," the woman said.

Toma met her gaze, and everything melted away, the other passengers, the seats, the walls of the aircraft, until only the woman stood before her. A friend would be nice—probably not the type of friend that the woman had suggested. She was a hot little thing, with golden skin as if she worked outside. Maybe she was Latina, or Native American like Toma. The woman had long, wavy, jet-black hair held in a loose ponytail that rested on her shoulder. She had almond-shaped brown eyes, huge eyebrows that nearly connected, dark eyelashes, and high cheekbones. She had full, kissable, lickable, inviting lips. She was a pocket-sized woman compared to Toma's six-foot stature. The friend also had a nice plump backside, a great rack, and, best of all, cowboy boots. The combination of the woman's boots, her gentle smile, her touch, and her concerned gaze ripped Toma open yet again.

Toma dropped her focus to the floor. She didn't bother to hide her tears. She couldn't. Something about the woman hinted that she probably didn't care, and so Toma let them fall, let them stream from her eyes, etching a familiar path. She felt the woman touch her bicep, then travel the length of her arm to her fingertips and gently squeeze them before letting go.

Toma shook her head and said something that she hoped sounded like, "rough week," when she intended to say, "rough year, rough life." Toma filled her life with more manufactured excitement than anyone in their right mind, courtesy of her job as a stuntwoman and overall adrenaline junkie: extreme sports, extreme skiing, extreme power walking, extreme everything that she did, always to the nth degree.

Toma focused on the stitching on the woman's boots. It wasn't as if the world was going to end; no one had died. *Everything is going to be okay,* her brother had said to her on the phone call that prompted her to purchase a one-way ticket from Los Angeles to Idaho—to home.

Dad got kicked, working with a stallion, a son of a bitch with big balls, were her brother's exact words. *Got Dad in the shoulder, pushed him into the fencing; he broke his back. He'll be okay, but we need help until Dad gets on his feet again. He can't travel with us on circuit; we need help running the horses and the ranch…can you come home? Please?* A home that she had seen a total of three times over the past twelve years. Add to that the abrupt end of an intense relationship, the end of her work on the set of *Vikings*, and not knowing what was next for herself and there it was, a full-blown existential crisis, Toma Rozene style.

"There's an open seat next to me; want to talk?"

Toma could only manage a shake of her head indicating that she wasn't interested.

"We don't have to talk. We can just sit together."

"Okay. Thank you." She sniffled.

"I'm in twelve A." The woman shifted her weight from one foot to the other. "But first, do you mind?" She eyed the lavatory. "I really need to go."

"Sorry." Toma moved out of the way, walked to row twelve, buckled her seatbelt, rested her head against the headrest, and closed her eyes. The woman returned a short time later with a cup of cold water. When she sat, she lifted the armrest between them and let her leg rest against

Toma's. The simple feeling of the woman's touch, her warmth, and the comfort of her body helped calm Toma's nerves more than she thought it would.

The woman rested her hand, palm side up, on Toma's thigh. Was she offering Toma her hand to hold? Toma thought so. She took hold and held on, hoping that the firmer her grip, the deeper she inhaled, the less she would ache and that she would eventually stop feeling.

Toma jolted awake when the flight attendant announced that they were preparing the cabin for arrival. A short time later they touched down, and the passengers began deboarding. Toma's heart raced. She shifted in her seat. She swallowed a lump in her throat and tried to calm herself before she caved all over again.

"We still have time." The woman continued to hold her hand.

"What's your name?" Toma asked as she watched the last of the passengers file out. She suddenly felt as though she had wasted the flight not learning a thing about the woman, her savior, her comforter.

"I'm Eva. What's yours?"

"Sorry, ladies, but we really need to get ready for the next flight," a flight attendant said, his hand on his waist and annoyance in his eyes. They were the last two passengers on the plane. "Captain's orders."

"Sorry."

"So sorry. We're going," Eva assured. She unbuckled her seatbelt and grabbed her carry-on from the overhead compartment. "You okay?"

"I'll be okay." *I'm so not okay.*

"You sure?"

"Positive." *So not positive.*

"Want to walk out together?" Eva asked.

"No, please. Go ahead." *Don't leave me!* "Thank you, Eva."

"Anytime." Eva left Toma with a parting smile and walked out of her life.

Once in the terminal, Toma headed for the women's bathroom to clean herself up. She was careful to avoid the mirror. She emerged a long time later, feeling as though she was ready to face her new world. She found the baggage claim and five older brothers and their kids, who smothered her with hugs and kisses. There was no sign of the woman who'd held her.

CHAPTER TWO

"FIRST UP TO KICK OFF the women's barrel racing competition, she's riding her four-year-old filly; Frida's the name, a dapple-gray quarter horse who's already proven her worth. In the hot seat is a local Idaho legend, a farm girl who knows a thing or two about being in a saddle. She hails from Canyon County, from the beautiful town of Wilder, if you're not from these parts, and I am guessing you are judging by the whoopin' and the hollerin'. All right, folks let me get this out and get her on her way. I know she's crying to go. She's a two-time world champion, top money earner, being courted yet again for the invitational finals in Las Vegas later this year. She squeezed out winning times at the Riggins Rodeo earlier this summer and again in Jerome just last week. She's already got most of the ladies in the circuit beat. She's ready for the world. Let's give it up for this gem of the Gem State: Miss Eva Angeles and Frida!"

Eva tuned out Pierson Price, the self-proclaimed voice of the rodeo. Tuning him out never proved difficult; he was cheesier than gas station nachos. The roar of opening night at the Caldwell Night Rodeo, with its bright lights and cheering fans, proved harder to ignore. If she wanted to put in a decent effort, she had to turn the dial to zero. Complete focus on her horse, with her horse, and for her horse would get her a decent run.

She settled into the saddle on Frida, her champion horse that she trained herself, one that had already earned her an impressive one hundred and eighty-three thousand dollars in prize money that year along with several sponsorships, a new truck, and a top-of-the-line air-conditioned trailer for her three horses. The Caldwell Night Rodeo was one of sixty-plus opportunities in the Southern Spark circuit that included Idaho, Oregon, and Washington. She was in the saddle this night because she knew she could win. It also held another place in her heart. It was the first rodeo she'd attended with her dad as a little girl where she told him she wanted to ride horses and be a queen, and here she was years later, the queen of them all. Winning a third time would cement her place in barrel racing history.

In her periphery, she spotted the rest of the rodeo cast: the gate crew, photographers, reporters, and judges. Most importantly, she spotted her saviors, bullfighters and pickup men there to protect downed athletes when they dismounted or were bucked off an animal and to escort bucking broncos and bulls to safety after a ride. Her favorites were the barrel men, who performed thrilling, lifesaving, unique moves with a barrel to distract a bull hell-bent on kicking a cowboy when he was already down. The entire team of bullfighters worked as a coordinated unit, providing distraction and safety. All of them were ready to put their lives on the line in case something went wrong. At this point in the show, they were cooling off. Their big moment came during the bull riding, calf roping, steer wrestling, and bareback riding competitions.

"Give me the nod, Eva," the guy working the chutes instructed.

Eva bent over Frida's neck and twirled her fingers through the coarse hair of her mane. She inhaled her scent, her sweat, the oils of the leather, and the fresh, rich dirt in the arena—an intoxicating mix that fueled her senses, breathed life into her, and whispered words for champions. In fifteen seconds or less, it would all be over. Eva closed her eyes. The roar of the crowd and Pierson Price's commentary combined and created a dull buzz in her mind.

"Let's go, girl. Me and you." Eva gave a clear nod, the gate opened, and a blast of wind hit her. Frida's signature move. As quick as lightning in a bottle, the start to life, they were out of the gate in an all-out attack on their first barrel. The money barrel. Hitting that one hard and fast set the tone for the entire run.

"Heya! Girl!" She leaned forward and dropped to her side, helping Frida around their first turn, clearing it with ease. Onto the next. Another tight, twisted loop, and then they thundered toward the last barrel, which they cleared in a hurry.

Eva squeezed her legs against Frida's stomach, clicked her tongue, and sent her wishes. "Home, girl home!" They cracked toward the finish line. Eva's eyes never strayed from her goal. Her blood rushed in her ears and pounded through her body, from her fingertips to her toes. Her heart beat in tandem with Frida's. And they were done.

She turned her horse back toward the arena for a couple of cool-down laps. People stood and waved their hats in the air. The bright lights of the arena brought everything into focus: the white fencing, the sponsor logos, the rich color of the arena dirt, and, flashing above, her image on the arena's Jumbotron. Eva gripped the reins hard while she waited for their time to post. The sweet arena was her dance floor, where she laid everything on the line night after night, her heart, along with her mind, her horse, and three barrels.

"Folks," Pierson announced. "We got the baseline from which to start. Take a look at the time on the board. Fifteen seconds, point one! That was a stellar run! Best of luck to the other ladies that'll be chasin' that lead tonight. Better hold on to your hats!" Pierson Price, the voice of the rodeo, good ol' Price, his voice sounded like music to her ears.

"Yes!" Eva yelled. She pumped her fist into the air. "Good girl! We did it! You did it! That was all you, Frida baby!" She leaned onto Frida's neck and kissed her. "Not too shabby for opening night, huh?"

Eva trotted her horse one more time around the arena to settle her spirits before going back through the gate. She waved her Stetson hat and shouted her thanks to her fans. Eva gripped the reins with both hands when Frida started whipping her head every which way. She squeezed her knees, letting Frida take the lead.

"Easy girl," she said while trying to spot the problem but only saw barrel men scattering, yelling, and rolling barrel distractions. The whirlwind of activity caused Frida to rear. Eva hadn't time to brace herself before she fell onto her back and got the wind knocked out of her. She winced and tried to catch her breath.

"Uh oh, guys and gals, cowgirl down!" Pierson's voice cut through her confusion. "We got a bull on the loose, and he does not look happy. No siree. Folks, this isn't uncommon that a bull breaks free; they're so damn rowdy and hell-bent on raisin' heck. Look at him go! Dang, he's a big boy! I pity the bulldogger that's gotta ride him!"

"Frida!" Eva croaked as she became aware of the unfolding scene. Her breath came in short spurts as she tried to ease the tight feeling inside. A pickup-man sprinted on his horse to catch Frida. Grabbing her reins, he made for safety. Her eyesight sharpened in time to see the spray of clumps of dirt and two thousand pounds of bull, four angry hooves, and two blunted horns heading straight for her. She closed her eyes, held her breath, and braced herself for impact. Instead, she felt the weight of a body atop her own—a bullfighter to the rescue. He used his momentum and rolled them out of the way.

"Let's move, cowgirl." Eva locked eyes with her savior. It was a woman. She knew all the bullfighters on the circuit; not one of them was a woman. It was Wonder Woman. The woman with the belt buckle. The woman from—

"You good?" Wonder Woman shouted.

Eva nodded that she was.

"Come on then!"

Eva could only stare; could it really be her?

"Up and at 'em, cowgirl. Up! Up! Up!" Wonder Woman got to her feet, then pulled Eva up and spun her around so she was holding her from behind. She lifted her into the air, then shoved her into the outstretched arms of a pickup-man atop his horse. He grabbed Eva by the waist, and they headed away from the chaos. Out of Eva's peripheral vision, she caught sight of a crushing impact: Wonder Woman being knocked to her feet, taking horns to her body, being rolled again and again, and then the gate shut and she saw no more.

"Whoa ho ho, folks. That was a close call…" Eva heard Price saying over the speaker. His voice sounded light, she thought. She hoped that meant Wonder Woman had survived. "Hope that one's got extra padding on tonight. My oh my, wasn't that somethin'. You want to play with bulls, sometimes they win; and they ain't playin' chess, folks. You saw it here." The spectators laughed.

Eva had heard that line time and time again when Price was commentating, *you want to play with bulls, sometimes they win; and they ain't playin' chess.* As much as it made her eyes roll, it was the truth, and such was life in the rodeo.

"You okay, Eva?" Tito, the rider who rode her to safety, asked as she slid off his horse onto shaky footing. "Damn way to end a try."

"Holy crap!" Eva brushed the dirt off her body and righted her clothing. "What the hell was that?"

"I don't know, but the bull's name is Hell Raiser, if that says anything."

"It says everything." She turned her attention to her horse, which Tito's brother Benji had saved. "You okay, girl? I'm so sorry I couldn't hold on. You okay?" She took the reins. "Thank you for getting to her so quickly, Benji. Thank you so much." Eva's entire body shook with the reality that both she and her horse could have been beaten into early retirement or worse.

"S'my job." Benji gave her a tip of his hat and trotted back toward the arena.

"Who was that, that woman?" Eva asked. She already knew the answer. She was Wonder Woman from the plane; she hadn't been able to get her out of her head since they had met. She'd recognize her anywhere, not because of the belt buckle, but because the pain that emanated from her soul painted a canvas of hurt, so complex, that it stilled her, dropped her to her knees, and drew tears of her own.

"That was my sister."

"You have a sister?" Eva scratched her head.

"My twin."

"Since when?"

Tito laughed. "I'll introduce you later." He started trotting back to the arena. "You okay?" he yelled as he left.

"I'm fine!" *A twin? Could it really be the woman from the plane?* "What's her name?" she asked, but it was too late. He was gone. She turned her attention to her surroundings, searching for the woman who had saved her. Eva felt relieved when she saw the woman walking toward her, then defeated. The woman favored her right arm but held fire in her eyes and Eva's hat in her other hand.

"What the hell was that all about?" Tito's twin yelled and threw Eva her Stetson.

"What are you talking about?"

"You know what I'm talking about."

"I'm sorry but I don't." Eva wanted to hide from the looks of those passing by.

"You hesitated when I was trying to do my job. Why?"

"I'm sorry."

"When I say move, you can't just stand there." Wonder Woman winced and ran her hand through her thick black hair.

"I know. You're right. I'm sorry. I don't know what happened to me. I'm so sorry." Eva stroked her horse's mane. Her cheeks burned with embarrassment as the woman she had comforted only days ago now reamed her out because Eva had done something stupid. "Hey," she said, trying to keep up with the retreating woman, to explain herself, but it was no use. The woman disappeared inside the medical tent.

Eva had hesitated, and stupid moves like that could have deadly consequences.

She walked with Frida to her stall and inspected her for injury. She removed Frida's boots, ran her hands down her legs, felt her strong muscles, and inspected her hooves and tendons.

"There you go; you're okay," Eva whispered as she removed Frida's saddle, saddle blanket, and bit. She took her time while she brushed her down. She would run Dolores tomorrow and take Frida home overnight. She texted Rosie, her vet and long-time friend, to come over for a checkup in the morning, just in case.

"You going to make it?" she asked as she kissed Frida's neck.

Frida nodded. She understood Eva, sensed everything that she said and everything that she didn't say with words. The trust that Eva built with her horses was a large part of why they worked so well together and why they won races.

"Brilliant run out there. I messed up, didn't I?"

Frida gave a soft whinny and shook her head.

Eva groaned and pressed her forehead into her horse's neck. "Do you think she's calmed down by now?" Her horse gave her support by digging into a bucket of oats.

When Eva was satisfied that her horse was okay, she summoned the courage to find Wonder Woman.

"Hey, Beth," Eva said as she opened the door to the medical tent and swept the area with her eyes.

"Hiya." Nurse Beth looked up from her iPad and over her glasses. "Come in. What's up?"

"I was looking for that woman. The female bullfighter that was hurt, the one with the Wonder Woman belt buckle."

"Toma?"

"How many other female bullfighters are there?"

"Good point. She went back out," Beth said.

"She looked hurt."

"She had a partially dislocated shoulder. I popped it back for her."

"And she went back out?" Eva's eyes widened.

"She's a Rozene through and through, stubborn, hardheaded, thinks they're bulletproof. I told her to sit out the rest of the night, but she didn't agree."

"Oh, no." If Toma wasn't already furious, she was now. It was common rodeo practice to tape the shit out of yourself and hide anything and everything from Nurse Beth and, if you couldn't avoid her tent, to do what she ordered.

"Defy my recommendations, get sent to the hospital, can't come back until I see a doctor's note."

"Where are you sending them?"

"Valley Medical. Move," Beth said the moment a limping bulldogger hobbled in.

"Thanks, Beth."

When the night was over, Eva tried to find Toma but learned that she and Tito had already left. Eva headed to Valley Medical, found a parking spot that accommodated her huge truck and trailer, and went inside.

"I'm looking for a woman." Eva grimaced at her choice of words. "A patient, her name's Toma, sent from the rodeo nurse, Beth Joseph."

"Last name?" The nurse at the front desk shuffled papers and looked around Eva to the automatic emergency room entrance doors.

"Rozene?" Eva assumed. Unless Toma was married and had a different last name than her brothers, she thought. Toma had been wearing a ring. Eva wondered if her partner was with her. She bit her lip and second-guessed her decision.

"Room twelve." The nurse motioned in the general direction. Eva followed her directions and heard the familiar voice that had let her have it. Eva sat in a chair outside of the room. She tried blocking out the details, but everything echoed in the linoleum-laden hospital corridor. A nurse had told Toma that she had suffered a subluxation or partial dislocation, no nerve damage, no torn ligaments. She'd be fine. She'd be sore. She needed to apply heat and take it easy. Eva heard Toma piece together an impressive string of expletives at that last bit.

"Such a waste of time," filtered out of the room and, "if every little bump and knock is going to send me here, I'm out, Tito," and "calm down, that *was* a hard hit, Toma," and "sit still," followed by swearing and then bickering between the twins that stopped the moment the doctor went in and closed the door.

Eva watched the hands on her wristwatch move slower than molasses in winter until finally the door opened and the medical staff came out with the twins.

Eva popped to her feet and tried for words, but her tongue felt heavy. *Hello,* she imagined herself saying, but couldn't form the word. Toma's striking presence commanded eyes upon her at all times. The languid way that she moved, her grace when she ran a hand through her short, thick black hair, was enough to freeze Eva all over again. This time, she noticed more details. Toma had high cheekbones, full lips, kind eyes, a smear of dust on her right cheek. Seeing her and Tito side by side, she indeed looked like a female, more toned, taller, darker-skinned version. Toma wore a white tank top tucked into her well-worn blue jeans. Her arms were long. And her hands, though Eva couldn't see them, she knew what they looked like and what they felt like. She had touched them, caressed them, and studied Toma's long tapered fingers, until the moment they were forced apart. Eva gasped when she saw that Toma wore a blue sling and held a white paper bag. Toma looked at her phone then bumped into her brother. Eva swallowed a knot in her throat.

"Jesus, Tito," Toma said. "That hurt."

"Oh, *that* hurt?"

"I jammed my finger."

"You big baby. Oh hey, Eva," Tito said. "Damn, did you get banished by Nurse Beth too?"

"No. I mean yes." Eva closed her eyes and took a deep breath, then locked eyes with Toma.

Tito turned his gaze between them. "Eva, this is Toma, my little sister by two minutes. Toma, this is Eva, former Miss Rodeo Idaho and world champion barrel racer."

"On my way to a third title," Eva said to prove that she wasn't a clueless amateur in the arena. She held out her hand. "Eva Angeles." She realized her blunder immediately.

With her arm in the sling and juggling the paper bag and her phone in her free hand, Toma hadn't a free hand for a proper introduction. Instead, she acknowledged Eva in that same piercing way that had frozen her in the arena. Toma's eyes were no longer brimming with tears and heartbreak, but were keen, attentive, apt, and able.

"Gimme a sec, Tito." Her voice was barely a whisper. "I'll be right there."

"Hurry up. Dad's been texting all night about the show, wants all the deets. The guys are already there. We're beyond hungry."

"Don't get your panties in a—" Toma looked upward. "Gimme a sec," she said through clenched teeth.

"Great ride tonight, Eva," Tito said as he left. "See you tomorrow?"

"Yeah. Thanks. Tomorrow." Eva sent him off with a wave while continuing to focus on his twin. She swallowed hard. Usually a woman with a talent for conversation, she didn't know where to begin. Eva saw only a trace of the hurt and broken woman and only if she looked closely. Toma seemed masterful at hiding that side from her brother.

"You okay?" Eva's eyes trailed along Toma's sling. She so wanted to touch her again, with both hands this time, to press up against her and show her how sorry she was.

"I'll live. You?"

"I'm good." Only the rustling of the white paper bag and random beeping sounds registered. "I'm really sorry you got hurt because of me." Eva shook her head and looked at the ceiling. "You caught me off guard. I wasn't expecting to see you again. It's not every day that you run into Wonder Woman at the rodeo." Eva hoped Toma found some humor in her remark.

Toma fumbled with the sling before taking it off and chucking it into the nearest trash receptacle.

Eva opened her mouth, then closed it. She scratched her forehead, and moments crept by.

"That bull would have ended you."

"I know, and I'm sorry for putting you in its path. I don't know what my problem was back there."

"You froze. It happens."

"It was more than that." Eva exhaled.

"How so?"

"Weren't you surprised? A little? When you saw me?" Eva felt as though her words were a fully loaded pistol in the kill shot.

Toma cupped her chin in a mock pondering of life, then dropped her hand, giving up the charade. "Everything's a surprise and everything always feels off when your coworkers are two-thousand-pound bulls. Kind of comes with the job. My job is to protect everyone or everything that gets in their way or does stupid…who…seconds count, *you* know that. Sorry if I'm coming across like a total dick and reamed you out in front of everyone, truly, I am but I've been on the job for all of one day, and you're the reason I've spent the last two hours here." She pinched the bridge of her nose and took a deep breath. "It's been a long night; I have a screaming headache like you wouldn't believe; and you heard my brother. My dad's dying to know how tonight went. To top it off, I'll not live this down easily—hurt, day one on the job. Do you have any idea how stupid five brothers can be?"

"It won't happen again." It *will* happen again if Toma looks at her with eyes that had once let her in, all the way in, and were now closed.

Toma opened her mouth as if wanting to say more but only nodded. She crumpled the bag and tossed it into the trash receptacle. She strode out of the hospital.

Eva sighed, went to the trash can, and pulled out the elbow sling and the white bag, which held painkillers.

CHAPTER THREE

"YOU NEED TO GO TO bed, Dad," Toma said for the third time in an hour. "I'm serious." She hoped that overdramatic clanking while putting away the dinner dishes hinted that it was time to wrap up their dinner-slash-opening-night-at-the-rodeo play-by-play-by-play. "I need to go to bed; Tito needs to go to bed." She yawned. Her other brothers had left long ago. Pierson Price's Rodeo Radio broadcast and aftershow were officially over. "It's past midnight. We're wiped."

"She's right, Dad." Tito put his hands on the back of their dad's recliner and gave it a gentle jostle.

"I know. I know." Red Rozene was six feet, six inches tall, a brawny man whose full head of raven black hair was streaked white at his temples. He acted more like a teenager at times than his seventy years of age—with the strength to match. "You kids don't have a clue how hard this is for me. I've only missed one rodeo in forty-seven years. One rodeo."

Toma had heard that boast before. Her dad was blessed. Careers in the rodeo, especially for bullfighters, were fast, hard, and usually short. Career-ending injuries and sometimes death weren't uncommon. Most old-timers were working youth rodeos, coaching, retired, severely injured, or dead.

"When was the last time you were grounded?" Tito asked.

"When I busted my jaw." Red rubbed his chin. "The time the bull hopped the fence."

"That's right," Tito added with a laugh. "The bastard rode around the arena with the gate on his head like a hat."

"Hurt like a sonofabitch." Red laughed hard until he began coughing and he rubbed at his chest.

"Dad, take it easy. The doctor said you need to relax," Toma said.

"I am relaxed. What I need is a good dose of rodeo." He grunted and shook his head.

"Not until you get the orders. It stresses you out," Tito reminded him.

"It stresses me out in a good way."

"Your body would beg to differ. Speaking of, time for bed, let's get you into your PJs."

"I like it better when the nurse helps me. She's gentler than you are."

"That's 'cause you're nicer to her." Tito laughed. "Don't make me wrangle you to your bedroom." Tito circled the recliner and helped Red to his feet. Red groaned as he stood. "There you go, Dad."

"I'm fine, Son," Red said after catching his breath. "I'm not a damn invalid. It wasn't a month ago that I wrestled a full-grown bull, saving you from horns in your ass."

"I know, Dad," Tito said as if he had heard one too many similar reminders. "But you need to rest; we all do. Maybe by finals you will be ready to go, maybe help strategize, but now, take it easy; it's only been a month since—"

Red put his hand up. "Does everything have to be about that?"

"Until the doctors say so, yes, everything is going to be about that."

"Speaking of strategy, I have some ideas I wanted to run by you kids. I got them written down, play for play. Let's review tomorrow. You should start incorporating them into your work, like now."

"Sounds like a plan, Dad," Toma heard as the two retreated down the hall toward her father's room.

Toma could only watch their interaction. She wasn't sure how to help her father, aside from cooking, cleaning, and running the horses. She'd been away from the family for so long, she felt like a stranger. She wondered if she'd ever feel as though she'd fit in And what about her place in the circuit? Would she make friends? Did she want to make friends—was it even worth it to try? The larger question was what the hell was she going to do after the rodeo season ended. Would she have another gig by then? If she did, could she leave? Would her dad be healthy enough to be able to maintain their ranch and work at the rodeo? Judging by what she'd seen thus far in her short time home, not likely.

Her thoughts floated back to the embarrassment of her mental breakdown on the airplane, and then to her shitshow of a save, and from that to her public berating of former Miss Rodeo Idaho. "Eva Angeles," she whispered. Toma had imagined meeting Eva again, had fantasized about how she'd properly thank her for being there for her. She imagined thanking her over a drink, maybe dinner, maybe with a kiss, maybe more. Toma rolled her eyes. She cringed at how her second meeting with Eva had actually transpired.

She massaged her forehead. Horrible didn't begin to describe how she felt. She squeezed her eyes shut and groaned at her poor behavior. She wasn't in any state to become involved with another woman so soon after everything that had happened with the last one. Her heartache at everything that had transpired back in L.A. was beginning to turn to anger. *Good, that's good*, she thought.

She continued clearing the kitchen of the aftermath of six grown men. She readied the coffeepot—one less thing to do in the morning. She closed all the windows and slipped into her sweatshirt. She had been home from L.A. for a little over a week and was still adjusting to the cool of the Idaho nights. Goosebumps all over her body told her fall and winter weren't going to be fun.

"How is he?" she asked when Tito returned.

"He may look like an old bastard, but he's strong. Had to wrestle him into his nightshirt," he said and stomped his foot on the tile like a WWF wrestler.

"You're so good with him."

"It takes stubborn to fight stubborn." He slumped into the chair, stretched, and yawned. Toma considered her twin and how much he had changed since the last time she'd been home. He'd successfully grown an honest-to-goodness mustache, albeit not very thick. No one in their family could grow impressive facial hair. She liked his longer, shoulder-length hair; it fit him. He mussed his thick black hair, clearing it from his eyes. "I'm glad you're home. It's been a lot on my own, even with Nurse Jackie. The guys can only do so much with everything they've got going on, the kids and stuff."

"I'm sorry it's been so long."

"What's twelve years?" Tito said.

Toma heard no bitterness in his voice but knew that it had been hard on everyone, Tito, especially. She bit the inside of her cheek and wrapped her arms around her stomach, shoving down the ache.

"Sorry. I didn't mean it like that," Tito said in a softer tone.

He didn't mean for it to come out like that, but it did. Toma guessed her other brothers felt the same way too. She had kept her distance physically and emotionally. She rarely came home, not for holidays, or monumental birthdays. She had only returned for the births of her brother's children. It took her dad almost dying to bring her home for more than a few days. "Even if you didn't mean it, it's still true."

"No it's not. We get it. Your career took you all over the world. I wish I would've followed my dreams instead of chasing bulls. But I love it, so there's that."

"What was your dream, Tito?"

"The circus."

Toma laughed.

"You think I'm kidding?"

"I know you're serious. I can see it, really I can. You have the hair, the body, everything about you says circus."

"You know we're twins, right?" he joked.

Toma threw a leather coaster at him that he swatted away.

Toma hadn't simply left home to follow her dreams. She'd taken the first out she found.

Toma would always remember the day that her mother had had her stroke. Mom had told her to hurry and find her dad. Looking at what happened on rewind, it was clear that her mother had needed her. The look in her eyes, the panic and fear, would always haunt Toma. But at five years old, she hadn't understood that her mother was dying.

A fight with her dad came years later. He had said he couldn't bear to look at her, that it broke his heart every time because, as she grew older, she looked more like her mother. He never apologized, but over the years he'd tried in his own way. Toma didn't make it easy for him. She had always been too busy, thanks to insane production schedules. There was always a job, traveling, being out of the country. There was always something else and the perfect excuse.

"I wanted to help, and the timing was…" She looked down. "Sorry, that did not come out right. I would have dropped everything to be home and help. I'm sorry it took Dad's accident."

"Me too. But Pops is strong. He's doing good, and you did good tonight too. Dad's not overly fond of your acrobatics," he said with air quotes. "Gave me an earful. Says you're too dangerous."

"It's basic stunt work. Wasn't it exhilarating?"

"Totally. Let's do that diversion thing again tomorrow." Tito pushed himself from the chair and began folding a throw blanket. "What did Eva want?" he said through another yawn.

"Eva?"

"Eva? The hospital? What did she want?"

Toma groaned. "To apologize." It should have been the other way around. Toma was indebted to Eva for helping her endure the flight home, for holding her hand, for comforting her in her time of need.

"For what?"

For nothing. She did nothing wrong. "She hesitated when I went in for the save. I kind of reamed her out in front of everyone." *Then brushed her off at the hospital.*

"Why would you do that?"

"I don't know." She knew she sounded defensive.

"Sure you do."

"I don't." Toma shoved her hands in her pockets and stared at the floor.

"I know why."

Toma kept staring at nothing and hoping he'd drop it.

"Want me to enlighten you?"

"Not really?" Toma met his gaze.

"You're a major a-hole."

"What?" She gasped. "No, I'm not."

"Sounds like an asshole move to me."

"She cost me time. I got my ass kicked by that bull." Toma winced at her pathetic attempt at an excuse.

"Getting your ass kicked by a bull is literally our job."

Toma groaned, and Tito patted her back.

"You're right," she relented. "I should have been more patient."

"You think? She was your first save, of, like, ever."

"I know. I know. I overreacted." In truth, she'd acted as any normal woman would act when seeing someone who had seen *her* in the raw bareness of flesh and bone. "I'm the one who needs to apologize, no doubt about that."

"That would be a good first step." He resumed tidying the living room.

"Do you know how to get ahold of her?" Toma asked.

"You'll see her tomorrow."

"I know, but in case I don't get time to talk to her. Do you have her number?"

"No, but I know where she works."

"I'm not going to go to her work. That's a little stalker-like, don't you think?"

"Kinda."

"Where does she work?" Toma couldn't help wanting to know as much as she could about Eva Angeles.

"They own a restaurant and a farm. She, like, heavy-duty farms with her family. Operates big combines." He showed her how big with his hands. "Big, big combines." His eyes grew wider, and he laughed at himself.

"I feel like crap." Toma's hand went to her shoulder. She wished she had kept her painkillers, instead of throwing them away like an idiot.

"You should. She commands a ton of respect. She's not your standard rodeo queen airhead hottie."

"I don't think that. Not at all." *The hot part, yes.* Well-endowed and fearless on a horse were two of Toma's favorite things.

"She's the reigning barrel racing world champion, a community advocate, volunteers all over the place," he said through another yawn. "I'm going to bed." Tito started down the hallway toward his bedroom.

"Goodnight."

"Do the right thing."

"I will." Doing the right thing was the reason Toma had booked her flight home. It was the reason she'd broken down midflight, the reason her family needed her. Suddenly, after being gone for so long, she felt like a linchpin that held everything together. There was no way she could go back to stunt work anytime soon. Being a stuntwoman demanded everything from her: her mind, her body, and every second of her time. A clean break, for now, would leave her in one piece. Her family needed her, and her father's health was her utmost priority.

She filled her water bottle, turned off the lights, and pushed through the back door of the house, stopping short at the sight of her dad's loafers, worn leather with the heels pushed in for easy access. She remembered how she'd wear a similar pair to get to and from playing in the barn and, when she was older, for chores like taking out the trash. She slipped a foot inside—still too big. It felt familiar, felt like home. *What the hell.* She used them to walk to the barn and to the old ranch hand's apartment, where she felt she'd have the most privacy and also be closer to the horses and their needs. It was the family's once-upon-a-time bullfighter-training facility, complete with an outdoor regulation-sized arena they now used for practicing.

With the new twins, Danny can't commit. We can't manage everything. We're closing the school down, sending people to Weiser. She remembered reading Tito's email while sitting in makeup, reading it as if it was another random family update, when the update was one of the most important parts of her dad's life, her family's life. A chapter had closed and a new one began, which she better understood because she was home.

Her dad was older; she saw it in his eyes, in his weathered skin and his joints. He'd never do another season in the rodeo. Except for Tito, her brothers were married or in serious relationships. They had families and kids, whom she'd last seen when they were babies. All of them adored her, looked up to her because of her job in the movies as if she was a movie star instead of seeing what she really was, a stuntwoman who made other people look good.

She opened the door to the barn. She avoided turning on the large overhead light in favor of going straight to her room so she didn't have to see the extent of what her family had given up, didn't have to look at the barrels, ropes and tack, posters, old schedules, and other equipment that sat wondering that its next role would be.

CHAPTER FOUR

EVA DROVE HOME IN SILENCE, preferring to listen to the sound of the wind through the window and the rhythm of the spray of the sprinklers in the fields as she drove past, absorbing the smell of sweet mint fields and rich soils through the pores of her soul. She peeked in her rearview mirror at her precious cargo, her horse Frida. She prayed she was okay after the night's wild ending. She made the turn into her family's property and drove down the long gravel driveway. She pulled into the barn; her dad was still up. He gave her a wave. She waved back.

"Hi, Papá." Eva closed the truck door behind her, then stretched, reaching toward the sky, feeling a couple of vertebrae right themselves. Her hip felt sore from where she'd landed on it when she fell.

"Hola, mi reina." Roberto, her dad, wore his usual after-work uniform: a white T-shirt, khaki knee-length shorts, and socks that reached mid-calf. Her mom would tease him about the tan lines on his legs by the end of the summer.

"You didn't need to wait up for me." Eva had called her dad to let him know what had happened and that she was bringing Frida home for the night. Usually, they stayed on the arena premises during a competition, but, with the scare, she wanted Frida home.

"Quería esperarte, mija." Roberto put the tool he'd been holding on his workbench, wiped his hands on a rag, kissed her on the side of the head, then pulled her into his arms for one of his comforting bear hugs. He smelled like the outside and of home. She closed her eyes and sighed. He always knew when she needed a big hug, and, after tonight with its mountain highs and ocean lows, it felt good.

"Mom closing tonight?" she asked. In addition to farming, her family owned a popular Mexican restaurant that catered to the area's farmers, seasonal workers, and anyone looking for authentic Mexican cuisine. *Aleida's* was named after her abuelita who, in her early eighties, still pulled shifts when she could, kicked like a mule, swore like a sailor, and spit like a cowboy.

"Si. Preparándose para un gran trabajo de catering este fin de semana."

"Oh, that's right, the funeral."

"¿Si? ¿Pues? Aside from the scare, dime?"

"You know how it went, Papá." She eyed the radio. He always listened to Pierson Price's Rodeo Radio show when he couldn't make it to a competition.

"Claro, pero me gusta más cuando me lo cuentas."

"I got top time." She injected more excitement into her words than how she truly felt.

"I'm so proud, mija."

"I also set the benchmark for the circuit." She couldn't force the accompanying smile. She should be ecstatic. No other rider came close to her time. She and Frida would have to run blindfolded to lose.

"Bumps or bruises?" her papá asked. He lifted her Stetson and gave her a good looking over.

"I'm fine." No visible bruises, only one major pain in her heart from seeing the woman that she had thought about nonstop since her trip from Seattle. Toma. Toma Rozene. Toma Rozene, bullfighter, Wonder Woman, tough as nails, but with a thin shell that barely held her together, who had embarrassed her in front of half the arena staff. Eva didn't hold it against her. She'd probably react the same way if she fell apart in front of a total stranger she never thought she'd see again.

"¿Y Frida?"

"Rosie's coming over tomorrow; we'll know after that." In addition to being Eva's vet, Rosie was her longtime friend and team member and accompanied Eva on most of her out-of-town competitions.

"You sure you're okay, mija?"

"I'm fine," she said, hoping to alleviate his concerns. "That fall didn't settle well with me." They opened the gate of her horse trailer. She patted Frida's rump, then went into the trailer, hitched a lead to her harness, and talked her out. Her dad got a broom and started sweeping the inside of the trailer.

"Thanks." She kissed Frida. Her horse's prickly muzzle against the side of her cheek calmed her.

"Abuelita left enchiladas in the oven for you."

"Good. I'm starving." She circled Frida a few times before settling her into her stall.

"Give to me your keys. I'll put the trailer away. Then go eat."

"Gracias, Papá." She tossed him her set of keys.

"Buenas noches, mija." He jingled her keys in his hand as he left.

"Night, Papá. ¿Oh, cual es el plan para mañana?"

"Maru's crew is running the combines in the upper section, so I need you weeding with Carlita's team."

"I'll be there."

While Eva would have liked to make her entire living from the rodeo, that wasn't feasible. Her full-time job was helping run the farm. She worked alongside two sisters, Maru and Carlita; a slew of aunts and uncles and cousins and nieces and nephews; and seasonal laborers. The money was good but hard-earned, especially during the summer when her days started at four in the morning. At least they ended at noon, leaving her time to rest, train, and compete.

She'd worked on the farm since she was in elementary school, through high school, and summers during college. Her family had been fortunate enough to get a loan to buy an established farm from a childless widower. With the income from their restaurant and the farm, they did well, and she always had their support. Horses and competitions were the opposite of cheap: vet visits, lessons, equipment, gear, association fees, travel, clothing, food. Eva's sponsorships helped with all of that now. She never forgot the hard work and the sacrifices her family had made for her along the way. She never forgot how hard it'd been when she was up-and-coming, so she provided mentoring and free lessons to two or three young barrel racers who didn't have the robust support system she had enjoyed.

Eva walked Frida to her stall and looked into her intelligent eyes before slumping against the wall. "I'm tired all of a sudden."

By this time of the year, Eva led the other circuit contenders in terms of money earned. She could choose her competitions; she no longer had to take anything and everything. She already ran upwards of fifty races, and came out on top with healthy horses.

All of a sudden, she felt more overwhelmed than ever, and not because she spent all her spare time volunteering, organizing events, and doing public speaking or because, in addition to her training, she had commitments to the farm and the restaurant. A week ago, she'd felt able to manage all that and more. Enter a certain dark, broody, mirthless, downtrodden woman who had gotten into her head and thrown her a sword when she was juggling tennis balls.

*   *   *

EVA SAT ATOP THE ARENA'S fence along with a handful of other competitors who were watching the bullfighters practice. The addition of a certain woman bullfighter was taking their practice sessions from entertaining to exhilaratingly frightening. Toma was easy to spot in the arena. She moved with a distinctly female grace, like a ballerina, flitting and floating over the dirt. Her every move seemed calculated, purposeful, and easy. She seemed to be everywhere at once and capable of doing everything as well as, if not better than, the guys. Her brothers seemed to know it but didn't seem to mind, judging from their constant laughing and teasing, especially between the twins.

Toma mounted her horse and sent signals to her brothers via a series of high-pitched whistles and hand signals. They moved into their respective positions before a gate guy opened the chute. A massive bull burst through the gate horns first, heading straight for their decoy downed cowboy. Tito, one of the barrel men, rolled a barrel in front of the decoy to cut off the animal. The bull sent the barrel for a ride, leaving a bullfighter plenty of time to save the downed cowboy and get him to safety.

The spectators clapped. After another series of whistles, the team moved into another formation. This time, Toma lay on the ground while Tito sent a barrel her way. She climbed atop it, one leg on either end.

"What is she doing?" Julie, one of Eva's barrel racing friends, asked.

"I don't know." Eva shook her head and sat up straighter. She didn't want to speculate. She could scarcely keep her eyes focused.

"She is…"

"Fearless," Eva said.

"I was going to say crazy," Julie corrected.

"I'm just glad her pops isn't here to see this," said Cody, a cocky son of a bitch with a record to back himself up. "Doing stuff like that'll end your career in a minute, and maybe someone else's." He shook his head. "Reckless woman. She won't last the season doing shit like that; mark my words." Another cowboy clapped Cody on the back and shook his head.

The rodeo was a macho sport; bullfighting was the most macho. Seeing a woman coming in for the save, doing what some old-timers and rigid-minded people thought was a man's job and doing it better, didn't sit well with a lot of them—males, mostly.

"You sure had a different opinion of her when she saving your ass last night, Cody," Eva said.

The cowboy resettled his hat atop his head and hopped off the gate.

"That's what I thought," she scoffed.

She redirected her attention to see Toma standing on top of the barrel waving her arms overhead, yelling. The bull took one look at her. Two brothers on their horses circled him, confusing him, causing the beast to snort and dig his hooves in the ground before he charged straight for Toma. Eva and the spectators took a collective gasp when

Toma jumped into the air and over the bull, landed on her feet, and hopped into another barrel while the bull charged the fake barrel, giving even an elderly person with a walker enough time to scoot out of the arena and get a beer while they were at it.

"Oh. My. God." Eva proclaimed.

"I think, with old man Rozene out, they're experimenting. He's not here to crack the whip anymore. This season will be fun with her here," Julie said.

"I've never seen anything like that," Eva said. "That was absolutely nuts." She laughed. "How the hell…"

"Tito told me she worked years in the movies, did TV shows and stuff."

"Doing what?"

"Equestrian stunt work."

"Ah." Eva shook her head. Toma made a little more sense: the way her body was all hard muscle, her fearlessness, and her athleticism. The woman didn't throw caution to the wind. She packed it in a box, as if it were a glass bowl without protective wrapping, and sent it to Siberia, letting fate determine its destiny.

"I'm going to get my horse ready." Julie hopped off the gate. "You coming?"

"I'll be right there. I want to keep watching. It's cool. Everything they do is amazingly choreographed, each move, a dance, like an all-out—" Eva looked around and saw that her friend had left. "Okay, I'm officially talking to myself."

She readjusted her Stetson and continued to focus on Toma, her moves, her dangerous confidence, her lightning-quick reactions, on the way she rode her horse, on how she squeezed her legs to steer, on that tight, beautiful backside when she stood in her stirrups and on the way she handled the bulls, using their energy against them.

"Damn it," she whispered. As much as Eva was hurt by Toma's behavior from the night before, she was also intrigued.

Warning bells went off in her head. *Don't do it, Eva. Don't get involved. Turn around. Look away. Leave. Now!* Toma seemed like a woman on a collision course with life and hell-bent on knocking everything over that wasn't bolted down. Too late. Toma made eye contact, then trotted toward her on her horse with that perfect, erect posture.

"Hi again." Toma readjusted herself in her saddle. Eva so wanted to let her gaze wander to the seat of that saddle, but focused her attention beyond Toma to her brothers. Hopefully, that would distract Eva long enough to let the wave of heat pass.

"Hi." Eva gave her a tight-lipped smile.

"Well, what do you think?"

"About what?"

Toma motioned over her shoulder. "Our stunts."

Eva gave her two thumbs up. "Solid."

Toma lifted her hat and ran her hand through her hair. "I wanted to say that I'm sorry about last night and wondered if you—" A high-pitched whistle interrupted her.

"What the hell, Sis!" Tito came trotting up. "We only have twenty more minutes of arena time. You can talk later. Hi, Eva. Sorry, Eva." He circled around.

Toma alternated her gaze between Eva and her brother before deciding to do as Tito asked. She left Eva with a once-over look at her body. *Why would she do that?* The look stole Eva's breath. She hopped off the fence to prepare for the evening's events.

After a good night's rest and a long day of working on the farm, she had finally exorcised that nagging feeling that had consumed her since her flight. It returned in full force. Toma emanated pain, anger, passion all at the same time, and it seemed as though she hid it from everyone but Eva.

CHAPTER FIVE

"FOLKS, HERE WE GO AGAIN, riding her three-year-old filly, Dolores is the name, a midnight-black quarter horse with a lone white sock on her hind leg. You might remember the rider from last night, who just happened to set the benchmark for all other ladies in this competition. Now let me get a show of hands." The crowd groaned. "Okay, all right, okay. How about a whoop and a holler if you were a witness to the greatness last night when this little lady came out and did her thang! Let me hear it, folks!" Pierson Price hollered, and the crowd followed suit.

"Fifteen seconds point one was the time she put on the board. Take a look at all her stats front and center on the Albertsons Jumbotron. Albertsons, home of the Whole Bird, five ninety-nine roasted chicken. Now, can she do it again?" Pierson asked. "Let's see what she's got tonight. Let's give it up for the one, the only, Miss Eva Angeles and Dolores."

Toma grinned as the crowd went wild. She'd anticipated this moment all night, waited for Eva, just to see her again. Everything else that she had done so far was simply work.

Eva wore all black, matching her all-black horse. Eva's clothes had silver fringe, which shimmered in the arena's lights.

Tito laughed. "You like all that fringe, don't you?"

"Shuddup," she said, then thwapped Tito's leg with one of her leather reins. She and Tito were on bullfighter duty. Two other brothers were staffing barrels, and another two brothers were pickup men. From Toma's vantage point, she could see the rise and fall of Eva's chest. Eva blew several short puffs of air between her lips and bobbed up and down atop her prancing horse. Eva bent forward and wove her fingers through her horse's mane. The connection Toma felt between woman and horse was brighter, more electrifying, than the lights of the arena. Rider and horse were one. Eva's total focus could still the Roman Coliseum.

A calm blanketed the arena. Then Eva came out of the gate like a bolt of lightning, faster than reaching the ground after a base jump. They attacked barrel after barrel, turn after turn, hugged them tightly, as in a dance with each partner knowing their role, having practiced a thousand times. The only things that registered to Toma were the spray of dirt and the silver fringe kissing the wind.

"Wowza! How do you like that, folks? Isn't she a delight? I can't get enough of her, and, judging by what I'm hearing, neither can you. Let's give it up!" As soon as the display board lit up, Pierson had the audience roaring and standing, having just witnessed Eva break the record she'd set the night before.

"No one else is even close," Toma said to her twin.

"Did you like that?"

Toma didn't respond. She was captivated by all things Eva: the way she waved her hat in the air, the way the wind caused the fringe on her sleeves to dance, her wavy black hair, and the sparkle of the stadium lights in her eyes. She rode past Toma and tipped her hat. Toma smiled and tipped her hat back.

"She prefers the company of queens, you know," Tito said.

"Well, of course."

"No, I mean *prefers* the company of queens."

"What are you talking about?"

"You're hopeless."

"Oh. Got it. She's a lesbian."

"Ding. Ding. Ding. You're smart, Sis."

Toma rolled her eyes.

"Just sayin'. I know you all like to band together and play softball." He swung an imaginary bat and clicked his tongue as he hit an imaginary ball.

Toma shook her head. She could finally relax the moment Eva trotted to safety behind the gates; she was glad that a bull hadn't decided to play chess with her again. The nervousness she felt at her brother's queen comment added an extra layer of complexity to the woman and made her that much more tempting, but Toma remembered her place, remembered her situation and her commitments

"Did you apologize to her?" he asked.

"I was trying to before the show when you came over and demanded that I return to practice."

"Is that what you were doing?" he said, and they trotted over to help the crew reset the arena for the bareback completion. They jumped off their horses. "'Cause it sounded like you were flirting."

"I didn't even say three words to her." Toma felt as though she had no right to flirt. She was still embarrassed at how she'd acted: crying on the flight, the save, reaming Eva out; the list went on.

"Hi, Polly." Eva's voice over the loudspeaker stopped Toma in her tracks.

Toma turned to the Jumbotron to watch Eva being interviewed. Her horse stood behind her.

"What a ride tonight, and yesterday too. Great way to start the circuit," said reporter Polly Gonzalez. Toma liked the way Polly pronounced Eva's last name *Onghelles*, as a native Spanish speaker would, versus the way Price spoke it—and most other people, for that matter. "How do you feel?"

"I feel pretty good."

"Pretty good?"

"I feel really good." Eva kissed Dolores's muzzle. "I wish I could take more of the credit, but my horses are the stars."

"We're excited to watch you putting up the best times and earning that purse. Do you feel like you're headed to the pros again in Las Vegas?"

"We only want to get through each night, one ride at a time. That's how we work. If we get the invite, come hell or high water, we'll be there."

"One last question: Do you have any advice for the young rising barrel racers watching?"

Eva looked directly into the camera. "Hi, girls," she said with a wave. "Hang on to your dreams, learn from them, never stop riding, find a hero and—" The feed was cut, and the crowd cheered.

"There you have it, folks. From the mind of one of our state's greatest, a former Miss Rodeo Idaho and the reigning world champion! Now for the bareback riding competition. I'd like to introduce a local good boy, hails from Middleton..."

That fucking asshole. How dare he cut her feed! Toma looked up at the announcer's stand and shot them a look; she was moments away from flipping him her middle finger.

"So that's what gawking looks like," Tito said, bringing Toma back to their task. She looked around to see her brothers already in position, waiting for her.

"And this is what rolling my eyes looks like," Toma demonstrated.

"Smartass! Ready when you are."

Everything went as smoothly as it could for the rest of the night until, not two riders into the calf roping competition, a bull crashed into the scene and charged through the gate, one that her brother Benji was holding. The commotion knocked him off and onto his back.

"Help Benji with the gate! I'll get Maverick," Toma ordered.

"Got it!" Tito yelled, and cantered on his horse to secure the opened gate while Toma pivoted on her horse, spurred into action, and raced toward the fallen cowboy. His knee twisted at an odd angle and he gritted his teeth in pain. She dismounted and helped him stand. When she was back atop her horse, he hoisted himself up and clung to the horn of her saddle while she rode them to safety.

"You okay, Mav?" Toma jumped from her horse. He wrapped an arm around her shoulder as they inched their way to the nurse's station.

"This ain't nothing." He grimaced and limped. "Calf pinned me good. Didja check those gates today? Your daddy always did b'fore each set."

"I checked them all myself. Double-checked them after last night's bull incident."

"Better check 'em again," he said. "Not blaming you, this ain't the best arena on God's green earth. Your daddy always brought his own lumber and tools with him, always said that this venue never did give no rat's ass about the wood 'round here. They spent more money on that Jumbotron. He advocated like heck against it in favor of better equipment, but no."

"Sorry, Mav. We'll check them again." Toma guided him into the nurse's station and deposited him in a chair.

"Thanks, kid. Tell your daddy hello and that we miss him and you're doing real good. Tell him Mav said so."

"I will. Thanks. Come back quick, all right?"

"Can't keep me down."

"No doubt about that, Mav." Toma felt for the guy. He'd probably busted his knee but, knowing these cowboy types, he'd tape the shit out of it and try again tomorrow.

Toma left the nurse's station feeling off; something wasn't right. The one thing that had often saved her in her career as a stuntwoman was that she acted on instinct. Listening to her gut had always been a more secure safety line than any harness or inflatable stunt bag. She rounded a corner, bypassing the area where the barrel racers got ready. She stopped and backed up. She wondered if Eva was around so she could better apologize for being dumb.

"Do you know where I can find Eva?" she asked a contestant wearing red fringe.

"Stall twenty-three," the woman said.

Toma headed to Eva's area: three stalls assigned to her for Frida, Dolores, and Vivian. She spotted a roll of tape on a small table along with a hoof pick and a currycomb. There also sat a pair of silver-fringed leather gloves. She picked them up, marveling at how small they were. Remembering the power of those small hands when they held her own, she set them down.

A photo was tucked inside the frame of a mirror. Toma looked around before picking it up. It showed Eva, standing between two other women. All three wore sashes and held bouquets of roses and wrenches in their hands. A vinyl DeWalt Tools banner hung behind the trio. Eva's smile, her full lips, and her caring eyes set her apart from the other women in the photo. Toma put the picture back. Fresh roses sat inside a metal bucket. A horse blanket was folded on the metal chair. Toma lifted a rose from the bucket, closed her eyes, and held it to her nose. Feeling the soft velvet of its petals, she sighed.

"Can I help you?" a woman asked.

"Hi. No. Sorry. I was looking for Eva. Angeles."

"She went home. You're Toma, right? New bullfighter?"

"Yes. Hi, nice to meet you."

"Likewise. I'm Julie. Cool moves out there." The woman extended her hand for a shake.

"Thanks," Toma said. "Okay, well. I guess I'll catch Eva tomorrow."

"We're not racing tomorrow."

"Damn." Toma sighed. She wanted to set things right with Eva, sooner rather than later. She hated that Eva might be feeling bad about herself because Toma had been a dummy. Then again, maybe Eva wasn't thinking about her at all. She thought about asking if Julie had Eva's number, but that didn't feel right.

"I have her number." Julie pulled out her cellphone. "Let me text her and see if she minds that I give it to you, or I can give her yours." Julie's fingers wove over the screen.

"Are you sure?" Toma rubbed the back of her neck. "It is kind of important."

"No prob. She's super quick at responding." As if on cue, Julie's phone dinged. "See? She's super quick."

"No doubt." *What'd she say? What'd she say!*

"She's said it's cool that I give you her number. Here it is." Julie held the phone out for Toma as Toma recorded the new contact in her phone.

"Thank you so much."

"No problem. See you out there." Julie walked away.

"Yeah. Thanks. Thank you." Toma waved her phone in the air before typing out her text message to Eva on her flip phone, which suddenly seemed archaic.

CHAPTER SIX

TOMA DROVE HER DAD'S PRIZED 1959 Tiffany-blue GMC pickup toward the Angeles farm, where Eva had said she'd be able to find her during the day. Probably not the wisest decision to drive the antique truck on a twelve-mile round trip. With her brother using the other one for work, she didn't have an array of options. She was careful to keep her speed right around fifty so as not to push the truck beyond what it could do. The old blue truck proved her worth and delivered Toma to the small town of Wilder without issue.

She hadn't been there since she was a kid. She had no recollection of the place. The landscape, however, seemed familiar. Its charming roads were dotted with warped hardwood branches of stone-fruit trees, and lush green grapevines lined the landscape. Hopvines grew skyward and seemed ready for harvest.

She cranked down her windows and inhaled the fresh, warm wind that blew through the cab carrying scents of mint and onions and, at times, traces of dust floated on sprinkler spray—an earthy delight that was the essence of southern Idaho.

Eva said to not follow the Google directions, that they led to an administrative office, and that Toma could find her at a field at the intersection of Roswell and Red Top Road. She coursed through the small-town with no sidewalks; the adobe buildings had signs written in Spanish. Old men with huge cowboy hats sat outside a tiny brick building with red-and-blue striped poles awaiting haircuts. She passed seasonal-worker housing with pristine green lawns, plastic toys, and picnic tables in the yards. A vivid turquoise building with beautifully depicted imagery of Día de los Muertos and other Mexican symbolism caught her eye. *Aleida's de Mexico*. A restaurant. Maybe she'd stop afterward and bring lunch home to Dad and Tito.

She continued through the town until she began seeing farmland. Fields of potatoes, onions, corn, and other crops. Her heart sped up as she approached the intersection. She saw white tents and green outhouses and recognized Eva's truck.

Toma slowed and pulled to the shoulder and onto the gravel road. She parked behind a string of dusty old trucks and sedans. Coolers sat on opened tailgates or in front seats. Toma picked up her Stetson, settled it on her head, and got out of the truck and walked down the embankment. She spotted people in the distance dotting the field. Their backs hunched, they were weeding.

"Hi," Toma said to the approaching migrant worker who was covered from head to toe in billowy white cotton: long-sleeved button-down, worn cotton pants, work boots, and a huge straw hat atop her head and sunglasses on her face. "Sorry to bother, I'm looking for Eva Angeles, she's the farm owner, the farm family, the Angeles' Farm. Farms. She operates combines, big combines." The woman stared at her. "I saw her truck over there." Toma motioned over her shoulder. *What the hell am I doing? Bad idea coming to her work!* "¿Si habla, hablando Ingless de Eva?" Toma tried again, but her pronunciation was embarrassingly bad. "Okay. Sorry. Hasta la vista." She turned around, feeling dumb for coming all this way just to say sorry. It had felt important that she say it in person.

"Toma," came a familiar-sounding voice.

Toma turned and looked the woman up and down.

"It's me." The woman took off her sunglasses.

"You look, *really* different." Toma did a double take. "Sorry. I was caught off guard."

Eva laughed. "I know the feeling," she said. "So, you found me."

Toma looked around. "Great directions."

"Thanks."

"Are you allowed to take a break? Can we talk?" Toma put her hands into her pockets.

Eva looked over her shoulder. "Carla!"

Toma's eyes widened, and she froze at the level of Eva's voice.

"¿Mande?" said a voice in the distance.

"¡Yo ya me voy!"

"¡Andele!" Carla yelled.

"Follow me."

Toma followed Eva toward her pickup and stood directly in front of the tailgate.

"Here, let's…" Eva motioned to the tailgate. "…the tailgate, here, let me…" Eva reached past Toma and brushed against her hip, causing her to jump. Eva released the hatch on the back of the truck and immediately went to the cooler. She rummaged inside, fished out a giant thermos of water, and took a drink. "Are you thirsty?" Eva asked. She pulled out another bottle of water and handed it to Toma. It dripped onto Toma's jeans, wetting them. "Sorry 'bout that," Eva said before hopping onto the tailgate.

"Thanks." Toma hoisted herself atop the tailgate and swung her legs back and forth in tandem with Eva's. The sun on her arms warmed her, as did sitting next to Eva.

"So." Eva pulled the handkerchief off her neck and wiped her brow.

"So."

"How are you?"

"Fine. Good," Toma said, suddenly tongue-tied. *Where to start and how to say it?* "And you?"

"Busy. We're making good time today. We'll have most of this section done before long. Then off to the next."

"That's good."

"Yeah, well the days are getting— Sorry, what did you want to talk to me about?"

"My turn to apologize and to give you a long-overdue thank you." Toma turned to Eva and saw a mix of confusion and curiosity upon her face.

"An overdue thank you?"

For holding me together on the flight home, thank you for your touch, for allowing me to bare my soul to you, for… "Um, the flight. That was really hard for me."

Eva's strong and sure hands gripped the water bottle. She met her eyes and earned a sweet smile.

"I'm glad I was there. You okay?"

"Life felt entirely too real suddenly. Piss-poor timing, I guess."

"I think it was good timing," Eva offered.

Toma warmed at Eva's eager spirit. "I also wanted to say sorry, I'm so sorry, for reaming you out when you got thrown off your horse and for brushing you off at the medical center. You caught me off guard too. I didn't think I'd ever see you again. I mean, I hoped that I would, if anything, to say thank you. What you experienced wasn't my anger, but more my utter embarrassment."

"You don't need to be embarrassed." Eva's voice was gentler than the warm breeze that kissed Toma's skin.

"I am though. I don't usually cry… I haven't cried like that in…" Toma didn't know how long it had been since she'd had a good cry, never probably. She wasn't a crier; she never showed anyone how she felt, preferring to keep feelings inside, where they belonged. "I don't remember the last time I lost it like that."

"Isn't it funny how we can go through life thinking we're on top of the world only to realize that we've had our zipper down the entire time?"

Toma laughed.

"Forgive me for being presumptuous, but I imagine that it had to do with your dad?"

"Mostly. Partly some other things too. A bad, *bad* breakup." She took a chug of water. "I'm sorry yet again. I don't mean to put all this on you."

"No need to keep apologizing, okay?" Eva patted Toma's leg. The feeling shot straight to Toma's groin. She sat up straighter and took another gulp of water. "You obviously need an ear and a friend. I am happy to be both if you want."

Toma nodded. "A friend would be, that'd be, I'd like that." Toma shifted her weight on the tailgate, feeling shy in the presence of the other woman, this stranger who already knew her intimately.

"How's he doing?" Eva asked.

"Better. Thanks for asking."

"I bet he's itching to come back, huh?"

"Yes, but I don't think it's going to happen."

"Really?"

"I think so," Toma whispered.

"Damn. That's the end of an era, isn't it?"

Toma nodded. "It's for the best; he's seventy."

"Is he really?"

"Yeah. It's nuts. He's nuts."

"So that's why you're here?" Eva sounded as if she finally understood one of life's great mysteries.

"I'm filling Dad's spot for the season."

"So we'll see a lot of you this summer?" Eva said, less as a question than a comment.

Toma nodded. "No doubt. I'm on for the circuit, doing the Snake River Stampede, Pendleton, Ellensburg, Las Vegas, and whatever exhibitions I can pick up in between."

"Word is that you used to be a stuntwoman?"

"There's word about me?" Toma wondered if Eva had been asking about her. The idea made her tingle with excitement. She took a drink of water.

"It's a small town, and you're quite the talk of it. A rough-and-tumble female bullfighter, a long-lost Rozene that nobody knew about."

"The rumors are true." *More like perpetually hidden, always-on-the-run, long-lost Rozene.*

"Your work is impressive." Eva's eyes lit up as she spoke, and she added her hands to help emphasize her points. "The way you move around the arena is so cool and so terrifying at the same time."

"Thanks." Toma grinned and looked at her own hands as she started peeling the damp label off the bottle of water. "You're quite the competitor as well."

"I am, aren't I?"

"Modest too."

Eva laughed. "How's this?" Eva quickly brushed her fingers against Toma's arm.

Another burst of tingling shot through Toma. She held out her arm and bent it back and forth. "As good as new. Are you okay? Did you get hurt when you fell? I'm sorry I never asked until now."

"I bruised my ass." Eva looked over her shoulder, and Toma followed her line of sight. "But it's okay; I got a lot of padding back there."

Toma laughed, then turned her attention to a dancing whirlwind making its way toward them until another gust of wind blew it off track.

Eva looked at her watch.

"Sorry, do you have to go?" Toma sat up straighter.

"I should, soon."

"There is something else I wanted to talk to you about." Toma cleared her throat.

"What is it?" Eva's expression turned serious.

"When you fell from Frida that night, did you get the impression that something was off?"

"Off?" Eva asked.

"Like, do you think it was more than just the shock of seeing me?"

"Why do you ask?" Eva shifted her body toward Toma.

"Midway through the calf roping competition, a bull came charging through the gates, gates that I checked before the show. He came raging through as if the locks were made of twigs, but the locks were fine. None of the wood splintered at all."

"That's weird, but not entirely. Are you okay?" Eva asked. Her eyes ran Toma's length before making eye contact and settling, as if seeing inside her.

That gave Toma goosebumps despite the heat of July at ten in the morning. "Benji got knocked on his backside. Got Maverick good; busted his knee."

"Damn. Poor guy," Eva groaned.

"No doubt, but, aside from that, we're okay," Toma said.

"What do you think's happening?"

"Hopefully, nothing."

"How can I help?"

"Can you tell me what you remember of the night you fell from Frida?"

Eva sighed and chewed the inside of her cheek, then took another swig of water.

"Did you hear or see anything out of the ordinary before you fell?"

"I heard whistling, but you guys use whistling as signals, right?"

Toma nodded.

They sat in silence for a few moments. "I'm sorry. I don't know. I'm not very much help."

"You're being really helpful."

"What are you going to do?"

"I don't know, but rule number one in my profession is to trust your gut. If something feels off, it's because something *is* off."

"What do you do in that case?"

"Take a break. Demand a gear check. Sit out if I have to."

"We can't quite do that."

"I know." Toma agreed.

"So now what?"

"Wait and see I guess, develop a theory."

"A theory?"

"Try to nab the guy. Catch him in the act." Toma rubbed her hands together.

"Catch him in the act?" Eva gasped. "You think someone's doing this on purpose?"

"I don't know. Maybe. Is that crazy? Am *I* crazy?"

"Well, no, but maybe let's slow our roll. For all we know a twisted kid thinks it's funny, wants to see some action."

"What do you mean a twisted kid?"

"A couple of years ago during the Snake River Stampede, a family brought a stallion, a wild thing that needed medical attention. They needed a place to keep him during the competition until they headed back to Montana or wherever they were from." Eva turned toward Toma and began talking with her hands. "This little girl, she must have been five or six, opened his stall door, just slid open the lock open." Eva demonstrated with her finger. "Didn't even open the gate. The horse figured it out, damn smart horse. He came charging through. Scared the bejesus out of everyone; took five of us to catch him and calm him down. Poor animal."

"How did you know it was the little girl?"

"Her mother said she had done it before."

"But to let a one-ton bull out, guide him to a chute, and pop the gate mid-competition without anyone noticing?" Toma countered.

"Yeah, that's farfetched." Eva hunched her shoulders.

Toma bit the inside of her cheek and sighed. "This could all be a coincidence, standard rodeo bullshit," she said with air quotes, "but it doesn't feel like it."

"What do your brothers think?"

"I haven't shared any of this with them. I wanted to hear what you had to say first."

Eva cocked her head. "You said you checked the gates?"

"We check them pre- and post-show. It's part of the job: check gates and check them again. Its standard protocol, even if you're not on gate crew."

"Maybe you can give the gate crew a little reminder tonight and see what happens? It's early in the competition; people are rusty. The arena isn't the best, not by a long shot, and it's old and long overdue for a major rehaul. Everything's probably all held together with duct tape."

Toma's eyes widened. She wasn't used to second-rate gear or equipment. She worked with the best of the best. She knew the rodeo wasn't a film set, but still. Eva's hand on her arm brought her back. "Not really duct tape, Toma."

"Thank goodness."

"Don't you'all have a meeting before each show? Maybe bring it up and see what they know."

"Good idea."

Eva shifted her body to face forward again. Toma immediately missed her attention. "Let me know what they say."

Toma hopped off the tailgate. "I will."

"When?"

"When what?"

"When will you let me know what they say?"

"How about one of these nights after the show? Maybe over drinks? A drink?" Toma offered as she remembered her fantasy part-two meeting with Eva.

"Did you just ask me on a date?" Eva kept her eyes focused on the water bottle in her hands.

Toma shook her head. The reality of her situation hit her square in the nose. She couldn't do this again. "I uh, wasn't...friend, friends, we're—just a drink to say thank you for the uh, plane and sorry about... we don't even have to—"

"Too early in our friendship to be joking?"

Toma exhaled and gripped her water bottle. The crumpling of plastic was a fitting sound to accompany the awkward moment they shared. Her cheeks burned. She resettled her hat, nodded, and walked away. She turned around. "Oh, I have one more question."

"Yep." Eva still had a little smirk on her lips.

"What was that thing you were saying…" Toma inspected the crumpled water bottle in her hands. "…with Polly before the feed cut out?"

"Hey girls, hang on to your dreams, learn from them, never stop riding, find a hero, and hang on to her." Eva punctuated her statement with her radiant smile.

"Beautiful." Toma wore a smile all the way to her truck. She was thinking back to how she had held on to Eva on that flight home. Toma had found her hero. She just hoped that she could return the favor one day and be there for Eva if ever she needed someone to hold on to.

CHAPTER SEVEN

EVA AND TOMA SAT IN the local townie bar-turned-happening-place thanks to the influx of people the Caldwell Night Rodeo brought from all over the northwest—cowboys and cowgirls all with the same goal, the finals in Las Vegas in a few short months.

"To flukes." Eva held her bottle in the air.

"I'll drink to that." Toma clanked her bottle against Eva's. These were their second beers of the evening.

Toma reported that a newbie on the stock team hadn't been checking the inner gates that connected the bullpen to the individual chutes. "Likely, that's how the bulls kept busting through. The poor kid looked on the verge of tears when Tito reamed him out."

"Isn't that's how you learn? Through a thorough scolding?" Eva gave her a smirk.

"Touché." Toma laughed but kept focused on her beer bottle.

"To thorough scoldings!" Eva held her bottle in the air once again, forcing eye contact, if only to see Toma's soft chestnut-colored eyes. "May those flukes be the last flukes at this competition and the competitions to come."

"No doubt." Toma clanked her bottle against Eva's.

"Salud," Eva said before she leaned against her side of the booth. Toma's smile magnified her already striking features: her high cheekbones, her bright eyes, the curl of her lips. It was such a distinct turnabout from the creature on the plane and from the woman who'd scolded her in the arena.

"To friends," Toma echoed. She peered at Eva over her beer bottle as she took a drink.

"I like the sound of that," Eva said.

Toma nodded. "Me too."

They continued to share shy glances and lingering stares. Eva took another drink, drinking way too fast. A group of drunk bulldoggers who were trying to carry a tune crashed into their table and caused Eva to fumble her bottle. It clanked on its side and foamed all over the table and right into Toma's lap.

"Hey!" Toma said as she stood. "Watch it!"

Eva shoved her napkins her way.

"*You* watch it, clown!" The guys kept moving, laughing and bumping around the bar like a set of pool balls after a break.

"Say that to me tomorrow in the arena when I'm saving your ass! *If* I save your ass," Toma yelled. She took the napkins and blotted her crotch area. Eva looked up at the tin ceiling tiles she'd never noticed. *Such a unique pattern up there, really vintage, really cool.* She settled her focus on Toma in time to see Toma run her fingers through her hair. Eva loved it when she ran her long, slender fingers through her thick, beautiful black hair and resettled her hat. "You owe her a beer!"

"It's fine."

Toma sat back down and jumped back up. "And the bench is wet, and so is my ass."

Eva laughed and scooted over. "Come here," she ordered.

Toma joined Eva on her side of the booth. "Thanks." She finished blotting her jeans.

"You okay?"

"Just a little wet."

Eva's alcohol-loosened demeanor turned her self-conscious, introspective, and shy. She sat up straighter, giving Toma as much space as she could, which wasn't much, since Eva's back was flush against the brick wall. Toma angled her body toward her and hung her arm across the back of the booth. It meant nothing. Toma had made it very clear that she needed a friend. Eva would respect her wishes and be the best friend that she could be. A friend, an honest-to-goodness friend, sounded great to Eva too. One would think that a former Miss Rodeo Idaho would have a ton of friends, and she did. But most of them were acquaintances. She couldn't think of anyone she could call to talk about real-life stuff, until now.

"Where were we?" Toma took a swig of her beer.

"I don't remember. Oh!" Eva said, "to my winning streak." While Eva didn't beat her record from her previous runs, neither did any of the other ladies. "Couple that with no more bulls or broncos on the loose, and I'd say it was a good night."

"A wonderful night." Toma held Eva's gaze. "Thanks to your intuition."

"And to yours."

"You still look worried," Toma stated.

Toma's closeness made Eva nervous. Eva sat straighter even though she wanted to lean into Toma. God, this was hopeless. She felt like a sex-deprived, horny teenager, which wasn't entirely true. She wasn't a teenager anymore. Everything else was one hundred percent true. "Showtime jitters, that's all."

"You get nervous after you run?"

"Sometimes." She picked up a bottle cap and spun it like a top. "So, how long are you here for?"

"However long my dad and the boys need me. At least through the end of the summer."

"And your stunt work?" Eva finally relaxed and angled her body toward Toma.

"Another thing I don't know. Working in film is a twenty-four-seven job, more so behind the scenes like I am, or was." Toma smiled, but it didn't seem to reach her eyes. "Between you and me, it's nice to be away from it temporarily. I've missed out on a lot. My dad, he's aged so much since I've seen him. It's good to spend time with my brothers and their kids. I've missed a lot. I wasn't the best sister."

"I'm sure you were the best sister you could be." Eva watched Toma peel the label off her bottle of beer and shake her head.

"I wasn't."

Eva wondered if Toma's guilt was part of the reason she fell apart on the plane. "I bet they love having you home."

"They love having me around to help cook for them and help run the ranch. There's so much work right now, but it's okay. I'm enjoying it and enjoying the rodeo. It's a different type of feeling, the life of a bullfighter; it's a wilder, more unpredictable thrill than the precision stunt work that I'm used to."

"But you're going to miss it."

"No doubt." Toma dropped her eyes. "It's more the comradery, the lifestyle. The girls I worked with were like sisters to me. As you can imagine, coming from a family of dudes I'm experiencing a little bit of a shift in my family dynamic and I never thought I'd live in Idaho again, of all places. Not sure how long I'll last before going insane. Sorry, no offense."

"None taken. I feel like I'm going crazy sometimes too. I've managed to figure a few things out," Eva assured her.

"Then I definitely need you close at all times." Toma scratched the back of her neck. "How do you do it?"

"The key is to travel. A lot. Seattle isn't that far away, as you know, and neither is Portland or Canada, for that matter. There's a ton of stuff outdoors, too, in the mountains. Hiking, camping, white water rafting, skiing—that is, if you like that sort of stuff." Eva grew excited at the thought of enjoying those activities with Toma, if Toma stuck around long enough. Eva hoped that she would. She liked her. Toma was easy to talk to, though Eva felt as though she understood Toma without using spoken words.

"I love the outdoors," Toma said.

"Me too."

"I figured."

"Can I ask you a personal question?" Eva asked.

"Ask away."

"Are you married?" Eva eyed the band of gold on the ring finger of Toma's left hand.

Toma held her hand in front of her own face. "This was my mother's."

Eva knew that Red Rozene was a widower, but that was the extent of what she knew.

"She died when I was five."

"I'm sorry." Eva couldn't imagine what that was like. Her mother was always there and her aunts, her two sisters, her grandmother, countless cousins, second cousins, cousins of cousins, always there, even when she didn't want them around.

Toma twisted the thin gold band between her fingers and looked beyond Eva as if remembering something.

"What's your favorite memory of her?" Eva asked.

"Riding horses together and when she'd sing to me. She used to sing this song when she'd help me get up in the morning."

"Sing it to me."

"God. No. I couldn't." Toma looked at the ring on her finger and spun it around and around.

"Please?"

"I only know like one verse."

"Sing it."

"Okay." Toma laughed and cleared her throat and leaned in. *"This is the way we wash our face, wash and scrub, rinse and clean, don't forget to brush your teeth, always remember to comb your hair, every single day."* She ended with a shy smile.

Eva clapped. "I love it. Very sweet."

"The tune or my operatic voice?"

"Both."

"What about you?"

"I can't sing."

"No, are you seeing anyone?"

Eva quit fiddling with her bottle cap. She shook her head.

"I find that hard to believe."

"I'll take that as a compliment." Eva felt her face flush.

"It was."

"If you do decide to stick around these parts, it won't take you long to realize there's kind of slim pickings." *Until now.* "I had a girlfriend, but she moved to New Mexico, inherited some land. I wasn't ready to drop my life here to go with her."

"Do you regret it?" Toma asked.

"Once she made me choose, I knew it was over."

"That's a shitty position to put someone in."

"Tell me about it."

"And you don't date?"

"I have a hard time breaking away, what with everything going on with the farm and training, especially once the circuit starts. I don't have much time for myself. I also don't get out much, so there's that." Eva laughed at herself.

"Makes dating pretty much nonexistent, huh?"

"Exactly." Eva took a drink. "You said that you were in a relationship before coming here. What happened?"

"She cheated on me."

"I'm sorry." Eva wondered what type of person would cheat on Toma. Then again, there were always two sides to the coin. Eva remained silent. Toma pursed her lips and looked at her beer bottle as though she had more to say; maybe she was building up the courage to voice the words.

"When I look back, there were signs; they were so obvious. And worse, all of our friends knew, and no one said anything. I'm beyond embarrassed. I'm more hurt that no one said anything. Then again, I imagine they were put in a situation they didn't want to be in, didn't want to be the bearer of bad news, I guess. Hell, I don't know." Toma groaned.

"I'm so sorry, Toma." Eva thought about asking her if she had loved the woman, but didn't. She knew that the pain hurt regardless. Toma's reaction when Eva had asked her if tonight was a date made more sense now. Toma was hurting and protecting herself.

Toma pursed her lips and shook her head. "It's over now. It's okay. I'm okay."

The bricks of Toma's wall began to stack again. Eva had seen a glimpse when she had seen Toma around her brothers. Eva nodded and patted Toma's knee. "I'm dying to ask…"

"Ask away."

"What films were you in?"

"I did a ton of horse work in *The Hobbit*."

Eva gawked.

"I take it you saw that one about fifty times too?"

"More like a hundred and fifty thousand times! I love the books and the movies. Were you in *Lord of the Rings* too?"

"A little before my time. But I know a lot of people that were in them."

"What else were you in?"

"The most recent was *Vikings* and then *Outlander* and then *Wonder Woman*."

"No way!" Eva swooned. "Oh, my God, that's so awesome." She settled her gaze on Toma's waist. "That explains the belt buckle."

"I was one of, like, seven stunt doubles for Gal."

"No way! Is she cool?"

"Very. But I worked more with Robin. She wanted to do her own riding, so I was on her training team."

"Robin as in Robin Wright."

"The one and only."

"Is she cool?"

"Very. She's also an interesting person when you get to know her. She's pretty down-to-earth as far as famous people go."

"Oh, my God! You're, I can't believe, wow. You are quite an interesting person." Eva forced herself to settle down, realizing that she might be making Toma uncomfortable.

Toma dropped her eyes. "Thank you, Eva. I think you are too."

"The wild and crazy life of a cowgirl." Eva gave a self-deprecating laugh.

"I mean it, you're a great competitor and two-time world champion? Do you ever lose?"

Eva laughed. "I've done my fair share of losing."

"Seriously, you're a fantastic horse handler. No doubt, if I had you on my stunt team, with your abilities and nerve, we'd do every scene in one take, and the world would be a better place," Toma said in a whimsical tone.

"Thanks." Eva took a drink to hide her blush. "You ain't seen nothing yet. You should see my hay bale tossing technique."

"There's a technique for that?"

"It's all in the legs." Eva slapped her thigh.

"I find it all…" Toma waved her finger in front of Eva. "…the entire package fascinating. Now can I ask a question?"

"Shoot."

Toma leaned over and whispered, "How many crowns *do* you have?"

Eva roared. "I've lost count. I can show them to you if you're truly interested. Maybe let you wear one." Eva chided herself for taking their conversation into flirting territory. It felt good, but scary and too close to the line they'd drawn earlier.

"Tito said you stay pretty busy this time of the year?"

Eva rolled her eyes. "I have my hands in way too many pies at the moment." Sensing Toma's eyes on her fiddling hands, she blushed at her choice of words.

"What do you do for fun?"

"I still work with the Miss Rodeo Idaho Association. It pulls me all over the place: charity breakfasts, galas, organizing community events, speaking to kids at schools. I mentor a couple of up-and-coming barrel racers, which is fun and inspiring, but a lot of work. I used to train them at your dad's."

"You did?"

Eva nodded. "Until it closed."

"It got to be too much for him and the boys."

"I get it. I imagine it's a lot of work maintaining a training center."

"It was." Toma shifted in her seat. "Where do you train them now?"

"Weiser, it's a pain in the ass drive but it's the closest one that meets my needs."

"You certainly manage your twenty-four hours quite well." Toma smiled. "But you didn't answer my question. What do you do for fun?"

"My favorite thing is tending to my mustangs."

"Your mustangs?"

"Technically they belong to the BLM, but the BLM relies on volunteers to help and I volunteer with the HMA."

Toma knit her eyebrows.

"Sorry, too many acronyms. The Bureau of Land Management has HMAs, Herd Management Associations. Basically, a group of us make sure the wild horses get care when they need it, vaccinate them, put out salt blocks, plant native plants so they have enough to eat, ensure people are respectful of the lands and the herds. Four-wheelers are the bane of my existence."

"Wait, back up. Do you do the vaccinations yourself?"

"I do. Another volunteer, Rosie, she's my vet, trained me on how to do it. She's great. She's on my racing team. Everyone that tends to this herd is beyond passionate. I've been saving all my winnings, *all* my money, to start a nonprofit. I want to build a center for us to work out of, complete with a place for me to live, an educational center, classes, the works."

"That sounds like a beautiful dream."

"It's all I've ever wanted to do. I just need the money, which I almost have. Just one more huge win, and then I plan to retire from this crazy lifestyle and focus entirely on that."

"You'd give everything up?"

"I love it, but it's time for a new chapter."

"Good for you for knowing when it's time."

"It's time," Eva confirmed.

"How often do you get out to your horses?"

"Whenever possible. We're heading out soon. Want to ride along? It's an overnight kind of thing, and you'll need a horse and a tent. If you want to come, you can. Sometime. Whenever." Eva held her breath.

"I would love to, really would love to. I miss my horse from the last show I worked on. Cindy, a battle-ax, seventeen hands. I trained her myself; she was so wild when I met her and now she's the sweetest little lady."

"There are plenty of wild mustangs waiting for you to love them." Eva was happy that she had planted the seed for another outing with Toma.

"When are you going?"

"After Caldwell Night, that week before the Snake River Stampede." Eva leaned back against her seat to study Toma aglow in excitement about the trip.

"Let me double-check with Tito to make sure Dad has coverage. He's starting physical therapy soon; they might need help."

"Of course. Cool and cheers." Eva lifted her bottle of beer. She was glad that the mystery of the loose bulls was solved so she could focus her complete attention on cultivating her budding friendship with Toma.

*   *   *

IT WAS FRIDAY AND TECHNICALLY Eva's day off from farming. However, instead of relaxing, she picked up a shift at Aleida's, covering for her mom and most of their staff, who were all-hands-on-deck catering the funeral. She hoped that Toma might text her, might want to talk, but Eva had heard nothing from her since they'd had drinks. Eva's phone chirped she felt a rush of adrenaline, only to be disappointed when it wasn't Toma. Eva could text Toma, but she didn't, thinking that maybe Toma needed space—room to breathe, decompress, and be there for her family.

Finally, the restaurant was manageable again. With only three active tables, their part-time waitress and full-time student, Leticia, easily managed the floor on her own, giving Eva time to catch up in the kitchen and run another flat of silverware to her grandmother, who was wrapping them in paper napkins at her favorite bar stool.

"Your head is filled with elote, mija."

"¿Perdón?"

"Look to what you brought for me," her grandmother Aleida said.

Eva inspected the flat of silverware, the flat of *dirty* silverware. "Dios mío."

"Do you want to me to use my spit to clean them?" Her grandma mock-spit on the tray. "What would the goberment say about that?" Her grandmother referred to public health as simply "the goberment." She referred to every public entity, the phone company, anyone in a uniform, as "the goberment."

"I'm sure they'd try to recruit you."

"Siéntate, mjia. ¿Que paso?"

"I'm tired."

"You lie to your abelita?" Aleida clutched imaginary pearls around her neck.

"I got a lot on my plate."

"Stop with the excuses in a can." Her grandmother's broken English and misuse of American idioms always made Eva chuckle.

"You mean canned excuses?"

"You doubt your grandmother?"

"Okay, fine, you caught me."

"Care to indulge a viejita?"

"No."

"Then quit crying."

"I'm not crying."

"Mira, te voy a dar algo para que llores de verdad."

"Your threats don't work on me anymore." Eva wagged her finger in front of her grandmother's face.

"If I was younger..." Her grandmother punctuated her statement with a shaking of her fist.

If I was younger was her grandmother's way of saying many different things, such as she'd beat her ass, if only she could get to her feet more easily.

"Siéntate, Reina."

Eva followed orders, sat on the barstool next to her grandmother, and stared at the dirty silverware.

"¿Que paso?"

"Just a new friend I'm thinking about."

"From the rodeo?"

"Yep. She's just a friend."

"If she was just a friend, you wouldn't keep insisting that she was *solo un amiga*."

Eva rolled her eyes. Her grandmother was right, but she wasn't about to admit that to her. She had been thinking about Toma entirely too much and not in a healthy sort of way, more like a head over heels, infatuation, going to get hurt sort of way. She didn't want to be friends with Toma; she wanted to be more than that, but it was entirely one-sided. Toma was a self-proclaimed woman at a crossroads. *Two roads diverged in a yellow wood, and, sorry, she could not travel both.* Though maybe, with the right signals, Toma could wander with Eva on an entirely new path, maybe take a tumble in the lush forest. Eva would ensure that it would make all the difference.

A chiming bell signaled that they had a new customer. Eva turned to see a tall, dark, and handsome hunk of a woman. The sound of clattering broke her trance. Toma had bumped their potted lemon tree, causing it to tip before she caught the thing.

"Sorry." Toma looked up and froze upon seeing Eva.

"My, my. This must be your nueva amiguita, si?" her grandmother said, entirely too loudly.

Eva shook her head and, with a menu in hand, she made her approach. "Hi. You okay?"

"You're asking the limones, right?" Aleida said from her spot on the stool and then cackled.

"Grandma." Eva shook her head and held her gaze on her grandmother before dragging her eyes to Toma, not quite able to meet her eyes.

Toma chose to focus on the potted plant and then the menu that Eva shuffled between her hands. "What are you doing here?" Toma asked. They finally made eye contact.

"I work here."

"What don't you do?"

"She doesn't do the dishes very well," her grandma admitted.

Eva shot her grandma a look. "Toma, this is my grandmother, Aleida."

"Aleida like Aleida's de Mexico?"

"Oh, this one is smart. Are you married? Mi Evita is muy single."

"¡Abuela!" Eva closed her eyes and took a deep breath. "Please excuse my grandmother; she knows not what she does."

Toma raised an eyebrow and alternated a glance between Eva and her grandmother. "Nice to meet you."

"Table for two?" Aleida asked and batted her eyelashes.

"Grandma," Eva warned.

"Takeout."

"Have a seat at the bar," Eva interjected before her grandmother could make another wisecrack. "Here's the menu. Want a coke or water or beer or something?"

"Sure, to the beer. So, you work here?" Toma asked again, then furrowed her eyebrows. Her cheeks flushed as if she realized that she had just asked Eva the same question twice.

"Sometimes, when she's not thinking about her new friend from the rodeo."

"Don't listen to this old lady; she's going senile." Eva raised her finger to her own temple and twirled it against her head as if indicating her grandmother was losing it. "So, how'd you hear about us?"

"I drove past the other day when I came to talk to you."

"Stalker much?" Aleida cackled.

"¡Abuelita, en serio!"

"I, uh, thought I'd give it a try."

"She's *so* glad you did." Aleida nudged Toma on the arm. "She was just telling me about you."

"True," Eva said, giving up and so wanting to run and hide.

"She was also saying that she was ever so lonely."

"Abuelita! Silencio antes de decirle a Mamá que estás tomando sorbos de tequila."

"You wouldn't."

"I so would."

At that, her grandmother gave her a look and made a show of getting up. Eva kissed her on the head before her grandma took the tray of dirty silverware to the back.

"She's hilarious," Toma said with a laugh.

"Oh yeah, she's a regular comedian."

"No doubt. What did you threaten her with?"

"I told her that I'd tell my mom that she's the one who's been swiping swigs of the primo tequila." Eva got a hearty laugh from Toma.

"I love the way it feels in here."

"Thanks." Eva watched Toma take in the place as everyone did their first time inside. The restaurant was a sensory overload: bright colors, photos of Mexican street vendors, close-ups of chili peppers, statues of the Virgin Mary, crucifixes galore.

"Are those wrestlers?" Toma pointed at the display of ironwork that hung on the wall and depicted masked Mexican wrestlers in various positions.

"My dad had those made. He's obsessed with lucha libre."

"It's cool." Toma turned her gaze back to Eva. The way Toma looked at her made her feel as if she was a work of art too. Eva cleared her throat. She popped the bottle cap off a beer and set the cold glass before Toma.

"Thanks." Toma lifted the beer and gave her a nod. "So, what do you recommend?" Toma opened the menu.

"We're known for our mole."

Toma flipped the menu over. "There are like seven different kinds. Which do you like?"

"The chocolate is my grandmother's grandmother's recipe, or so she says."

"I'll take that, please. I need to feed my dad and Tito too. What do you suggest?"

"Your brother likes three beef tacos—"

"I'll take that—"

"And two chicken tacos and a tostada. Your dad usually gets the fajitas."

"All of that sounds perfect." Toma closed the menu. "To go, please."

"I'll get right on it."

"Thank you."

Eva retreated to the kitchen and watched her grandmother resume her seat at the bar with a tray of clean silverware. She picked up a conversation with Toma. Eva hoped the side-eye glare of warning she gave her grandmother as she passed by would help keep her in check.

CHAPTER EIGHT

"Hey," Tito waltzed into their family's dressing room in the repurposed barn that was a mix of storage, media rooms, and a café that featured burnt coffee, soft pretzels, and bright yellow popcorn. Since there were so many of them, the Rozene's room was large, private, and quiet compared to the rest of the building. "I saw Polly on the way in; she wants to interview you."

"Interview who?" Toma asked as she pulled her pads and clothing out of her bag and stripped from her street clothes, starting with her boots. She was no stranger to undressing in front of people; growing up with five brothers and working in show business ensured it.

"You, silly." He plopped his bag of gear next to hers and joined her in getting ready.

"About what?"

"What the heck do you think. You're a female bullfighter in a world of rodeo queens was how she put it."

"You're such a camera whore," Benji said, eliciting an onslaught of torments and more teasing from the brood.

Toma pulled the Velcro of her chest padding several times to drown out the mocking of her five brothers. "I won't do it." She secured the wrap around herself, probably too tightly.

"Yes, you will," Tito said in a singsong voice.

"No, I won't," she sang back.

"You will break Dad's heart." Toma shot him a look. "You have to anyway. New rules. You have to participate in any and all interview requests," he said, "didn't you read the fine print when you signed the contract? You also have to let them use your likeness however they see fit." He slapped her shoulder. "Same section as having to go to Valley Medical when Nurse Beth says so."

"What the hell am I going to talk about?"

"Talk about Gal Gadot," her brother Danny interjected. "I can assure you that everyone will be interested in that."

"Shuddup, Danny." She didn't want to talk to Polly but it seemed she had no choice. She heard knocking. "What now?" she muttered. Eva had told Toma that Polly was the only Latina reporter in the area, and was probably the only Latina reporter in the entire state. Polly deserved more respect than Toma was giving her but she hated, *hated* talking on camera.

"Knock-knock. Hello." Polly Gonzalez flitted into their dressing room. "Am I interrupting?"

"Kind of," Toma said, avoiding eye contact.

"Of course not," Tito chimed in. "We were just talking about you. Weren't we, Toma? Weren't we?"

"Kind of." Toma did the courteous thing and shook Polly's hand. "I'm Toma," she said in a monotone, hoping to come across as boring so that Polly might reconsider.

"A pleasure to finally meet you." Polly looked Toma up and down as if inspecting potential goods for sale.

Polly was about Toma's height, with long hair; beautiful brown tresses framed her face, not a single strand out of place. She had an adorable dimple in her chin. Polly's entire face lit up when she smiled, revealing bright white teeth. The reporter wore snip toe boots, brand-new-looking blue jeans, and a button-up top with a hint of fringe on her sleeves.

"Can we get this over with?" Toma asked. "We've got like forty-five minutes before showtime."

"I don't want to interview you now." Polly's melodious laugher filled the room. "I was thinking more we could do it in two parts."

Two parts! Toma wanted to shout. "Why?" she blurted.

"I was thinking I could get you during a break in the show, fresh off one of those thrilling saves maybe, capture some of that high, and then later, when you are out of these baggy clothes, we can talk woman to woman, professional to professional, back at the studio. Build you up a little before the next competition."

"Build me up? For what? For how long?" Toma's chest wrap suddenly felt too tight.

"For however long it takes." Polly stilled Toma's fidgeting with a brief touch to her arm. "I won't waste your time. Besides, people want to know you."

"Why?"

"Female bullfighter." Polly walked around the room. "Gutsier than the lot of these boys." Polly turned toward them. "No offense."

"None taken," Tito said.

"It's true," the rest said in unison.

"Besides, you got a lot of people talking, especially after last night's little show."

Toma and her brothers had debuted a risky, look-no-look, aversion technique involving two barrels and several backflips.

"The crowd loved it they loved you."

"I was something, wasn't I?" Toma grinned and slapped Tito on the arm.

"Ouch."

"You big baby."

"Pierson Price spent half his aftershow talking about it and the new era of bullfighting, he called it."

"Is that right?" Toma swatted Tito's hand away.

"He spent the other half asking his listeners if women had a place in such a masculine sport. His callers didn't seem to think so."

Toma's eyes narrowed, and she turned her full attention to Polly. "Is that right?"

"Didn't think women had the stamina to last."

"When is good for you?" Toma asked.

*　*　*

PIERSON PRICE HAD THE CROWD roaring. Scratch that. Eva was the real reason everyone was on their feet. Every time Toma watched her, observed her skills on her horse, her respect for the woman grew stronger. Eva communicated with her horse with her entire body, no words needed. Toma wondered what her body and Eva's would say to each other if they ever got close enough. Toma shoved the thoughts away. She needed Eva's friendship, not her body. But it was not as if Eva wasn't into her too. She most certainly was. Eva's smoldering gazes had confirmed it on several occasions. But Toma couldn't get involved, not now, when nothing was certain and everything was up in the air. She knew that she carried serious baggage; seriously oversized, won't fit above or below the seat, needs special airline handling baggage.

"Not even close, folks. Look at her time on the Albertsons Jumbotron. Wowza! She came a-bustin' into the ro-de-o as the top money earner and leaves that way too. She'd adding another seven thousand dollars to, get this, folks, a total year-to-date purse of one hundred and ninety thousand ducats. Not too shabby. A whole bunch of other ladies from across the West will get another opportunity to catch up to her at the Snake River Stampede, which kicks off in seven days. You'll find us all there, and me, Pierson Price, the voice of the cowboy, on my aftershow, Rodeo Radio on Sirius 990. Can I get a whoop and maybe a holler for our cowboys and cowgals that show up every night and put their hearts into it?"

Toma joined the crowd and applauded the fifteen barrel racers who trotted onto the scene. She couldn't help but smile at the queens cantering around the arena doing their one-handed waves to all their fans while balancing their bouquets of flowers. The top money earners sported their brand-new belt buckles and wore sashes over their shoulders. They were a tour de force of fringe and glitter that shimmered under the bright lights of the stadium.

Toma smiled because she felt as though she belonged and fit in with her brothers. There was no place she'd rather be—well, maybe one other place; maybe meeting Eva's wild horses on the range.

Eva did another victory lap around the arena and waved her Stetson in the air and gave Toma a wink as she galloped past her. That wink made Toma's stomach do funny things, as if she were going for a ride in a barrel and it wasn't because a one-ton bull had sent her for a spin.

Toma shifted in her saddle with a big stupid grin on her face. "What?" she said to her brother.

"I didn't say a word."

"Shuddup." She trotted to Eva and joined her on her way out of the arena. "That sash looks great on you. Nice run tonight. Congrats."

"Thanks! You're looking pretty great yourself." Eva tossed Toma her flowers.

"You like my baggy clothes?" Toma pressed her nose into the flowers and inhaled deeply.

"Oh yeah. God, and that one thing you did, with that crazy bull, with the lasso, so very Wonder Woman, by the way! That was so cool and so frightening. What were you thinking?" There was no judgment in Eva's tone. Her eyes were wide; she was high on her ride.

Toma's nerves frayed knowing that Eva had been watching her.

"That's one of my signature moves." Toma dismounted at the same time Eva climbed off Frida.

"From the looks of it, you have several signature moves." Eva wiggled her eyebrows. Eva handed her reins to an arena hand in exchange for another horse, whom Toma learned was named Vivian. Vivian carried what looked like a change of clothing for Eva over her rump: silver chaps and a matching leather jacket with fringe. "What are you doing out here?" Eva asked.

"Interview." Toma worked to avoid homing in on Eva's stripping. Granted, she was only swapping out chaps, removing her sponsor vest, and changing into a new button-up shirt. Toma watched Eva mount her horse, settle in and adjust her position in the saddle of her new mount. Toma took a deep breath through her nose and closed her eyes.

"With Polly?"

"In, like, five minutes." Toma kept looking over her shoulder.

Eva followed her gaze. Her brothers were waving and blowing loud kisses at her from atop their horses in the arena. "Are you nervous?"

"A little."

"Says the woman who moments ago jumped off a horse right into the path of a raging bull."

"Totally different."

"You'll be fine." Eva joined the other ladies lining up for their next act.

Polly arrived with her cameraman in tow. He handed Toma a headset. Toma tried to put it on. "Gah…" She lifted her hat with one hand, then settled the earpiece. Pierson's voice came in a little too loud and clear.

"Folks, now would be a great time to get an ice-cold brew. We're in for a special treat. Your reigning Miss Rodeo Idaho and your formers from years gone by have a special performance for all of you lucky people. Sit back while we reset the arena. You're gonna wanna get settled, 'cause these little ladies put on a show, and then it's everybody's favorite, the bareback competition. I'm sure those boys, tough as all get out, won't mind a bit more time to loosen up b'fore getting all shook to heck." The crowd laughed with him.

"You ready?" Polly asked. She placed her hands on Toma's shoulders and moved Toma so she stood in front of the vinyl Albertsons banner that hung on a gate.

"Folks, we got something fun planned for you. KIBO TV's Polly Gonzalez is about to interview one of our own, Toma Rozene, the new kid on the block. She's joined her family in her father's absence this summer, and, while she is a thrill to watch, we sure do miss Red, don't we folks?" The crowd clapped and cheered. "I know he's listening tonight; he'd never miss a show. You done good, Red, your kids are doing real, real good. You should be proud, and I know that you are. Feel better and come back soon, ya hear!" Pierson had the crowd going wild at that tribute. "Take a look at the Albertsons Jumbotron, and let's learn a little bit more about Toma Rozene."

The cameraman held up three fingers and then two and then he pointed at them for one—and showtime. A bright light nearly blinded her.

"Toma Rozene, bullfighter, looks like you are having a lot of fun out there," Polly said.

"I am." Toma looked beyond Polly to see Eva and the other women on their horses getting into position for their act.

"I understand that you used to work in movies as a stuntwoman. What was that like?"

"It doesn't compare."

"How so?"

"Um, there's not as much prep time before each show, each rodeo show, that is." Toma scratched the back of her neck.

Polly nodded her head, which encouraged Toma to keep talking.

"And here, I mean at the rodeo, we practice, but when you're filming, you get shot after shot to perfect it, to nail it, and there are pads and harnesses everywhere, and sometimes it's just intense physical scenes over and over, which, no doubt, isn't anywhere close to working with bulls or wild broncos."

"What's running through your mind when you're in the arena with a bull running after you?"

"A lot of things, uh, stuff."

"Like?" Polly nodded.

"You got a one-ton bull running after you, and one wrong move could mean serious injury not only to yourself but to someone else, which is way more stressful than doing stunt work. But, like stunt work, it's all about that team, and I got the best team on the planet. Shout out to my brothers; my brother Tito is single, by the way, and he is loaded, ladies." Toma heard the crowd's laughter through the headset.

"What's your favorite part about the rodeo thus far?"

"No doubt it has to be the barrel—"

"Holy smokes, folks!" Toma heard Price yell through her headset. "Take a look at that! We got a bronco loose, two broncos running amok, and they're raising heck. Watch out, girls!" Toma ripped off her headset and spotted a bucking bronco kicking up dirt and hooves and heading toward the Miss Rodeo Idaho women, who were doing their best to keep their horses from freaking out.

The kid they'd reamed out earlier in the week ran onto the scene wide-eyed and out of breath.

"What happened?" Toma asked.

"I checked the locks." He pointed to the locks. "Just plain busted."

"Another fucking fluke," Toma muttered. She spotted Tito heading toward her on his horse at full speed.

Pierson's play-by-play included her grabbing onto the back of Tito's horse, hoisting herself atop it, then leaping onto one of the bucking broncos and riding him away.

"No way," Price shouted. "This woman is absolutely fearless, folks. Holy heck."

CHAPTER NINE

Eva's ears perked up when she heard Pierson's raised voice and the collective groan of the audience filter through the radio. "Let's send our thoughts and our prayers to that brave-as-heck barrel man. That was that a hard hit. Haven't seen a barrel split open like that in a long time, folks, dang it."

Eva raced from the stable, where she was listening to the whole thing unfold. She hoped the injured barrel man wasn't Toma.

"What happened?" she asked in a breathless burst upon entering the nurse's station. Relieved when she met Toma standing beside Tito, who was on the examination table, she said, "Oh, geez, Tito." A rag was doing nothing to sop up the blood that spilled from his nose. Nurse Beth was going through concussion protocol. Toma bit her nails; her forehead was knitted.

"I'm fine," Tito mumbled. "Clean me up and let me get back there."

"Like hell," Beth said.

"What happened?" Eva asked.

Toma grabbed Eva's arm, and they went around the corner and waited for a couple of cowboys to pass before she started talking. "Tito's going for a ride in a barrel, nothing crazy, and then boom, the barrel splits, he's flat on his back, and a bull takes him out."

Eva groaned and rubbed her forehead. "Jesus."

"There is no reason that barrel should have split like it did." She lifted her Stetson and scratched her head. "The thing cracked in half. They are made of rubber." Toma leaned against the side of the building and slapped her hand against it. She hushed her voice at the concerned looks of people passing by. "Something's definitely wrong." Toma balled her fist and beat it against the wall.

Eva didn't know what to say. She ran her eyes up Toma's arm and saw a rip in her sleeve and red blood. Eva remembered when Frida was a baby, wild and jumpy at the slightest agitation, but easily subdued through a gentle touch and soft-spoken words. "What happened to you, huh?" Eva touched the blood-soaked fabric on Toma's shoulder and her hand lingered. Toma tensed when Eva touched her. "Sorry." She jerked her hand away. So much for taming the agitated woman.

Toma inspected the injury. "Damn it." She groaned.

"Let me take a look at that."

"I should get back to Tito, if anything to ensure he doesn't run back out there."

"He's in good hands right now. Let me take care of you before Nurse Beth insists you and Tito both get an order to visit the hospital."

Toma looked at her shoulder, then at Eva before conceding. She followed Eva to her area, bypassing several other barrel racing contestants, who gave Eva their congratulations and wished her good luck at future competitions. Finally, they were alone.

"Sit," Eva said. "Take your shirt off."

Toma unfastened her buttons, undoing only two of them before rubbing her forehead. "This is jacked." She slammed her body against the stable, startling Frida. "Sorry, girl." Toma turned around and gave Frida a pat on the muzzle. "I just noticed." Toma turned toward Eva. "Frida's totally got a unibrow, her markings. She's beautiful."

Eva watched Toma scratch her horse under the chin and kiss her muzzle. *Lucky beast.* "Isn't it the cutest thing?" Eva asked.

"No doubt. All of your horses are beautiful." Toma made her rounds, introducing herself to Eva's three horses.

"Thank you. I love them. Sit back down and quit moving. Be right back." Eva went to her truck, pulled her duffel from the back seat, and then fished her first aid kit from her glove box. "We're not quite the same size." Toma's torso was longer, her breasts smaller. *Perfect, beautiful handfuls...* "I'm sure the sleeves will be too short; you can roll them." She sat next to Toma and finished unbuttoning her shirt for her, in silence and with intermittent glances exchanged between them. "The padding," Eva said, in barely a whisper. "I don't want to get it all wet when I clean your arm." The sound of the Velcro filled the silence. "Hold this, please." Eva handed Toma the zipped-open first aid kit and stole a glance at Toma's washboard stomach through her sweat-soaked, thin white T-shirt. "Can you please lean in?" she asked and straddled the bench. Toma leaned toward her. Eva caught her scent: horse, cedar, and sweat.

"Looks worse than it is." Toma winced.

"Yeah, it's not that bad after all." Eva smiled, took Toma's arm into her hand, and poured water over it. Rust-colored water dripped into the straw on the floor. "This will hurt." Eva poured hydrogen peroxide on the wound.

Toma winced and sucked air between her teeth.

"Almost done," Eva whispered and glossed ointment on a gauze pad, pressed it against Toma's bicep, and held on to feel her hard muscle. She secured the pad with a bandage, and, though it was probably fine, Eva held on a little longer, just to be certain. "All set."

Toma ran her hand over Eva's handiwork. "Where's my lollipop?"

"I only have oats. You'll have to share with the girls."

"On second thought."

"You going to make it?"

"Yes. No. I don't know. The moment I arrive, shit starts going south for us and my dad. He's going to freak, and it's going to be my fault. It's always my fault, and this is the last thing he needs, the absolute last thing anyone needs right now. If we lose this contract, it will kill Dad, not to mention cause a major dent in his income. There's no more income from the training center, yet Dad is still paying the insurance. I didn't realize how bad it had gotten for him."

"Hey, slow down. This isn't your fault. This arena is shit, okay. I know it. I grew up here; it's always been like this. There's a reason why a lot of competitors, especially the big earners, don't give the Caldwell Night Rodeo a second thought. It's a shit arena. They don't want to risk it."

"Why are you here? Why are you risking your chance at Las Vegas, if it's so bad?"

Eva looked around. "This is my hometown, and if I pull out, others will pull out, and there won't be a Caldwell Night Rodeo anymore. I've seen it happen in other places."

"And, in the meantime, everyone's fine and dandy that there's the possibility of serious injury? Because it's me and my brothers, the gate guys, we're the ones..." Toma shut her eyes and rubbed her forehead.

"Your brothers, your dad, the gate crew, everyone knows the risk here and they come anyway and do the best they can. Every arena is different; that's the rodeo."

"I've been away from it for so long, I guess I forgot how it was..." Just when Eva thought she'd successfully calmed Toma, out came another burst of flame. "But that doesn't mean I can't take this to the rodeo association and demand changes. This arena is a work hazard." Toma popped up, almost spilling Eva on the other side of the bench.

"Toma!"

"What?" She spun around.

"You can't go out there like that?"

"Why?"

Eva held out her shirt.

"Oh." Toma looked at herself. She ran her hands over her stomach, then walked back. Eva held the shirt open. Toma fastened her own buttons this time.

"Hold up." The sexist comments that Eva had heard from time to time and that had increased the moment Toma entered the scene popped into her mind. "You can't just march out there and demand change from the association."

"Watch me." Toma turned around. She didn't get far. Eva held Toma's wrist tightly and pulled her back in a single motion.

"Listen to me. Let's take a deep breath, think about this. You're going to have a big fat target on your back, more than you already do. Rodeo is an old-school game, Toma. Some of these guys are complete assholes, sexist, homophobic, racist, you name it. I'm all for making change and using my voice for good and, trust me, I've tried and I've lost this particular battle more than once…" Eva placed both her hands on Toma's shoulders and pushed her gently back to the bench. "I'm sorry that Tito got hurt. I'm sorry that you got hurt."

"I don't want anyone else to get hurt or to constantly be thinking that something terrible is going to happen. We already have things to worry about, people's lives that we're responsible for, our own lives. I'd hate to see you hurt. There are so many ways you could get hurt, and your prize money, for your horses—"

Eva took Toma's hands into her own. "My record, the prize money, are the least of my concerns. Our safety, your safety, is the most important thing to me too. Got it? We watch each other's backs, okay, that's the rodeo through and through. And you know what?" Eva studied Toma's chestnut-colored eyes. They were kind, full of fire, compassionate. "This is the last night here, then off to the Snake River Stampede, which is, like, the primo arena in the entire state."

Toma squeezed Eva's hands. "Thank you."

"What are friends for, huh?"

Toma nodded in agreement.

"You gonna make it?"

Toma nodded that she would.

"Hey, I gotta ask," Eva said before letting go. "Before you got cut off, Polly asked you what your favorite part of the competition was thus far. What was it?"

"Oh, I liked a lot of things."

"Like?"

"I love the bareback competition. And the little kids riding the sheep, love those little guys. No doubt, that's probably my favorite thing." Toma nodded as if that was the final word on the topic.

Eva rolled her eyes. "Go. Be with Tito. Let's talk this weekend." She gave Toma a little pat on the butt to get her moving, which got her a parting smile from her friend.

CHAPTER TEN

"EVA?" TOMA LOOKED AT HER phone as if she'd called a foreign planet. "You there? I can't hear you. Eva, can you hear me?" Toma pressed a finger against her free ear to try to focus on Eva's voice.

"Toma!" Eva finally said. "Can you hold on? Give me a sec; hold on!"

Toma held the phone away from her ear when she heard Eva yell something in Spanish to someone, then silence. "Can you hear me now?"

"Much better," Toma said. "What the hell was that?"

"You caught me in the combine."

"In what?"

"Onions. We've started harvesting."

"Oh."

"How's Tito?"

"That's why I'm calling."

"Is everything okay?"

"Yes, he's okay; we're okay, but I need to stick close to home this weekend. I can't go with you to the range to see your wild mustangs. With Tito on his ass, I'm running the ranch alone and I have to pick up supplies for the horses, and Dad's PT starts this week, and there's too much going on." Toma thought she heard a sigh at the other end. "I'm sorry. I really wanted to go."

"Oh, my goodness, no, Toma. Totally okay. Your family needs you. There'll be other times."

"There will?" Toma realized that her voice had risen an octave.

"There is so much to do out there. I'll take you whenever you want."

"Cool. When? I mean, good."

"After the Snake River Stampede there's a whopping two weeks before the Pendleton Roundup."

"You're not doing any competitions between the two?" Toma asked.

"Don't need to risk running my horses. I'm sitting pretty good as top earner in the circuit, so no."

"That's great."

"Yeah—dame un segundo!"

Toma pulled the cellphone away from her ear at the change in volume.

"Sorry. I really gotta go. Harvesting is kinda a two-person job."

"See you when you get back?"

"For sure. Give Tito and your dad my regards and don't worry."

"I won't."

"Adios, amiga."

Toma ended the call just as Tito walked into the kitchen with a pizza box in hand and mumbled something incoherent that Toma took for an invitation to have a slice.

"Hey!" Tito said. He was no match for her pizza-napping abilities.

"Oh, pineapple my favorite." She took a huge bite.

He handed her a printout. "Here's where you need to go for the supplies."

"Mere da 'ell is dtar?" Toma mumbled.

"I have no idea what you're saying." Tito's pronunciation was no better than hers. His voice was still nasally because of his broken nose, which was still swollen and bandaged.

Toma swallowed. "I said, where the hell is Star?"

"Use the GPS," he mumbled.

"It's so annoying having to program it every single time I want to go somewhere."

"That's the entire point."

Toma groaned.

"Here's a better idea: ditch the flip phone and get a smartphone like everyone else."

"Nope. Never. I refuse." Toma was not giving up her tried-and-true, tough-as-nails flip phone for a mini-computer that was more fragile than a snow globe. "No way in hell." She finished her slice, then brushed her hands together.

"You better get going. Dad wants to talk to us after dinner. Wants to talk about our plan for the stampede and review the adjustments we're going to make."

"What adjustments do we need to make?"

"We gotta tidy up a couple of things, especially the cut-off route, since the Snake River arena is inside, twice the size, it's different dirt, and all hands on deck. Also, believe it or not, Dad wanted to hear about the new sequences you're teaching us."

"You're kidding." Toma lit up.

"Yeah, he says he wants to talk you out of it, but, between you and me, I think he's intrigued."

"Really?"

"Nah, probably not." Tito leaned back in his chair and gave her a lopsided grin through a bite of pizza.

She headed to the work truck and coursed down the highway. At least her brother had a CD player in the work truck so she could listen to music. She'd had the foresight to pack a couple of CDs in her carry-on to get her through long days like this one. She still awaited the arrival of most of her belongings from L.A.

Toma sang along to the music and kept herself company. She loved Motown and Gospel. The Chiffons, Irma Thomas, Kitty Lester, Clara Ward, and Aretha. She always sang along and replaced the words in such songs as "My Boyfriend's Back."

"My girlfriend's back, and you're gonna be in trouble, hey-la-day-la, my girlfriend's back."

But in real life, her girlfriend wasn't coming back; she'd fallen in love with someone else. A throbbing pain started in her chest as she relived the afternoon she'd come home early from work. She had hoped to crawl into bed, where Sofia would hold her and tell her that her dad was going to be okay and that life was going to work itself out. She had thought it was odd that Mandy's car was parked a few houses down from theirs. But after all, she and Sofia had been spending a lot of time together while working on their script.

Toma let herself in through the garage. She threw her keys in the tray and sat at the kitchen table, wondering why it was so quiet. She knew Sofia was home. Her car was in the driveway. Maybe she was taking a shower, getting ready for her shift at the bar.

The rest of what she saw was a blur. The sounds of their lovemaking were undeniable. They didn't see her at first. Toma cleared her throat. *My dad got hurt. I need to go home.* At least they had the decency to try to explain themselves. They said all those things that people say when they've been caught, and Toma shouted all the things that people usually shout when they're shocked, hurt, and confused. She packed everything she could into three suitcases and everything else into trash bags and left her house key on the kitchen counter.

Toma wiped away the tears as she popped in another CD: The Orlons. She belted the lyrics to "Everything Nice," the song that boasted trading rubies and pearls for love.

Toma wondered what she could have given Sofia for her total and unconditional love. Toma had given her everything she could spare, or so she thought. Looking back, it wasn't enough, otherwise, the little voice inside her head wouldn't be screaming at her at all hours telling her that she'd fucked up. Where and when and how did it go wrong? She had spent countless nights mulling over what she'd done to push Sofia away. In a recurring nightmare, she was a fearless athlete ready for her shot but with ropes made of paper and a harness made of lace. Had she been doomed from the beginning? Was her love as frail as lace? The answers felt so out of reach. The entire experience seemed so long ago. It felt like another life in another world and all she could do was watch the crash on repeat and in slow motion.

Later, after dinner, Tito had projected his iPad to a newly acquired monitor that monopolized a large portion of their kitchen table. Red pointed to an area on the screen. Everyone gathered around, silently cursing whomever their dad had convinced to send him digital recordings or, as he called them, tapes, of the rodeo. They had been reviewing the same stretch of film for nearly thirty minutes.

"I'm serious, Benji," Red said, "you need to tighten your moves when you're coming in for the save." Usually, when that happened, the downed guy struggled to get up. He was dazed and confused, and seconds counted, especially if the bull had his sights set on revenge.

"I know, Dad. Comanche was really antsy that day."

"Sure, blame your horse," came the jabs from the brothers.

"Shut up," Benji spat.

"Probably stayed out too late drinking with Gina," Tito added.

"And who were you drinking with?"

"Ohs" and "ouches" followed. The other brothers were quick to chime in and give Tito a hard time for being single.

Toma watched her brothers bickering. Once they got started, it evolved into an all-out pissing match, an overall display of machismo that only five brothers could create in record time. In the past twelve years, nothing had changed. Key among things that hadn't changed was their dad's ability to round them up with a simple, but stern, request.

"Boys, pay attention."

The brood quieted down, trading jabs for glares and refocusing their attention on an area that Red was circling.

They spent the rest of the hour reviewing plans and exploring modifications they would make and how they could avoid mistakes, improve their process, and work out all the kinks of working with their new, self-appointed leader, their oldest brother, Elroy, and their newest member, Toma.

Toma thought about her relationship with Eva. She wondered what Eva was doing: if she was with her horses; if she was asleep, or looking at the stars. Was she alone? How close a friend was this vet she talked about? It really shouldn't concern her if Eva was alone or with someone else. They were friends, pure and simple, and Toma would like to keep it that way. She had enough on her plate getting her own affairs under control, including figuring out if she should stay in the area after her dad recovered. She monitored her email daily for word from her stunt coordinator. There were jobs, none of them to go crazy over. Again her thoughts turned to Eva. She couldn't deny the fact that she looked for every excuse to talk to her.

"Toma."

"Yeah, Dad?"

"Walk me to my room. Let these guys do the dishes tonight."

Toma met Tito's gaze, wondering if hers was as perplexed as his. As her twin, Tito had always been her closest sibling, the only one with whom she semi-kind-of-sort-of kept in regular contact. Tito knew the real reason why she didn't come home very often. He knew that she and their dad had had a big fight and both were stubborn about it.

"Sure, Dad." She followed him down the hall and stopped short of walking inside his room. She was incredibly nervous to be alone with him because she felt guilty for being away for so long. She had long ago forgiven him for telling her that he couldn't bear to look at her because she reminded him so much of the love of his life. Her dad spoke before he thought, and so did Toma. In addition to their physical features, they shared an uncanny ability to fail at expressing emotions in a productive way. Her dad in his seventies still wrestled with bulls, and she, at the age of thirty-four, put herself in harm's way on purpose.

Their past was water under the bridge, but she still felt the accusation every time she looked in the mirror. She placed her hand on the doorframe and took in her dad's space: neat and orderly with one lone rug, a hand-woven colorful design, threadwork from their Shoshone-Paiute tribe, hung on the wall. A queen bed was centered against a wall. A photo of her mother stood on his nightstand. She closed her eyes at the memories that always flooded when she saw the photo of the woman she resembled.

It was in this room that her mom had told her to hurry and find her dad. Toma had had every intention of finding him as quickly as possible.

But she'd stopped along the way to look at the pollywogs in the pond, wondering when they would turn into frogs and how they would turn into frogs. Would their legs come first? What would happen to their tails? She had stopped to pick up her brother's volleyball. He said never to kick it, only use her hands. She wondered why. She tested it to see what would happen. It went far, farther than any ball she'd ever kicked. So she kicked it again and again until it got stuck in a tree. When she found her dad, he asked why she was crying. She admitted to kicking her brother's volleyball into a tree. They walked hand in hand to find her mother. The rest of that memory was a blur.

Her dad had never blamed her for her mother's death. No one did. At the age of five, she hadn't understood that her mother was dying. Her dad had never remarried—or even dated, as far as she knew. She hung her head and bit the inside of her cheek at being so out of the picture. She wondered how she'd be able to make up for lost time. *Time just flew by*, she repeated over and over to herself when that nagging feeling of guilt started to consume her.

"Come in," he said. "Stay awhile. Rest your brains." He motioned at the matching chairs that sat next to the open window, where the drapes billowed against a gentle breeze. They sat together and looked out onto their property. Their home sat on the outskirts of Caldwell, Idaho, nestled next to the Deer Flat Refuge, a hundred-thousand-acre wildlife preserve. As far as the eye could see, massive syringa trees towered along the horizon. In the near distance, brown, black, and white spots—horses—dotted the rolling, green pasture. The setting sun reflected off the stable's large windows and glimmered as if winking, wishing Toma good luck when she talked to her dad.

"Remember when you were a kid and you'd wake up and run outside and hop on the first horse you'd see?"

"I'd ride them bareback as far they would take me."

"I used to watch you from this spot right here." He patted his armrest.

"You did?"

"You'd flap your arms in the air like you were a bird."

She remembered the feeling, the freedom she felt while atop a horse running wild as far as the horse would take her. "I thought I could fly."

"You could fly." He chuckled. "Remember that one time you fell asleep on Boots?"

"The *one* time?"

"She took care of you, though, always brought you home." Her dad smiled at her.

"I loved that horse."

"She was a great horse."

"Yep." Toma drummed her fingertips against the armchair.

"Are the boys treating you okay out there?"

"They're easy to manage."

"They seem to be enjoying your management style." The look on her dad's face made Toma wonder if this was when he was going to ask her to dial things back, quit being reckless, and quit putting them all in needless danger because he didn't understand the mechanics of her style of stunt work. She was prepared to state her case and ready to describe why choreographed moves decreased mistakes, helped anticipate them.

"I almost lost Benji," Red said while looking at his nails. "Gabby almost didn't come back this summer; he's ready to move on. They've all been done for a while. I think if I hadn't had my accident, they all would have walked." He rubbed his chest.

"I thought they loved it." Toma turned her body toward her dad.

"They did at one point." Red rubbed the back of his neck. "They've wanted to do their own thing in the arena; I never let them. Guess it took seeing their old man wired up at Valley Medical to get them excited again. Though, between you and me, it's you bein' home that has caused them to love it again."

"Why couldn't they just tell you?"

"They didn't want to hurt my feelings, I suspect. This is what I've been doing my whole life, where I met your mother; it's where… it's my everything, you know?"

"Geez, Dad. I'm sorry. I didn't know they were going to quit." She stopped herself from going down that path of reviewing all the things she didn't know, couldn't know, hadn't wanted to know for twelve years. She observed him gazing at the old photo of her mother. He grew teary. Toma loved him for that. Her dad wore his emotions on the outside and he'd always been tough enough, even now, coming off a major injury, that he could still kick anyone's ass who gave him a hard time about it. Wearing her emotions on her sleeve wasn't something that she inherited from him. The only thing she got from him was his tall stature and dark skin.

From her mother, on the other hand, she got her features and her fearlessness, or so she had been told. Again, she couldn't remember. She and her twin relied on the accounts of others. They knew from photos that their mom had been a tiny woman who loved horses, a barrel racer like Eva. She had grown up on the reservation, grown up poor, and that, coupled with inadequate healthcare, left her with a lifetime of illnesses and health issues which eventually led to a stroke at the age of thirty-nine. Five more years and Toma would be thirty-nine too.

"When I met your mother, she couldn't keep her hands off me; I was too irresistible. I came in for the save, and she never let go."

Toma had heard her father say that before, and every time he told anyone that story, it sounded like the first time. Her mother was a green racer; she fell off her horse on her third turn. Red came in for the save, and she never let go. True to his story, in every picture Toma saw of her parents, her mother was hugging or kissing her dad. People who knew them supported the fact that their love was a romance. Toma wondered what that felt like. The closest thing she'd had to that kind of romance was how she felt when Eva had held her hand on the airplane: safe, no questions asked. Would her friendship with Eva be something worthy of holding on to? Was there something within herself worth holding in both hands? Her past told her: not likely.

"Well, Toma, I guess I'm what I'm trying to tell you is, thank you for coming back, keeping the guys together at least for one more season.

I know you have an excitin' life, travelin' all over the world and doing your stunt work, to have to come back and take care of the boys for me."

"I should have… home… sooner…"

"I'm sorry we never made time to see you, either. We could have made more of an effort."

"I was out of the country a lot."

"The best thing your mom and I did was to have a bunch of kids. That's the only thing Mom wanted."

"No doubt, you definitely did that." Toma laughed.

"Now go on, get. Better make sure the boys haven't burned down the kitchen."

Toma stood. "Good call. You coming?"

"I'm going to watch the sun go down."

"Love you, Dad," Toma said as she exited.

CHAPTER ELEVEN

A COUPLE OF DAYS BEFORE the Snake River Stampede, competitors and crew worked to get the arena ready for opening night. Out-of-towners with their trucks and trailers, horses and hopes, streamed single file onto the premises.

Eva pulled into her assigned spot and immediately spotted a few of the Rozenes. Elroy and Gabby were walking their horses out of their trailer. She saw no sign of Toma. Her heart thumped in her chest and not because she'd soon be challenged with maintaining her ranking and getting that coveted invitation to the finals in Las Vegas. The butterflies in her stomach, like her chipped and ragged nails, had more to do with a certain bullfighter whom Eva couldn't stop thinking about during her four-day break. More sleep would have been nice. She'd come home from her campout with an intense need to watch *Wonder Woman*, specifically the scenes with horses, specifically to spot Toma—a glimpse, something, anything. But Hollywood wanted her to see Diana and the Amazons, not Stuntwoman Seventeen Toma Rozene, whom Eva finally did spot in the closing credits.

Eva shut off her engine and stuffed her keys in the visor. No sooner did her boots hit the gravel than she heard a familiar voice that sent tingles all over her body, like drops of cool rain tickling her shoulder and inching down her back.

"Howdy, cowgirl."

Eva turned to see a grinning Toma, who looked as delectable as Eva remembered her. Toma wore snip toe boots, faded and worn blue jeans, and a hot pink tank top that complimented her dark skin and highlighted her toned arms.

"How are you? I watched *Wonder Woman*," she said, knowing that a hue of red overtook her complexion.

"You did?"

Eva nodded. "How was your time off?

"I forgot how utterly immature five brothers can be. I feel like I lost half my IQ this last week."

"With any luck, I can infuse some intellect back into your life."

"I was thinking about you." Toma looked at the ground.

"Oh, yeah? Me too, especially when," *gazing at the stars, going to sleep, waking up, riding my horse,* "lifting the salt blocks on my own."

"I thought you had a signature technique for that?"

"That was my hay-bale-lifting technique. Salt blocks are a whole other animal." Eva made her way to the trailer to offload Frida and Dolores.

"How are you? How was your trip?" Toma jumped to help.

"Amazingly amazing and peacefully peaceful. I counted, like, fifty shooting stars."

"Did you also make fifty wishes?" Toma asked in a quiet voice.

Only one. One very specific wish that involved a certain stuntwoman and a single-person tent. "Well…" Eva looked skyward. "…I wanted to relax, and that wish came true. It's just what the doctor ordered."

"Did she come? Your doctor, vet friend?"

"Rosie? No. She couldn't after all. It was only me and the stars, the herd, and the sound of their beating hooves that woke me up in the middle of the night when they got close. There's nothing quite as beautiful."

Toma smirked. "Now you're just rubbing it in."

"Next time."

"No doubt."

"Speaking of, how's Tito? How's your dad?"

"Both are good. Tito's back at it; he's around here somewhere."

"Did you do anything fun?" Eva asked.

"I had my interview with Polly."

"How did it go?"

"Fine. Hey, so, for some odd reason I chose to pack a couple of my *Wonder Woman* practice footage DVDs along with, you know, the toothpaste and underwear. Do you want to come over sometime and watch them?" Toma asked. "There's a lot of horse stuff you might find interesting."

"What? Yes. Of course. When?"

"Whenever. Well, I take that back, I need to ask my brother if I can borrow his iPad, but he'll say yes."

"Don't you have a TV?"

"Not in the barn."

"You stay in the barn?" Eva asked. Her mind flooded with images of Toma sleeping in a big, soft, fluffy bed of straw surrounded by horses, birds, cats, and other animals like a butch Snow White.

"It's more like an apartment where the old ranch hand lived. So tonight, after you settle in? We're practicing until eight; then I'm done."

"Can we make it tomorrow? There's a volunteer meeting thing I got to do tonight."

"Sure. No doubt."

Disappointment flickered in Toma's eyes. Toma shoved her hands in her pockets and nodded that she understood.

"Tell you what, let's make a dinner out of it. I'll bring something from Aleida's for us."

"Sounds perfect." Toma filled with energy once again. "Cool. Can't wait."

How about that. One of Eva's fifty wishes was about to come true: dinner and a date with Toma.

"HEY, EVA. WAS THAT TOMA you were talking to?" Polly asked upon entering Eva's dressing area.

"Hi, Polly. Yeah. She's a friend of mine."

"Me too. That woman is something else."

Eva could only nod in agreement.

"Did you see my interview with her?" Polly asked.

"Not yet."

"Check it out. It's on our social."

Eva opened her phone and looked up the KIBO Twitter handle to see their top post, titled "The New Heiress of Bullfighting. Clever title."

"Isn't it?"

"Holy shit! It has five hundred and thirty-nine retweets and, like, three hundred comments." Eva scrolled through. *"Toma Rozene, local Shoshone-Paiute Member, former equestrian stuntwoman, and the state's first female bullfighter discusses growing up in the rodeo, being raised with five brothers, and what it takes to be a bullfighter."* The image showed Toma sans her black hat, looking like the picture of elegance, wearing a tailored black blazer with a silk camisole. Eva sat on a nearby stool and started watching.

"Watch it later, I have a proposition for you."

"Sure." Eva couldn't tear her eyes from the video.

"I was kind of hoping I could interview you too."

"Heck yeah. I'm game."

"Like a duo type of thing."

"With who?"

"With her." Eva followed Polly's line of sight. "A hot new thing from Oregon. Former Miss Rodeo Oregon, Melissa Faye Jackson. She's already agreed."

"Count me in."

"Perfect! Thank you. I'm thinking of this title: Two Queens, One Crown."

"Brilliant."

"I know. Hey, Melissa! Yoo-hoo." Polly waved, motioning Melissa to come over. "She's in."

Melissa sauntered over. She wore a huge smile—perfect teeth. She was taller than Eva, Latina like Eva, but more of a glamour queen persona with great big hair and a ton of makeup, totally unlike Eva.

"Melissa, this is Eva Angeles."

"I know who this legend is." Melissa eyed Eva. "Nice to finally meet you." Melissa shook Eva's hand, maintaining her hold. "I've seen your name. A lot. Nice money earned this year."

"Thanks. It's not been without its challenges, that's for sure. Welcome to town."

"It's nice to be here." Melissa finally let Eva's hand go.

"So," Polly interjected, "I want to first interview the two of you together, after your respective runs on opening night, then conduct a more in-depth convo, after you've both had a chance to see each other in action."

"Sounds fun," Eva said. She welcomed a good old-fashioned melding of the minds.

Polly rubbed her hands together. "Think about your similarities and differences, hopes and dreams, and I'll do the rest."

"I can't wait."

"Not as much as me. Well." Polly turned her attention to a new flood of competitors who had entered the dressing area. "I've tied up too much of your time, so I'll leave you to it. Thanks again."

"This should be fun."

"Polly's great too."

"I can tell."

"She's made quite the name for herself around here."

"As have you. Looks like you'll get your invitation to ride in the Thomas and Mack Center in Sin City, huh?" Melissa nudged Eva with her elbow.

"Fingers crossed. How are you looking?"

"I'm sitting pretty good, not that far behind you in cash earned."

"I look forward to seeing what you're all about."

"Ditto." Melissa ran her eyes along Eva's body. "Rumor has it you're involved in the Buckaroo Breakfast fundraiser that's happening this week."

"I am. Yes, it's this Thursday." Eva clapped her hands together.

"I brought a saddle to donate to the silent auction."

"You did! Thank you so much."

"It's a vintage Hamley, should bring about five thousand or so."

"Holy shit. Wow. Thank you."

"What are the proceeds going to this year?" Melissa asked.

"The Worthy Competitor fund to help people who can't afford their association fees."

"A very worthy cause indeed," Melissa agreed. "Count me in. I'd love to get involved while I'm here and be totally immersed in the experience."

"Are you also, by chance, volunteering?" Eva held her hands together as if she was praying. "I'm head of the volunteer committee, and we need more help."

"I'd love to," Melissa said. "I can probably rope in a couple of my team members, too, if that will help."

"You're a dream. Thank you so much. I never turn down a pair of hands and a willing heart."

"My hands and heart are yours for the taking," Melissa said.

"Uh, thanks. We're all meeting tonight, in about an hour, upstairs in the Owyhee Room, can you come?"

"You bet I can." Melissa winked. "Come and get me when you head up?"

"Sure thing. Thanks again." Eva settled in to her assigned area in the arena. She looked over her shoulder and saw Melissa's eyes on her. They shared a smile. Competing in the rodeo was a mind game, especially this close to finals. The top money earners could choose their competitions. At the end of the season, they chose the races where they thought they could beat the other competitors. No doubt Melissa thought she could take the top spot. The only problem was that Eva thought *she* could take the top spot. Seducing a woman to get into her mind wasn't above some riders. Eva would keep her guard up until she knew for sure what Melissa was all about.

Eva joined the other volunteers scheduled to work the Snake River Stampede Buckaroo Breakfast charity fundraiser. After the group broke into its various committees, Eva called her team to order.

"Christina and Lisa, what's your group's volunteer count?" Eva asked.

"Fifteen so far. We're expecting another five or six to confirm this week," Lisa said.

"Can you try for thirty? I know that's a stretch, but we're way under where we need to be, especially with the silent auction, thanks to generous donations."

The two women looked at each other and nodded. "You can count on it, Eva."

"Perfect." Eva scribbled notes on her clipboard and continued checking off boxes. "How's the church group shaping up?" Eva turned her attention to Marge from the First Presbyterian Church, an elderly woman with a great head of white hair who'd never missed a Buckaroo Breakfast in thirty-seven years.

"We're bringing thirty-two volunteers this year," she said with pride. "Seventeen youth and fifteen adults including me, Pastor Gavin, and his wife."

"Perfect. How's the Youth League looking?" Eva asked.

"We have ten confirmed; I'll try to round up another five if I can," said Ginger.

"Perfect. Great job, everyone." Eva referred to her clipboard and quickly tallied the total number of volunteers, whispering as she counted, "Twenty-two, that's forty, fifty-seven... we'll be sitting pretty good and should have plenty of staff for the pancake and egg lines, and we're looking good for setup and cleanup, the auction, line management, yeah, we're looking solid. Anything we're forgetting?"

"What about the woman, the new female bullfighter we should include her," someone said.

"That's a great idea," another voice chimed in. "She should join us. We should get to know her better. Does anyone know her?"

"I'd like to get to know her brother better," one of the ladies chimed in.

"Which one? They're all hot." The comment garnered giggles and schoolgirl-like laughter from the women. Eva shook her head at their childishness. However, she also felt giddy and schoolgirly when she thought about a particular Rozene.

"Yeah, I wonder what she's like?"

"Did you see that video? She seems cool."

Cool? Thought Eva. *Yeah, that's a fitting word to describe Toma Rozene, along with broody, shy, sensitive, sexy, tall*—words that so wonderfully complemented her fearless exterior.

"Anybody, anybody," someone else said. "I'm happy to—"

"I can ask her," Eva blurted. "I know her. It's not a problem. I'll do it."

"See if you can also get a brother or two."

"Or three." The women laughed.

"I'll try." Eva moved them along to their next order of business, all the while thinking what she would have to do to get Toma to agree to volunteer to flip pancakes at the Buckaroo Breakfast fundraiser.

CHAPTER TWELVE

"WHERE ARE YOU GOING WITH that?" Tito asked.

"With what?" Toma said, after placing the last of her dinner supplies in a paper bag and setting it on the kitchen counter.

"All that beer? And why aren't you going to eat with us?" He knelt and looked into the oven at the lasagna Toma had put in there an hour ago. "It smells like it's going to be done soon."

"Mind your own business. I already told you I'm not hungry."

"You're such a bad liar."

"I have plans."

"What kind of plans?" Tito said in his signature singsong voice.

"You sound like a ten-year-old boy sometimes; you know that."

"So do you."

"Fuck off, I have plans, okay?"

"Fine, whatever. Don't tell me about your little date tonight," Tito said with a good dose of side-eye.

"It's not a date; how many times do I have to tell you. She's just coming over to watch *Wonder Woman* footage."

"Dinner and a movie? Kind of sounds like a date."

"I can have a friend all right. A friend that's not a dude. In case you haven't noticed, I'm surrounded by your kind twenty-four-seven."

"So, a girlfriend."

"A friend that's a girl," Toma insisted.

"You're being shifty." Tito smirked.

"You're being shifty?"

"You are."

"You are!"

They burst into laughter.

"Speaking of shifting, I need you to scoot." Tito placed his hands on Toma's shoulders and moved her out of the way so he could delve into the freezer and look around. "Did you get Rocky Road?"

"Of course, I did." Toma shook her head and watched him fish out a giant spoon. He practically ripped apart the carton of chocolate ice cream before digging in. "I got ice cream and cherry pie, Rice Krispie Treats, and Mexican sweet bread with the pink tops, and everything else you told me to get on that insanely long grocery list. The checker asked if I was stocking a fallout shelter."

"You're full of shit," he mumbled with his mouth full of ice cream.

"I'm serious. They said, 'Are you really going to eat all of this by yourself?' And I said, 'No, I'm feeding a wild pack of dogs.'" She loved teasing her brother; she had missed that. She had missed him, missed everyone, even her dad, especially because things were starting to feel better between them. She gave her dad way more credit, especially after their little talk the other night when he thanked her for coming home and keeping the boys together.

"Did you get Little Debbies?" Tito opened the door to the pantry, eyeing the Cosmic Brownies as if they were made of gold. "These are my favorite. How did you know?"

"I'm a mind reader. It was on the list!"

"You're a Little Debbie, too, you know that, a real—"

"Call me that one more time, and I'll—"

"Children," her dad chimed for the seventh time that night. They froze and met his eyes. "Bring me a bowl of ice cream, Tito."

"Sure thing." Tito reached over Toma and waved his arms in her face to get into the cupboard. She swatted him away and huffed. He pulled two bowls from the cupboard and scooped perfectly round mounds into each.

Once Tito and her dad settled into their respective recliners, she made her move.

"I see that everything is under control. When the little bell on the stove rings, one of you, Tito, needs to get up and take the lasagna out of the oven."

"We will," Red said.

"Eat the salad I made too."

"On it."

"Goodnight, Toma," her dad and brother said in unison.

"Thanks for getting dinner started," Red added.

"You're welcome, Dad." She made her way out of the kitchen. "You're welcome, Tito," she said over her shoulder in an annoying high-pitched voice. She heard a thank you through a mouth full of ice cream followed by an even more annoying kissing noise. She rolled her eyes, took a breath, and made for her apartment in time to hear tires on gravel and then see Eva's insanely large truck. Eva parked between her dad's GMC and Tito's work truck.

Toma held the paper bag in one arm and gave an eager wave, nearly spilling the contents in the paper bag as she did so. Ecstatic, over the moon, utterly content, and finally able to breathe deeply after anticipation of this moment, she gave Eva a goofy grin.

"Let me help you with that," Toma said, seeing Eva open the cab to her truck and lift onto the tips of her toes to reach the bags. *Or not.* She witnessed Eva's perfectly round backside wiggle in the air as she stretched to get her belongings.

"I'm good," Eva countered with bags in hand.

They moved to hug each other but couldn't quite make it happen. They both carried awkwardly-sized items. "Nice to see you." Toma gave a nervous laugh at their blunder. She wondered if Eva was nervous too.

"You too," Eva said. They stared at each other for what felt like five hours.

"What's in the bag?" they said in unison, then laughed.

"You first," Eva offered.

"I have a sixer of beer. I thought it would go good with dinner even though I don't know what we're having, but beer goes with anything, right?"

"Always. Do you have plates and silverware in that bag too? That's the only thing I forgot."

"Yep. I got it. But it's not real silverware, I'm sure the boys would have tried to pawn it a long time ago it if was. Ready?" Toma led the way to her apartment. She pulled open the huge sliding door, which created a wind tunnel since the westside barn doors were open. Toma caught notes of lavender and leather when Eva's hair blew in the wind.

"I haven't been here in forever. I forgot how cool it is," Eva said as she scanned the area. The sun shone through the barn's west-facing side casting a soft, orange glow. "It always reminded me of an airplane hangar."

"No doubt." Toma watched Eva taking everything in. "Wait, you've been here before?"

"Yeah, I used to ride here."

"Oh, that's right." Toma thought about the impact of her dad's decision to close the training center on other people's lives.

"Can I have a tour?" Eva asked as she looked around. "It's been a while since I've been here."

"Well, let's get you reacquainted. The first attraction, the pool table."

"This definitely wasn't here when I trained."

"After we closed, the boys made this their own personal party pad. I don't mind it. It makes a great table. Feel free to set everything on there." Toma set her bag atop the table. Eva followed suit. "Second attraction. Do you remember these guys? Patsy and Eddie." Two fat yellow labs lay on their sides in the sun. Their tails thudded against the cement floor. "Don't bother getting up and saying hi to our guest or anything."

"Hey, remember me?" Eva knelt and gave them belly rubs. "Look at their gray faces. How old are they now?"

"Eleven."

"They are adorable."

Toma smiled at the sight of Eva bumping heads with the dogs and giving them kisses. "They'd be more adorable if they lost, like, fifteen pounds. Dad feeds them more than he should. I got them back on a diet."

"They're perfect." Eva laughed as she stood and clapped her hands free of dog hair.

"This is where we keep the horses." Toma led Eva through a door that led to the stable.

"Hey, Shazam." Eva petted the horse that Toma usually rode. Toma joined her in giving affection. They grazed each other's fingers more than once. Eva's touch sent flutters through Toma's body.

Toma fished an apple from a basket on the ground. "Feed him this." She handed Eva the apple. "It's really cute what he does."

Eva offered it to the horse. He promptly took it, chewed it, then stuck his tongue out while he sucked out the juice. Eva and Toma laughed at the sight.

"He's cute."

"He's a good boy."

"He's so huge."

"He's a little over seventeen hands."

"He's beautiful." Eva patted Shazam one last time. "I'm in love with your place."

"Me too. It smells like horse crap sometimes, but there are worse things." Toma laughed.

"I can think of much worse things."

Toma walked them through an area that held her dad's equipment from their school. They ended up at the west side of the barn, which opened onto a dirt path that led to their regulation-sized arena.

"Something just occurred to me," Toma said.

"What's that?"

"You are more than welcome to have your lessons here. We still have all the gear; Dad's still paying on the insurance."

"How much to rent?"

"What do you mean how much?"

"I can't use it for free."

"Says who? Seriously, it would make my dad so happy to see it being used again. Aside from us, it's open. Think about it, okay? Unless you like going to Weiser."

"I might take you up on that, but not for free. I know all this costs money."

"Okay, but you'll get the family discount."

"In that case, I might take you up on that."

"I hope you do." Toma led them to the other side of the barn, which held their saddles, tack, and tools and to her room, a converted office that fit a queen-sized bed, a dresser, a small closet, and pegs for her hats.

"I never figured you to be a cat lady," Eva said upon seeing two cats curled together atop Toma's bed in a patch of sun.

"They only like me for my bed," Toma said before closing the door and clearing her throat. "If you need the bathroom, here it is." She opened a pocket door to a converted area with a toilet, sink, mirror, a lone shelf, and a small shower with a glass window that was open.

"I love your place." Eva ran her hand along a wooden railing. "The openness, the huge rafters, the horses, dogs, and cats, it's so…"

"So what?"

"So, you."

"How would you know what is *so* me?" Toma crossed her arms and smirked.

"Wild guess." Eva mimicked Toma's stance. "You hungry?" Eva headed toward the pool table.

"Starving. What did you bring?" Toma peeked into the bag. "Oh shit, there's like a full-on hot pot in here. What is it?"

"Rigatoni." Eva lifted it from the bag using two potholders.

"Italian?"

"No, that's just what my grandma calls it. She made it for us. It's rigatoni noodles sautéed in chili powder and oil, then she adds water, simmers it until the water evaporates, then adds Monterey Jack at the end. I hope you like spicy."

Eva lifted the lid, and Toma inhaled. "I do. Smells wonderful."

"She made a cabbage salad thing too." Eva produced another small bowl.

"It's perfect." Toma cracked the caps off two bottles of beer and handed one to Eva; they clanked bottles. "Cheers, and tell your grandma thanks for me." Toma maintained eye contact with Eva and held on even after taking a drink.

"Cheers to your interview, by the way."

"Oh, God," Toma groaned, shook her head, and dropped her gaze.

"Seriously. You did a great job. I learned a lot about you."

Toma knew that her face was flushed. "I hate doing things like that."

"Why?"

"I just do."

"You did great. Polly said it was one of her most popular stories."

"Really?" Toma asked.

"Um-hum." Eva finished unpacking their dinner and plated equal portions onto their respective dishes. "It seriously was a great interview."

"Well, thanks," Toma said. "Are those tortillas?" she asked, seeing a foil package.

"Fresh off the comal." Eva uncovered tortillas. "Do you know what to do with these?"

"I have no idea." Toma laughed on seeing the wide-eyed expression on Eva's face. Toma tore off a piece of tortilla and picked up her food with it. Stuffing it into her mouth, she moaned. "O myy goff. Tis soogood."

"Good. I'm glad I don't have to demonstrate how to eat."

"Well, if you want to feed me, I won't say no." Toma cleared her throat and sat back, realizing that she was flirting. She didn't mean to, but Eva made her forget all of her own rules. She enjoyed their meal. They sat in comfortable and easy silence, no pressure, no awkward glances, just friends watching the sunset and sharing smiles once in a while.

"You ready for tomorrow?" Toma asked.

"I'm so ready. There's a new hot thing from Oregon everyone's talking about, supposed to give me a run for the money."

"What's her edge?" Toma asked before taking another bite.

"I'll know more after practice tomorrow."

They finished their meal and retreated to the couch that faced a white screen Tito had installed for her movie night.

"Long day?" Toma asked after a particularly loud sigh from Eva.

"Yeah. Sorry. Harvest season means waking up at four in the morning, but at least I'm done at noon. I had to pick up another shift at Aleida's, barely had time to practice with Frida today."

"You still okay to stay and watch the film? You can go if you need to, seriously."

"Are you kidding?" Eva patted Toma's leg. "I've been looking forward to it since you suggested it."

"Really?" Toma felt as though she'd been struck with a small dose of electricity. She so wanted to ask Eva to define the elusive *it* Eva had said she'd been looking forward to. Did *it* refer to dinner? Did *it* refer to Toma? Or was *it* simply it and nothing more? Toma shook her head; there was no doubt what Eva meant. "If you need to leave at any time, just say so. Seriously."

"I will," Eva promised.

Toma cued the film on the iPad and projected it onto the screen, then dimmed the lights.

"It's like we're in a movie theater." Eva looked around.

"You can thank Tito; he set this up for us."

"That was nice."

"He's a little rough around the edges, but he has his good moments."

They watched the film while Toma shared behind-the-scenes insights about her horse work. She wondered if she was rambling. "Sorry. Am I talking too much?" she asked Eva, who sat with her legs curled under her and was positioned toward Toma, resting her head on the arm she extended across the back of the couch. She had an easy smile. Toma added, "I tend to get a little excited about this stuff and I loved shooting that scene."

"No, not at all. It's fascinating to hear your side of the work. What was your favorite thing about *Wonder Woman*?"

"The team. I worked with the most badass women on the planet; the comradery between everyone was nothing short of inspiring. I've met good people on the job, amazing animal handlers and trainers. And *Vikings* was so cool, because we got to use the coolest weapons, forged onsite. Everything was intensely choreographed: a ton of fighting scenes, a lot of fake blood, and cool costumes."

"What's Amalfi like?" Eva asked.

"Great food. Beautiful people—you'd totally fit in there. Everyone's literally hot, seriously."

Eva blushed and shifted in her seat. "How long were you there?"

"For about two months, which is a lot longer than most people on my team stayed, but I was on the training team, so I had to. I miss the towns nestled in the cliffs, the swimming, cliff-diving; we'd go every chance we had. The tomatoes were to die for, the coffee…" She closed her eyes and smiled. "Have you ever been?"

"I've never left the continent," Eva admitted.

"You haven't?"

Eva shook her head. "All family vacations were in one of two places: California or México. I know. I need to travel the world more. Oh, wait, we went to Canada once."

"Where were you coming from when we met on the flight?" Toma asked but, still embarrassed at her breakdown, kept her eyes cast down.

"Seattle. I have friends with a sailboat."

"I spent a ton of time in Seattle when we shot in Vancouver."

"That is still so cool, you work in the movies."

"Worked."

"For now, right?" Eva inched closer to Toma as she spoke.

"I don't know yet. I monitor my email, try to keep up and see what's coming down the pipeline. There are some jobs of interest, but without knowing when Dad will be back on his feet and what's happening next year, I don't know when I'll be available. I'm trying not to think about it too much. I want to be here, be present for Dad and the boys while I can. Want another beer?" Toma asked.

"Sure."

Toma cracked another beer and handed it to Eva, noticed that she had goosebumps on her arms, and thought a good friend would do something about that. "Want me to close the door?" Toma stood after pausing the film.

"No, leave it. I love it. I have a sweatshirt in the car." Eva started to get up.

"No. Stay. I have one too. Mine's closer; just let me just grab it from my room." She left and returned with a *Wonder Woman* hoodie.

"Sweet," Eva said. "Thanks. I might not give this back to you." Eva snuggled into it. Toma loved that she had to roll the sleeves above her wrists.

"You might have to. It's my only hoodie, and I'm always cold. The weather here is a far cry from Los Angeles."

"I bet."

A buzzing on the wooden table startled them both. Toma looked from the phone to Eva. "Sorry. Do you mind? I'm waiting for a call from FedEx; they seem to have lost my boxes."

"No, go ahead." Eva waved her hand in the air as if shooing Toma away.

"Sorry, thanks." Toma walked toward her bedroom with her phone. "Hello."

"Toma Rozene?"

"Yes, it's me."

"It's FedEx.

"Any update on my boxes?"

"Yes. The issue was that the addresses were incomplete, and so they were delivered to our distribution center in Mountain Home."

"Incomplete?" Toma gasped. Then again, she wasn't surprised. She'd packed in a complete daze and written her labels while fighting back tears and anger.

"Sorry."

"It's not your fault. I'm sorry for the trouble. What's the address of the distribution center?" she asked, finding a pen. "Damn it," she whispered, and headed back to Eva.

Her mind relaxed when she saw Eva in a languid stretch. Eva put her nose inside her *Wonder Woman* hoodie, closed her eyes, and inhaled. Toma cleared her throat and made her presence known.

"Everything okay?" Eva asked as she turned.

"Found my boxes."

"Oh, good."

"I messed up the addresses, and they're at a distribution center in Mountain Home." Toma paced. She ran her hand through her hair. "I'll need to find a ride. I highly doubt that my dad's antique GMC will make it. Maybe Tito can take time tomorrow. He's supposed to go to Boise; that's close to Mountain Home, right?"

"Kinda. I can give you a ride."

"You can?"

"Yeah. Tomorrow, I get off harvesting at noon. I can take an hour or two away and give you a ride."

"Really? Thank you so much. I owe you. Thank you. Seriously."

"I got the perfect way you can redeem your you owe me," Eva said.

"Name it."

"Flipping pancakes."

"Pancakes?" Toma narrowed her eyes.

"We have this huge fundraiser later this week. The Buckaroo Breakfast. I'm the head of the volunteer committee and I need more volunteers."

"Okay, sure. Count me in."

"Can you rope in a couple of your brothers for me? I mean, that is if they can afford to take time away, with your dad and all?"

"I'll see what I can do."

"Thanks!"

"No. Thank you. It's a more than fair exchange," Toma said. "What time does it start?"

"Early. It's breakfast."

"How early?"

"Five in the morning."

Toma closed her eyes and took a deep breath.

"Not a morning person?"

"I am. On set, we had to get there super early, but living here, I've gotten entirely too used to sleeping in."

"So then it's another date."

"Look at us dating." Toma smirked. "Seriously, thank you. I'm getting sick of the same three pairs of jeans."

Between the two of them, they polished off the entire six-pack of beer by the time they finished the film. Toma glanced at the clock and noted the late hour, but she didn't say anything because she wanted Eva to stay, even though she knew that Eva had to get up at four. On the other hand, Eva didn't seem in any hurry to race away. Besides, Toma loved how she felt in Eva's presence. Eva was so easygoing, always animated when she spoke, and fun. Most importantly, Eva had an uncanny ability to make Toma feel as if everything she was experiencing, all the uncertainty, the confusion, and worry that seemed to cloud Toma twenty-four-seven, had melted away.

Eva stifled a yawn and looked at her phone. "Holy hell. How did it get to be eleven-thirty?" She stood and stretched.

"I have no idea," Toma admitted. "Sorry I kept you out so late. You okay to drive?"

"Totally."

"Are you sure? I can give you a lift, or you can stay here."

"I'm good. I ate a ton and drank a lot of water too. I'm okay, but thanks." Eva rounded up her belongings and started helping Toma clean up.

"Don't even worry about it. I got this."

"Are you sure?"

"No doubt."

"Thanks." Eva began taking off the *Wonder Woman* hoodie.

"No, keep it." Toma placed her hands on Eva's shoulder to prevent her from taking off the garment.

"I have one in the truck."

"But isn't it the worst to take off a warm hoodie, then put on a cold one?"

"True," Eva relented. "Can I use your bathroom before I get on the road?"

"Of course. Remember where it's at?" Toma pointed the way, then continued to collect empty beer bottles and caps.

"Thanks so much for tonight; this was fun," Eva said when she returned.

"It was fun; hopefully, my play-by-play commentary wasn't too boring."

"Are you kidding? I loved it."

"I have more film if you want to see more, sometime, anytime. Never before seen, rare footage." Toma laughed. "Thank you for dinner."

"That was all my grandmother," Eva said.

"Tell her I loved her rigatoni."

"I will for sure. She'll love you forever."

"Thanks for the company." Toma shoved her hands in her pockets.

"I enjoyed myself too," Eva said, meeting Toma's gaze.

Toma wasn't sure if she should shake Eva's hand or hug her goodbye. She followed her instincts and leaned forward for a hug. She closed her eyes when she felt Eva's body pressing against hers and Eva's arms around her neck. Eva felt so good. She never wanted to let her go.

Toma's smile widened when saw that Eva had to stand on the tips of her toes to hug her.

"Be ready by noon," Eva whispered in Toma's ear.

"I will." Toma walked her to her truck and waved goodbye.

*   *   *

"Sorry. I'm late." Eva said as she pulled up with her window down.

"I got your text. It's no problem at all," Toma said as she rounded the truck and hopped into the passenger's side. She smiled when she saw that Eva still wore her *Wonder Woman* hoodie. "Did you sleep in it?" she asked, taking the moment to run her eyes over Eva's compact little body driving her huge truck.

"Maybe I did."

"Thanks again for the ride." Toma buckled her seatbelt.

"It's an even trade, remember?"

"Oh yes, the pancakes." Toma mimicked flipping something with an imaginary spatula. "I got Tito and Danny to help too."

"You did!"

Toma warmed at the excitement Eva displayed. "Is it that easy to get you excited?"

"It's that easy," she said. "Did you sleep well last night?"

"Very well, until the cats started flicking things off my dresser onto my face. What about you?"

"Really well, but I could still take a nap right about now." Eva stifled a yawn.

"Want me to drive?" Toma offered.

"I'm good. Mind if we stop for a coffee?"

"Only if I buy. I insist. It's only fair since you're driving."

"Deal."

Eva drove them to a drive-through coffee stand.

"You're a cheap date, by the way," Toma said.

"Why?"

"A drip when you could have ordered something grander."

"I just need the caffeine, no-frills," Eva said as she merged onto the interstate.

"There are better ways to get it."

"Such as?"

"An Americano or espresso."

"I like drip. Are you judging me?" Eva laughed; she raised her eyebrows.

"Italy will do that to you."

"I bet."

"Thus far I haven't been able to find a decent cup of coffee unless I make it." Toma took a sip. "I take that back. These are decent beans. This may be the best yet."

"Glad I could broaden your horizons." Eva turned on the radio and began singing along with the song that was playing.

Toma started laughing.

"What's so funny?" Eva asked, after taking a sip of her coffee.

"You don't know any of the words. Like, not even close." Toma laughed.

"I make it up when I don't know the words."

"I can hear that." Toma turned toward Eva who began bopping her head in the air and tapping her fingers against the wheel as she sang her made-up words.

Eva turned up the volume and sang louder until the song was over. "All right, fine. I'll spare you." Eva turned down the volume and started humming when the next song played.

"Go ahead and sing. I don't care. I kind of like it."

"Well then." Eva turned up the volume and sang along. This time Eva knew the words, as did Toma. This time, Eva's singing filled Toma with memories. It was the song that her stunt team played on set to amp them up before a scene: Carly Simon's "You're So Vain." An inside joke about the stars who thought they were supreme deities but who'd crumble in fear at the thought of having to touch a horse. Memories of her former life came on fast and threatened to swallow Toma whole. She couldn't understand why she hurt or why she couldn't catch a deep breath.

Toma distracted herself by drinking her coffee entirely too fast. That was not a good idea, since it caused a burn down her throat and sloshing of the bitter liquid in her stomach—a fitting feeling for the emotional toll of losing that part of her life. She cracked her window, searching for a cleansing breath. Everything started fading to black.

As if Eva understood, she turned down the volume on the radio. "You okay?"

"I think the double was a bad idea." Toma closed her eyes at the jitters and dizziness that began overwhelming her. Her new reality, the closing of a beloved chapter in her life, the ending of her relationship, and the fact that everything fit into fifteen cardboard boxes brought her to a new low.

She'd stayed up long after Eva had left and continued watching her footage, missing the work. The good memories morphed into bad ones and then to Sofia and their breakup and her so-called friends who chose to protect Sofia. *Why didn't anyone protect me?* An onslaught of emotions swirled in her mind, and a physical ache in her chest took the form of a one-ton bull she couldn't get a handle on and that was moments away from taking her out.

She lowered her window more, hoping the rush of air would help her be able to breathe easier. Her hands felt numb; she realized she'd been squeezing her hands into fists. "Breathing is supposed to be easy, right?" Toma eked out.

"Sometimes it's the hardest thing in the world."

Toma nodded at the truth in Eva's words. She closed her eyes, searching for a moment of clarity and hoped to God she didn't lose it. Again. "I don't know what's going on with me."

"You might be having a panic attack."

"A what?"

"Panic attack."

"What am I supposed to do?"

"Just know that it's a temporary feeling. It won't last forever."

Toma nodded and closed her eyes. Eva rested her hand palm side up on Toma's leg. Toma took hold and held on with everything she had. "Thank you."

"Anytime." Eva didn't push her or try to make small talk. She didn't try to pull out information, or show Toma that life wasn't that bad if you thought about the big picture and remembered that everyone was healthy and no one was going to die. She just drove and gave Toma something wonderful to hold on to while Toma once again shed tears. They didn't last as long or feel quite as bad, because she remembered that she wouldn't feel like this forever.

The sound of the truck's blinker brought her back from her trip down memory lane, which was more like memory's slog down a six-lane boulevard during rush hour, complete with pissed-off people in cars taking out their frustrations via their annoying-sounding horns. "I promise someday I'll quit crying and get off this damn proverbial couch," she sniffled.

"I'm here, whether you're on the couch or not."

Toma wiped her eyes. "I figured out another one of your signature moves."

"What's that?" Eva asked.

"You know all the right words to say."

"I say what I feel."

They arrived at the FedEx distribution center. When Eva started to get out of the truck to help, Toma insisted on hefting all the boxes on her own. "I got it."

"Are you sure? It'll go faster with the two of us."

"No doubt, but I need to... I got this," Toma insisted.

With the last box packed into the truck, she accepted Eva's help securing the ropes and bungees.

"Ready to go?" Eva asked as she started the truck.

Toma only nodded, and they began their journey home, not speaking another word until she off-loaded the last box into the barn.

"Well, that's that. Thank you, and sorry I got all weird." Toma removed her gloves, stuck them in her back pocket, and rubbed her face with her hands.

"No need to apologize, okay? How many times do I have to tell you that, huh?"

"Human nature, I guess."

Toma thanked Eva with an embrace and held on longer than any friend probably should. Eva had been her savior from the moment they met. She felt like fresh air laced with peace—a positive charge to Toma's soul. Toma didn't want to let her go, but she had to or face losing her mind altogether.

Eva deserved more than the shadow of Toma's former self. Eva deserved more than a depressed, anxious waif of a woman who floated in an abyss, not knowing where she would land.

"Want to talk?" Eva pulled back and searched Toma's eyes.

"No," Toma blurted. "I'm okay, I mean, that's okay. I need to get back. I have six more horses I need to run today; one of them's a real pain in the you know what." Toma motioned over her shoulder with her thumb and tried for a laugh that wasn't at all convincing. "I'm sure you have stuff to do, horses to... training..."

"You have my number, right? Text me whenever."

Toma nodded. "I will. Thank you for everything."

Toma closed the barn door behind herself and slid against it and onto the ground. The cold cement brought about a shocking realization. She walked through life a closed book: untouchable, incapable of letting anyone in. She'd shown Eva more of herself then she'd ever shared with Sofia or anyone. Opening up with Eva, being seen for who she was, flaws and all, felt like an intimate gift, and it all started with a touch, a very powerful touch.

CHAPTER THIRTEEN

THE FIRST NIGHT OF THE Snake River Stampede started without a hitch—no loose bulls, busted barrels, or anything out of the ordinary except for one small point of concern. Melissa Faye Jackson did give Eva a run for her money. The speculation, the what-ifs, and an honest-to-goodness competitor at her level, along with the tension that swirled through the arena, fueled Eva's competitive nature.

"Isn't that somethin' else, folks, we got ourselves a ball game," Pierson Price's voice relayed through the arena, after Eva beat Melissa by one-tenth of a second. "Lemme hear what all you'all think about all our little ladies racin' tonight." The crowd clapped and hollered and lifted their beer cups and waved them in the air.

"We look pretty good, don't we?" Melissa said, as the group of contenders took a final run around the arena, waving to their fans, and she and Eva saw themselves on the Jumbotron.

"Not too shabby," Eva shouted to compete with the cheers.

"What are you doing later?" Melissa asked as they slowed to a trot. "A group of us are headed to this place called the Saddle Club. Ever heard of it?"

"Yeah."

"Want to join?"

"I don't know." Eva mused. "I have to work early."

"You have to eat, right?"

In Eva's thirty-four years, she hadn't figured out a way to wrangle her way out of that age-old line, *you have to eat.*

"Dinner and one drink, that's it. I promise."

"What the hell."

As they trotted past Toma, Toma made eye contact with her. Her heart galloped when she saw Toma's little wave and shy smile. Eva had thought about nothing but Toma since she had given her the ride to get her belongings. That smile was a welcomed relief after the hurt she'd seen when she dropped Toma off. Eva had wanted to stay and be there for her, hold her while she cried; Toma had seemed to be moments away from falling apart completely. But she had needed space. Toma would let Eva know when she needed more.

Eva and Melissa dismounted their horses and led them to where they saw Polly waiting for part one of their joint interviews.

"You ladies ready?" Polly asked.

"Born ready," Melissa said and winked.

"My sash is crooked." Eva righted it.

The cameraman counted down from three, lights went on, and Polly began.

"Polly Gonzales, KIBO TV. We are live at the Snake River Stampede with the top two money earners in the barrel racing competition in all the Southern Spark Circuit. We're talking with Idaho's own Eva Angeles and with Melissa Faye Jackson, who hails from Oregon. Both are former Miss Rodeos; they know this game inside and out. Ladies, thank you both so much for talking to us tonight. Great runs out there, both of you, wow."

"Thanks," they said in unison.

"What's going through your minds right about now? Eva, why don't you start us out."

Eva looked at Melissa before she began. "I'm a little bit worried. Melissa's the real deal. She's quick out the gate, gets around that money barrel hard and fast, has a great horse. I'm totally in awe at her technique. Your horse…"

"His name's Hop," Melissa interjected.

"Hop has some fancy footwork around those barrels, looks custom." Eva scratched Hop under his chin.

Polly turned the mic to Melissa, who said, "Thanks for asking. It is custom footwork, by yours truly." Melissa shot a big toothy grin at the camera. Her energy, along with the obscene amount of glitter she wore, sparkled under the lights. "Like Eva, there'd be something seriously wrong with me if I wasn't totally worried. Eva's edge is how she communicates with Frida. That's seriously how you're going to win this thing. If our partners sense even the slightest hesitation, they'll hesitate too. If we're anything less than confident, they'll totally know, and it will totally show in our runs. From what I see, Eva and Frida are in tune, making music out there. If Eva's nervous, she's good at keeping it out of the arena."

"Are you nervous, Eva?" Polly asked, pushing the microphone her way.

"You'll never know." Eva's response garnered a laugh from Polly, Melissa, and the cameraman.

"How do you calm your nerves before a run?" Polly asked as a group of people, one of whom was Toma, stopped behind her to watch their interview.

Christ, Toma looked sexy as hell with dirt all over her body. Eva's heart thumped as she imagined removing Toma's clothing, one item at a time, then washing Toma's sexy body and seeing the soapsuds coat her every curve. Eva licked her lips, then cleared her throat when she realized that Toma had waved to her. Eva knew she wore a huge smile along with flushed cheeks.

"Care to divulge your secrets to getting into the zone? Melissa, why don't you start," Polly directed.

"As cliché as it seems," Melissa began, "I let my mind go blank, try to be in the moment, as I take that first turn, then the next. That's how I do it."

"What about you, Eva?"

Eva tore her eyes from Toma. "Same. I tune in, try to tune, I mean, I try to tune everything out." She shook her head and cleared her throat. "It's harder than it seems for less than fifteen seconds. But I practice. It's like breathing." She settled her gaze once again on Toma. "Sometimes it's easy, and other times it's the hardest thing in the world."

Eva let her mind wander yet again, doing the opposite of being in the moment. Polly must have wrapped up their interview, because next thing Eva knew, Polly was trying to get Toma's attention.

"Hey, Toma." Polly practically threw her microphone into her cameraman's hands and waved Toma over. "Toma!"

"Hi." Toma's eyes lingered on Eva before focusing on Polly.

"You still game for dinner and a drink?"

Eva raised her eyebrows at Toma.

"Yeah. At the Saddle Club?"

"That's where we're going." Melissa waved a finger between herself and Eva.

Toma, in turn, raised her eyebrows at Eva, which caused Eva to blush.

"Such a small world," Melissa added.

"Maybe we'll see you guys there." Polly snaked her arm around Toma's, and they walked away. Eva averted her eyes at their display of affection.

EVA JOINED MELISSA AND HER team at the Saddle Club. A restaurant-slash-pub, it had several pool tables, dark paneled walls, stained glass windows, saddles on the walls, candles at every table, and individual restrooms with names like Mother's Bonnet, Tried and True, and Windsor's Bane. Melissa introduced her brother, who was her trainer; her vet; and her vet's husband, who helped with the driving. Like Eva, Melissa had a top-of-the-line truck and trailer and sponsors to make traveling easier.

"You have a great team," Eva said as they finished dinner and ordered another round of drinks.

"I couldn't do this without them."

"I know the feeling," Eva added. Competitions were a grind, a grueling slog, a year of upwards of seventy races. The lucky ones, the ones with money, had a team to help them drive or drive for them while they flew to their next race. The well-funded competitors also had several horses. If one favored running indoors or was better in an outdoor arena or if, God forbid, a horse broke down, they had a backup. Not everyone had the support that Melissa and Eva had.

"Who travels with you?" Melissa asked.

"My vet Rosie and usually my dad. My sisters and grandma may come to Pendleton this year."

"Bringing all your fans, are you?" Melissa teased.

"If I want a decent chance against the top money earner there, I'll bring whoever I need to get the advantage. However, between us girls, the local Pendleton hot shot ain't got nothing on me." Eva got a hearty laugh from Melissa.

"Cheers." Melissa raised her glass.

"Cheers, and thanks for the invite. This is nice," Eva admitted.

"I figured you needed to eat."

"You figured right." The opening of the door drew Eva's attention. Again. She eyed everyone who had walked into the place, hoping it'd be Toma.

"Expecting someone?"

"No. Sorry. Opening night excitement. I'm still a bit on edge, I guess."

"I know the feeling."

The door again caught her attention, and again it wasn't Toma. Eva realized she was being rude. She turned her full attention to Melissa. "So what does a girl like you do during the day?"

"I'm fully dedicated to racing."

"You're the real deal, huh?"

"Only because I'm lucky."

Melissa's story wasn't all that rare. A lot of competitors could afford to dedicate their entire year to racing. However, the norm was, ladies worked full-time jobs. Some of them worked nine-to-five; some were teachers, stay-at-home moms, or farmers—like Eva.

"I'm not a total schmo," Melissa admitted, "I help out on the family farm when I can."

"No shit, me too. What do you guys grow?"

"Hops and we have a vineyard."

"That sounds way more fun than what we grow."

"What do you guys grow?"

"We rotate, but at the moment we're growing onions, mint, alfalfa, and corn."

"Well, you have one ingredient for a mint julep. Speaking of, want one?"

"Are you trying to get me drunk?" Eva asked.

"Anything to throw you off your game tomorrow," Melissa said with a warm smile featuring two adorable dimples. Melissa was a beautiful woman, though, in Eva's opinion, she wore way too much makeup. Also in Eva's opinion, Melissa had a successful career ahead of her and a long one; she was only twenty-seven years old. Melissa's sense of humor kept Eva laughing. She was energetic and animated, and they shared a lot of the same interests.

"You play?" Melissa asked.

"Play?"

"You keep eyeing the pool table. Want to hit some balls around?"

Seeing the pool table reminded Eva of Toma, reminded her of Toma's huge barn, where she lived surrounded by horses, leather and saddles, and tears at maybe closing a beloved chapter of her life and at being cheated on.

"Oh, sure. I haven't played in a long time, but what the hell." She followed Melissa and watched her rack the balls, then went to select her cue.

"Hey, girls." Polly's distinct voice alerted Eva. She turned in time to see Polly wave. Eva smiled the moment she made eye contact with Toma.

They headed straight for each other. Eva hoped it didn't seem as though she rushed to Toma, but she did. She couldn't help it, and besides, Toma was the one who headed straight for her. Eva gave Toma a huge hug. It's all she'd wanted to do since letting go of her that last time. She loved that she had to stand on the tips of her toes to wrap her arms around Toma's neck. She sighed when Toma's arms wrapped around her waist, pulling Eva into her. It felt as though Toma lifted her off the floor. She pulled away, knowing she was blushing.

"Fancy seeing you here." Toma looked at the floor.

"Want to play doubles?" Melissa asked. "Unless you're here to eat."

"Oh no, we enjoyed a lovely dinner already. We're here to play," Polly said, smoothing her hands together. "Does everyone know each other?"

"I don't think we've met." Melissa approached Toma. "I'm Melissa." She extended her hand, which Toma shook.

"Toma."

"You're the bullfighter, right? The female bullfighter?"

"Last I checked," Toma laughed.

"It's an honor, seriously. I totally loved your interview. You're a total badass."

"Polly made me look good."

"You needed absolutely no help in that department." Polly placed her hand on the small of Toma's back.

Eva dropped her eyes at seeing Polly being so damn handsy, especially because Toma and Polly made a stunning couple. Polly was a gorgeous woman. She dressed in designer clothing that hugged her every curve. She was wearing high heels, tight black jeans, an emerald-colored sleeveless, silky, button-up blouse, and matching gold bracelets and earrings. Her perfectly styled locks of brown hair covered her back. She was an elegant woman with an outgoing, vibrant personality to match. And Toma, Toma looked amazing in whatever she wore.

What did it matter? She and Toma were friends. Toma had said that she wasn't looking for a relationship. Maybe she meant she wasn't looking for a relationship with Eva. In either case, it was none of her business what the woman did or whom she dated. Eva searched inside herself for the appropriate emotion and realized that it was jealousy.

"You're from Pendleton, right?" Toma asked.

"Born and bred," Melissa said. "Are you and your brothers coming to work the arena at the Round-Up?"

"We'll be there."

"Get ready for a wild time. You think Snake River is rowdy; Pendleton Round-Up will make the Stampede seem like making cookies."

"It's true," Eva added. Many of the rodeos in the Southern Spark Circuit paled in comparison to the Pendleton Round-Up. Contenders came from all over the United States, some with pipe dreams, other with true shots at the finals in Las Vegas—a shot that Eva wanted. Thus far in the competition, Eva had been the favorite everywhere she went, but that would change in Melissa's hometown. The home-field advantage was insanely strong in the rodeo, especially if a competitor was good.

"Shall we get this party started?" Melissa asked.

"Toma's on my team," Polly stated. She hooked her arm with Toma's.

"Go easy on us," Eva said as she walked with Toma to the wall where they selected their cues. "Enjoying your date?" Eva said while avoiding eye contact.

"I couldn't get out of it."

Eva met Toma's eyes and saw Toma glaring at Melissa. "Me neither."

"Sixty-one?" Melissa suggested.

"Someone's going to need to explain that to me," Eva said, walking to the table with her cue in hand.

"The first team to score sixty-one points wins."

"So hit the high balls?"

"Hit the high balls."

"It's that easy."

"That sounds and looks promising," Eva pointed out, after Melissa's hearty break sent the balls scattering across the table.

"Side note," Polly said, "I've never played pool before."

"You're kidding!" Melissa laughed.

"Nope. Never even held a pool cue before." Polly held the cue upside down. The whole thing reminded Eva of that scene in *Gone with the*

Wind when Scarlett purposely put her bonnet on backward to get Rhett to pay attention. Eva hoped that Toma would see just how ridiculous Polly was being.

"How is that even possible?" Toma looked wide-eyed, and shook her head as she approached Polly.

"You're going to have to teach me." Polly smirked.

It took all of Eva's concentration to avoid rolling her eyes at Polly's blatant flirting. Eva wished she had never picked up a pool cue after seeing Toma wrap her body around Polly to help her with her form.

"Things are looking good for us, Eva, wouldn't you say?" Melissa said after getting them well onto their way to winning game number one.

"Do you ever get sick of winning, Melissa?"

"Nope. You?"

"Nah." The group erupted in laughter at their back and forth.

"How about the loser of game one buys the next round of drinks?" Toma suggested.

"You are so on," Eva agreed.

After Toma sank the last ball on the table for their third straight win, Melissa groaned. "This is bullshit."

Polly wore a mischievous look. "We're winning fair and square."

"Like you had anything to do with it." Eva laughed. Toma was the only reason they were getting their asses handed to them.

"I honestly haven't played in forever."

"Says the woman who has a pool table at home," Eva said.

"Oh, my God. I, like, just realized you're one of those girls who's good at everything." Melissa drank the last of her beer.

"Tell you what," Toma said, "no need to buy us that third round."

"Good, 'cause I'm broke." Eva crossed her arms.

"We'll settle for bragging rights," Polly added.

Polly's obvious attraction to Toma intensified the more she drank. Cue *Gone with the Wind* yet again and that scene when Rhett takes Scarlett into his arms and the camera lens fogs over. Eva knew the feeling. Toma did those things to her too; she did those things to all of them, especially when she leaned across the table to make a shot. Every time she stuck out her hot backside, Eva felt terribly hot and bothered. Fiddle-dee-dee! Eva had to do something to save face and the night. She did what any other losing woman would do. She tapped Toma's cue with the edge of her own pool cue just before Toma's shot, causing Toma to miss.

"Oh, now you're resorting to cheating!" Toma laughed, turned around, and took Eva's cue.

"Whatever it takes to get ahead." Eva reclaimed her cue and sat on her barstool.

"No doubt. I know what might help you, what might help all of you to improve your accuracy," Toma suggested, her expression turned serious as she eyed each of the women.

They turned their complete attention to Toma, awaiting her wise words of advice.

"Maybe if you'all would quit staring at my butt whenever I went for a shot, you'd be able to concentrate!" Toma laughed.

"Were we that obvious?" Melissa asked.

"Yes, you *all* are that obvious." Toma settled her eyes on Eva and then giggled.

"Was that a giggle?" Polly asked.

"Might have been."

Toma's girlish giggle ignited an inferno inside Eva that she couldn't ignore but knew that she needed to. "I should go," she said noticing the late hour.

"Already?" the collective said.

"Farm living is the life for me," Eva sang as she gathered her stuff.

"I should call it a night too," Melissa said.

"No, no. You stay. Maybe you'll have a killer hangover tomorrow, and I'll finally be able to get more than a tenth of a second on you." Eva hugged Melissa.

"In your dreams, princess."

"Thanks for the invite. This was fun. See you, ladies, tomorrow." Eva gave Polly a hug and then hugged Toma, which she swore seemed longer. "Anyone need a ride?"

"Do you mind?" Toma practically jumped from her stool. "I need to check in with Dad. I literally just got a text from him. Sorry, Polly, do you mind?"

"Of course not."

Eva suppressed a smile when she saw the look on Polly's face as they left.

"I think Miss Rodeo Oregon wants more than your crown, Miss Angeles."

"I think Polly wants another exclusive with you."

"I like them together," Toma stated. "They're perfect for each other."

"How so?" Eva asked, wanting to be exactly clear on what Toma meant.

"They're both glamour girls; they both love the camera, just different sides of it."

"I'm imaging the photoshoot now." Eva splayed her hands in front of her. "They should totally hook up."

Toma laughed. "They totally should."

*　　*　　*

LATER THAT WEEK, EVA GATHERED with her Buckaroo Breakfast fundraiser volunteers. They huddled around the park's lantern-lit picnic tables. The sun had only begun to light the sky. Five o'clock was an ungodly hour for some of them, especially the kids. Thanks to the coffee and donuts, people slowly began coming alive, even laughing.

"Hey, guys. Thanks so much for coming," Eva said, seeing Toma, Tito, and Danny. They headed straight for the coffee.

"Happy to check volunteering off my bucket list," Danny said. He mimicked writing a checkmark into the air.

"Me too. Happy to help," Tito echoed as he poured himself a cup.

"Thanks for coming too." Eva stood on the tips of her toes to wrap her arms around Toma's neck. Touching her was all she wanted to do every time she saw her. Judging by how long Toma held on, it seemed she felt the same way.

"Morning," Toma said against Eva's ear before pulling away.

"Hi, everyone." Melissa joined them at the coffee station. "Thanks for involving me." Melissa seemed overly perky for five in the morning; then again, Melissa was a farm girl too. Eva hugged her.

"Thanks for your time today."

"I'm all yours," Toma said and slapped her hands against her own thighs.

Something about the way Toma said that caused Eva to drop her clipboard. Melissa picked it up. "I'm all yours too," she added before handing it over.

"Me too." Tito eyed Toma and wiggled his eyebrows.

"You're all going to regret saying that after flipping a thousand pancakes and frying a hundred thousand dozen eggs." Eva gave the morning's marching orders.

The morning went surprisingly well. The lines were long but moved fast. People went back for seconds and seemed to be enjoying themselves. Best of all, silent auction bids were high and continued to roll in. It seemed they would surpass what they had raised the previous year.

Eva assigned Toma to work one of the pancake lines with her grandma. They both looked adorable wearing their matching aprons. Toma towered over Eva's five-foot-tall grandmother. Every time Eva looked their way, Toma was laughing and shaking her head, likely at Eva's grandmother's inappropriately funny antics. Finally, Eva was able to break away. She headed toward them, since they had a break in their line.

"¿Estas siendo buena, Abuelita?"

"Claramente no," her grandmother gasped.

"I'll assume, since I've had no complaints, that you are, in fact, behaving yourself."

"What is the point to living if you can't have fun at other people's expensive?"

"You mean other people's expense?" Eva clarified.

"All is the same," Aleida stated. "Ay, mis piesitos." She groaned.

"Sorry, Grandma, let me get you a chair." Eva looked for one, trying to inch her way between the tables.

"Let me," Toma said, placing her hand on Eva's arm. Toma wrangled a folding chair from another tent, then helped Eva's grandma to it. Toma's tender care of her grandmother, who meant so much to her, warmed Eva's heart.

"Thank you, mija." Aleida patted Toma's hand. "Evita," Aleida yelled from her spot under the shade, "take note, ella es para las gallinas."

"Did she just say I'm a hen?" Toma asked as she walked back.

Eva laughed. "She means you're a keeper. Thank you so much for putting up with her."

"She's hilarious. It made getting up at four in the morning totally worth it."

"I appreciate you being here and bringing your brothers."

"Yeah, sorry about that. I brought the two most talkative ones at that." They looked at the egg line, where Toma's brothers were assigned, in time to see Tito deep in conversation with a young woman, with the spatula in his hand helping him prove his points. The other brother was talking to an older man with his hands as if he was demonstrating how he would bring down a calf and cinch its feet.

"I saw them working earlier; not all is lost."

"Oh, good." Toma worked her way to the other side of the table to join Eva.

"Everything going okay?"

"Yeah, your grandma told me all your embarrassing stories."

"Oh, God." Eva shook her head.

"I've been meaning to ask—Jesus H!" Toma yelped when her twin came up behind her and shook her by the shoulders "Tito! You're so immature."

"Oh, that was good. I got you good."

"You're lucky I didn't beat your face with my greasy spatula!"

"Hey, Eva," Tito said after recovering from his fit of laughter.

"Hey, Tito," she said, sending Toma a look, trying to tell her she would have warned her, but she didn't see him in time.

"What do you want?" Toma asked, still looking visibly shaken and moments away from swatting her brother with her spatula.

"Party. Day after the Stampede. Everyone's coming. It's a surprise for Dad. All the guys want to see him, so we're having a bonfire and barbeque at our place." He punctuated the statement by pointing to himself with his thumbs. "We'd love to have you there, Eva. In fact, Melissa said she'd come if you would."

"I'd love to see your dad, that is, if it's okay with…" She eyed Toma.

"No doubt, it's totally okay; please come. In addition to being a complete ass at times, Tito's actually good at cooking food. Outside," Toma clarified.

"Great, then it's settled. I'll let Melissa know." Tito sauntered off.

"You do that," Toma yelled.

"Well, I for one am looking forward to it," Eva said.

"Me too."

"Thanks again for volunteering."

"A trade is a trade," Toma reminded her.

"Speaking of. Did you get unpacked?"

"Not quite, but I've made a good dent in one of the boxes."

"Just one?"

"The one with the underwear."

Eva joined Toma in laughter. "Did you find any more *Wonder Woman* stuff?"

"*Wonder Woman* underwear?" Toma's eyebrows near met her hairline.

"No! Oh my God." Eva covered her eyes. "Not how that was supposed to come out." She shook her head. "I should get back. In fact… " She looked at her watch. "…it's almost time to close the silent auction."

"How's it looking?"

"Good. Thanks for donating the arena time."

"It was Dad's idea; he does it every year."

"Also, there's an all-out bidding war on the training lessons you donated."

"You're kidding."

"It's the highest bid so far. You're an amazing horse handler, Toma."

"People just want to know how to do a handstand on a horse."

"I was going to ask if you'd teach me."

"Any time. Have you given any more thought to my offer of using the arena?"

"I have, and I think I might take you up on the offer if it still stands."

"Of course."

"I'll email you some times."

"Great."

"I better go. Thanks again for your help today. Adios, Abuelita!" Eva waved to her grandma and walked toward the auction tables. "Text me later?"

"Sure."

CHAPTER FOURTEEN

"Must be nice," Tito said as he came trotting atop a horse he'd been working. He tied her to a post, then sat down next to Toma. He removed his hat, tossed it onto the ground, and drank the entire contents of his water bottle in one gulp.

"I've run like six horses already and mucked the stables. I can take a break," Toma said.

"Oh, my God. What is that?"

"You smell like sweat. Get away."

"So do you. What is that?"

"Nothing." Toma felt like a little kid in her attempt to hide her new phone. It was no use.

"Need help?"

"No. Yeah." She presented her new iPhone. "I'm not used to Apple products."

"Look at you, Little Miss High Tech." Tito wiggled his eyebrows.

"Shuddup and show me how to send a damn text message." Toma had caved and gotten a new phone when she and Eva started texting. It took Toma way too long to text, and that wasn't any way to maintain a friendship.

"Demanding much?"

"Pretty please?" She batted her eyes.

"Here is where you go to start typing a message." Tito pointed at the little green box. "See, it says messages, right here. Look. Messages." He drew out each syllable.

"Shuddup." She laughed.

"You shuddup and pay attention. Watch me type." Tito started typing words.

"Oh wow, that looks much easier than cycling through one key for the letters."

"That's what I've been trying to tell you." He mock-slapped his forehead.

"What did you send?" Toma attempted to retrieve her phone, which he held just out of reach. "I texted Dad and said you were making tabouli tonight."

"Tabouli? That takes forever."

"I know." He smirked. "Now you try. Send me something." He handed the phone to her.

"What's your number?"

"You don't have it?"

"I'm still transferring my contacts."

"How many do you got in there?"

"Like a hundred." Toma eyed her old phone, which sat next to her gloves.

"Sucks to be you." He took her phone and input his info. "There."

"My hot brother?" She laughed at how he programed in his number. "You're crazy."

"Text me something."

yo.

She looked at her brother's phone. "Did you get it?"

"You have to send it." He pressed the send key for her. His phone chimed. Then hers did.

"Oh! I got a message."

"That was me, silly."

"Wow, you're fast."

"Because it's that fast. Aren't you going to read it?"

"So so suck your toe all the way to Mexico, while you're there, brush your hair, don't forget your underwear."

"Remember Mom used to sing that to us?"

"I loved that."

"Why the sudden interest in joining the twenty-first century?" Tito asked.

"Nunya."

"Uh-huh," he said. "Tell Miss Rodeo Idaho hola for me." He left her with a little wave.

Toma rolled her eyes and watched him leave the barn with his horse before she programmed Eva's number into her phone and started a text message.

good luck tonight. not that you need it.

Toma sent the text to Eva before she had a chance to chicken out. She shoved the phone into her back pocket and immediately pulled it out when a chime sounded.

Thanks! Eva texted.

are you nervous? or is the fact that i'm asking you if you're nervous making you nervous?

LOL. Nope and nope.

lol?

Serious?

i have no idea what that means.

LOL = Laugh Out Loud.

clever!

You kill me, Toma!

i hope not!

How are you? What are you doing?

i unpacked a box of wonder woman stuff and thought of you.

You're sweet. :)

break a leg tonight. can't wait to see your final run!

I can't wait to see you.

Smiling at Eva's responses, Toma reread their exchange for the fiftieth time that day. *You're sweet. I can't want to see you.* A ball of anxiety tumbled inside at the thought of acting on her desire to be more than friends with Eva. They'd grown so close so fast—too fast. Her earlier revelation, while insightful, also caused her trepidation and left her even more confused. Should she stoke their friendship when it was almost certain that it was headed somewhere else? Shouldn't she reevaluate her life a little more before jumping into something with another woman? Probably, but Eva felt so good and their connection so different from anything she'd felt before. There was also the small matter of Toma not knowing what was next career-wise. She might leave after the end of the year. She cared too much to start something she might not be able to finish. More importantly, Toma might fall too deep to be able to climb out when—if—Eva realized there wasn't anything in her worth holding on to.

Another chime came from her phone. She whipped it from her pocket like a gunslinger in a duel. It was Polly, wanting to know if Toma was free for a late dinner. How had Toma's life become so complicated so quickly?

It WAS THE LAST NIGHT of the Snake River Stampede and it showed in the way the bulldoggers walked, some stiff as boards, others limping from their weeklong fights to their cut of the prize money. Toma returned from escorting the last bull riding contestant out of the arena after he took horns to his ribs when he fell.

"Guys and dolls, we have a predicament now, don't we?" Pierson Price's voice echoed through the arena. "We got seven ladies crying for that prize money. Seven ladies and three big purses o' cash. Ain't that some math?" Toma called Price "the annoying voice of the rodeo." He had the crowd in tears with his cheesy-as-hell jokes.

Everyone was laughing with Price, everyone except Toma. She didn't like him. Maybe it was because he'd cut Eva's feed during her interview. Maybe it was how he described female contestants, *little ladies running high on emotions, crying for the top spot*, versus how he described the males, *tough as heck and fueled by fearlessness*. Maybe it was because he kept interrupting Polly, who sat beside him in the announcer's booth for the last night of the Stampede. She was a guest commentator thanks to her series, "Her Story, Her Way." Toma knew that having to share his spotlight annoyed Price. He had no choice. She brought good ratings, and the crowd knew that too.

Polly's work garnered a huge following. It piqued the interest of the usual professional rodeo outlets and many non-traditional groups as well. Women's groups loved it, calling it the new era of rodeo. Multicultural groups shared it as they were interested in Eva and Melissa's Latina heritage and Toma's Native American roots. Polly's work garnered so much attention that she was in talks for her own radio program.

"If you had to guess, Pierson, who would you say will have the three best times?" Polly asked.

"If we're goin' by the digits, the top spots will go to our very own Eva Angeles…" He broke for healthy applause. "… and Pendleton's Melissa Faye Jackson. Those two little ladies have a one-second lead on the next gal. The rest is a toss-up."

"I won't be surprised if the number three spot goes to Suzanne Westbrook. She's made significant gains since the first night. She gets better every time she tries. She needs to get her horse to the money barrel quicker. Otherwise, watch out for Stevi Albright. The two of them are neck and neck, both have promise and heart and a shot at good money tonight too."

"Promise and heart only go so far, Polly; time and try count in this game," Price interrupted her yet again.

"And of course home-field advantage, Pierson," Polly added. "Let me explain."

Toma smiled when Polly dominated the rest of the conversation talking about home-field advantage and the correlation between distance from home and time. She was glad that Polly still wanted to be friends after Toma had said she wasn't interested in anything more than that.

"It's electric tonight." Tito pulled Toma's attention back to resetting the area for the barrel racing competition.

"I'm nervous for her," Toma admitted. She rolled the last barrel into the arena and climbed atop her horse. Thus far in the competition, Eva and Melissa had traded spots at the top, but only by a few fractions of a second.

"I got my fingers crossed for her and my toes," Tito assured her, "but she doesn't need no damn luck. Frida's better trained, and this is their hometown." Eva also had the edge over Melissa because she was a few years older, which brought more experience. "First or second spot would work."

"I want her to win that first-place prize money." Toma wanted to see Eva doing her victory lap, wearing her sash, balancing her flowers while doing her one-handed wave, and wearing a beautiful smile.

"You just want to help her celebrate, don't you?" Tito laughed.

"Maybe."

"Look at you!"

"Shuddup. Five dollars says she throws her flowers at me."

"Make it fifty, and you're on. Look at you! I didn't know you were such a, a…"

"Gambler?" she asked.

"A hopeless romantic."

"I am not."

"You're swooning already!"

"No," Toma said, though a few moments later she ate her words when she spotted Eva enter the chute. She wore a smoking-hot all-black outfit: black boots, black jeans, black button-up; everything trimmed in gold fringe. Her entire being glimmered under the arena lights. Eva readjusted her black Stetson and settled into Frida's saddle. The image caused Toma's body to tingle.

Eva's chest heaved; she blew out air; she closed her eyes. She gave a nod to the gate guy, and boom! Frida, gray lightning, attacked the first barrel hard, and then they were off to the next, skirting it with ease. Frida's featherlight step made it seem as though they were flying or hovering atop the dirt rather than running through it. Frida and Eva danced in total sync. The determination on their faces and the trust between them, told Toma both rider and horse believed that they'd win. Another crack of lightning to the finish, and they were through.

"That was…" Toma placed her hand over her heart.

"Yep, a hopeless romantic."

"Whoa ho ho, folks, take a look at the time she just put up: fourteen point two seconds of fire! Holy smokes," Price hollered, "hold on to your seats. Listen to this, folks. Listen. To. This. For the hundred and three years we've been keepin' track of this sort of stuff, we have an arena record! You saw it here!" The crowd erupted in wild cheers and chanted Eva's name. Toma laughed as Eva yelled and pumped her fist in the air as she circled the arena waving her hat and hugging her horse.

As Toma had hoped, Eva won the top spot. Melissa came in second, and, as Polly had predicted, Suzanne Westbrook got the third-best time. At the end of their runs, the contestants made their celebratory laps, doing their one-handed waves, wearing their satin sashes, and carrying their bouquets. The arena crackled with excitement. Eva rode past with a well-earned smile. She tossed Toma her bouquet.

"You owe me fifty bucks," she said to Tito. Her eyes did not leave Eva.

"Now you can afford to take her on a date."

"We're friends," Toma said.

"Not for long," Tito sang.

Toma wondered if there was truth in Tito's proclamation, especially because Eva had texted earlier to remind her that she was going to see her wild mustangs, and to ask if Toma was able to join.

CHAPTER FIFTEEN

EVA TOSSED AND TURNED UNDER her bed covers. Her to-do list with everything she wanted to accomplish in the week before the Pendleton Round-Up kept growing longer. She ran through all of her chores she needed to complete before her three-day camping trip to see her mustangs: pick up the plants, salt blocks, spools of wire, lumber, food, and hopefully, Toma.

Maybe she could force herself to sleep for another couple of hours. Eva pulled the covers over her head more tightly, but that didn't help. She reached for her phone, again, to reread the text exchange with Toma that had started around one-thirty in the morning, while Eva was at the Snake River Stampede after-party. Eva had wanted Toma to join, but Toma said that she needed to get home to relieve her dad's nurse. Eva and Toma had settled instead on texting all night.

You're missing out. There's pool here, Eva texted.

you just want me because i can help you win drinks.

That's not the only reason! How's your dad?

he's good. he says congrats.

Can't wait to see him. It's not quite the rodeo without your dad.

tell him that when you see him tomorrow. it'll make his year.

I will.

we're both excited to see you tomorrow. I can't wait to congratulate you properly.

Wondering what a proper congratulations feels like from you.

it'll involve cake.

LOL. Then I can't wait.

shouldn't you be enjoying yourself instead of texting me?

I know. I'm probably being rude.
get out there. enjoy yourself, Miss Angeles, record breaker!
Can't wait to see you tomorrow.
me too.

The rest of their exchange consisted of Toma promising to let Eva know if she was able to get away to see the wild mustangs. Awaiting Toma's answer was the real reason Eva couldn't sleep.

"Mija." Her grandmother had the courtesy to knock, which sounded more like pounding from a catapult than from a hundred-pound, eighty-something, five-foot-tall woman. "¿Tienes el día libre para desperdiciarlo soñando?"

"I'm up," Eva groaned. She couldn't remember a time when her grandmother, her mother, a sister, or someone from her family didn't wake her up. She needed to get her own place. The first thing she'd do was sleep in.

"¿Pues?"

"It's six-thirty, Abuelita."

"¿Y?" Her grandmother entered without permission as per usual. Her long white hair was worn in a bun atop her head. She wore her uniform: a flour-covered rose print smock with a dish towel draped over her shoulder. She had been making tortillas.

"It's my day off." Eva disappeared under her covers.

"Fine. Spend the day getting wasted, Evita, see if I care."

"I'm not going to waste the day." Eva yawned, then squinted when her grandmother opened the curtains, blinding her.

Her grandmother eyed Eva's newly won sash and belt buckle. "I'm proud of you, mija."

"Thanks, Grandma." Eva relented, sat up, and stretched.

"Your mother is going to miss you when you give this up to live with horses."

"My mother or you?" Eva had had many similar conversations like this. Whenever her grandmother had qualms, was worried, or wanted to challenge Eva, she pretended that it was Eva's mother who harbored those reservations.

"Your mother refuses to believe you would leave all this glory behind."

"I won't be that far away." The mustang herd was a two-hour drive from their farm.

"Your mother is also concerned that you won't be able to take care of yourself, to feed yourself, do basic things. Do you even know how to washing your own clothes?" Her grandma busied herself gathering Eva's dirty clothes. Eva was spoiled, she knew it.

"I'll figure it out. Worst case, I'll just buy new clothes."

"If I was younger." Her grandmother waved her fist in the air. "I'm proud of you, mija." She sat next to Eva.

"Thanks, Abuelita."

"What are you doing on your day off?"

"Give the horses a bath, run Vivian, pack for camping. I need cabbage. Oh, that's another thing I need to add to the list."

"Cabbage?"

"I thought I'd bring your coleslaw dish to the party tonight." Toma had gone crazy for it the night that Eva brought her rigatoni.

"Leave the cabbage to me; you do your horse stuff."

"You will?" Eva said.

"Si, claramente."

"Thank you, Grandma." Eva lay back down.

"Just because I will to making your cabbage doesn't mean you can be lazy and wasted."

"I'm up. I'm up."

"Over easy or scrambled for breakfast."

Eva popped back up. "Can I have burritos, please?"

"Si. Pues, put some peppers in your step." Aleida left with Eva's dirty clothes in hand.

"Thank you, Grandma."

EVA USED HER MOM'S SEDAN to drive to the Rozene's ranch so her dad could change the oil in her truck before her trip. She slipped into a spot amongst all the huge pickup trucks and trailers. With the coleslaw dish in tow, a sixer of beer, and a potted plant, which was a housewarming gift for Toma, and with the *Wonder Woman* sweatshirt draped over one arm, Eva headed toward the party. The thought of seeing Toma made her nervous. She laughed at herself and her nerves of steel in the arena that turned to free-floating pussy willow branches swaying to-and-fro at the whim of the wind when she was around the tall, dark, and handsome bullfighter.

She shook away the thought when she saw people she recognized: arena staff, gate hands, other old-timers. She spotted Red, who waved at her when they made eye contact.

"Hey, Eva!" Red gave her a great big hug when she caught up to him. "Congrats. Heard you broke an arena record. Damn, wish I could have seen you doing your victory lap, kiddo."

"Me too. Thanks, Red."

"Need a hand?" he asked.

"I'm good. You look great!" He wore his standard attire of cowboy boots, faded blue jeans, and a blue and white-patterned, short-sleeved button-down.

"Do not. I've put on twenty pounds just sittin'. I'm going mad doing nothin' all day."

"You do look great, and it's great to see you. I've missed you. It's not quite the same without you."

"Gee, that's a nice thing…" Red's eyes brimmed with tears. "Thank you Eva. I miss it like hell, damn it."

"It misses you too, Red." Eva eyed the neck brace in Red's hand, he spun it round and round. "I see you're following doctor's orders." She laughed, remembering Toma chucking her sling into the trash at the medical center.

"Hate this thing. Makes me feel sickly. Don't tell Nurse Ratched." He looked over his shoulder. "She's around here somewhere."

"She's got her hands full, I can tell."

"You enjoying my daughter?"

Eva blinked. Of course, she *was* enjoying his daughter; she enjoyed everything about her a little too much. "Uh-huh." She swallowed the lump in her throat.

"I'm glad she's here. Darn proud of her. She's good for the boys. They're glad she's home. We hope it's for good."

"Me too." Eva thought about asking probing questions in case he knew more about Toma's future, but decided not to invade her privacy.

"Toma said you're interested in training your students here, using the arena again?"

"Maybe, if the schedule works out, and it's not too much of a hassle for you."

"Ain't no hassle at all. I'd love to see people using it again. Just got too busy; couldn't manage everything alone."

"Maybe it's time to slow down a little, huh?" She patted his arm.

"You sound like my kids." He laughed, then turned his attention to a particularly loud friend who wanted to say hi to him.

"Enjoy your party, Red," she said. "Great to see you."

"Good to see you too, Eva." He squeezed her shoulder before he left.

Eva scanned the scene, spotting Melissa and members of her team engaged in conversation. She also spotted Polly, who gave her a little wave. Eva tried to wave back, but her arms were full. She smiled instead and nodded her head.

"Hey, Eva. Take that for you?" Tito motioned to the bag.

"Thanks." She hefted it over.

"What'd you bring?" He sniffed into the paper bag.

"My grandma's coleslaw and a jar of salsa."

"Sweet. Thanks," he said. "Any special instructions?"

"Nope. Just take the tops off; there should be serving spoons in there."

"I think I can manage that. Oh, and beer?"

"Carta Blanca."

Tito's eyes widened. "Awesome. That stuff is so hard to find. I'm going to go ahead and take that into the house and tuck it in the back of the fridge for personal consumption."

"Good call."

"What's that?" Tito asked, seeing that Eva held a small potted ficus.

"It's for Toma, kind of a housewarming thing, I guess." Eva felt her cheeks get warm.

"You mean a barn-warming thing."

"I guess so. Where is she?"

"Around here somewhere. Probably hiding out in said barn."

"Cool. Well, need any help?"

"Nah. I'm good. Food will be out soon. Grab a drink; coolers are over there. Let's toast your win later!" he yelled as he retreated.

"Sounds like a plan." She made her way to where most of the people were gathered. She learned why: a table full of appetizers and beer, and lawn games.

"Hey!" Melissa said. "I was wondering when you'd make it."

"Here I am." Eva hugged her. "Did you get any sleep after last night's craziness?"

"I spent the entire day sleeping; it felt so good."

"I'm so jealous. My grandmother woke me up at, like, six this morning."

"God," Melissa groaned. "I guess being on the road has some perks, sleeping in. What's that plant for?"

"It's for Toma. A housewarming thing, I guess." Eva felt silly carrying the thing around and explaining it to everyone.

"That's sweet. Get you a beer or something?" Melissa motioned at the coolers under the tree.

"Oh, sure. Surprise me." Eva sat on a picnic bench and put the plant in the center of the table.

"What's that?" Toma asked, making her way toward the picnic table, eyeing the plant.

"If I have to explain this one more time." Eva knew she had a huge grin on her face. "It's for you, kind of a housewarming thing, I guess."

"Thank you. That was sweet. Fair warning, I might kill it." Toma sat next to her on the bench. They looked at each other and shared a smile. "I didn't see your truck."

"I used my mom's car. My dad's changing the oil in mine."

"I see. Did you get any rest after your night of celebrating?" Toma asked.

"A little, my grandma—"

"Hey, Toma!" Melissa returned with Eva's beer.

"Hi, Melissa. Congratulations," Toma said.

"Thanks, and thanks for the invite. Want a beer too?"

"I'll get my own. You're the guest, sit down." Toma went to the cooler, fished out a drink, and barely beat Polly to the seat next to Eva. That forced both Melissa and Polly to the other side of the table. Eva thought they looked good together—totally, one hundred percent, without a reasonable doubt, a much, *much* better match than Toma and Polly.

"Cheers." Toma tapped bottles with Melissa, Polly, and Eva. "I'm glad you're all here."

"So," Melissa said, "rumor has it your parties get a bit out of control."

"Do they?" Toma alternated looks between Polly and Eva.

"They usually end with your brothers and a beer bong and then a pissing match. A literal pissing match." Eva enlightened them.

The group laughed.

"It's like I came back to their high school years." Toma shook her head.

"How long had you been gone?" Melissa asked.

Toma dropped her gaze; her hold on her beer bottle turned into a vise grip. Eva scooted closer to Toma and let their legs touch. Eva felt Toma exhale when Eva squeezed her leg gently. "It's been a while, twelve years. I didn't come home as often as I wanted or should have."

"You're here now; that's what counts," Melissa said.

"Cheers to your homecoming," Eva said.

The evening was a mix of great food, great company, and lots of laughter. Orange and crimson hues painted the sky, and a gentle breeze blew through. As the evening wore on, Eva and Toma drew closer together, sharing more than each other's body heat. Eva covered their legs with the *Wonder Woman* sweatshirt. Her heart somersaulted, especially when Toma's hand searched for hers under the fabric. Eva took it in her own. She touched Toma's fingertips as Toma explored too. Eva's feelings turned from friendly and supportive to lustful and incredibly aroused. Eva was certain that they shared looks that said they wished they were alone.

Every time she met Toma's gaze, Eva wanted to get lost in it. She shared Red's wish that Toma was home for good. Eva wondered what possible excitement a world traveler and former stuntwoman could find in the state of Idaho. Would anything, or anyone, be able to hold her attention and keep it?

Melissa's friends arrived with sweaters and bags in hand. "Well," Melissa said as she stood and stretched. "I think we're heading out now."

"You're not planning to drive straight through, are you?" Eva gave Toma's hand a gentle squeeze before standing up with the rest of their group.

"No. We're stopping in Baker. Picking up custom tack there in the morning," Melissa said, raising her eyebrows.

"Oh, custom. Fancy," Eva teased. "You're going to need it."

Melissa laughed. "Thank you so much for everything. You've all been totally great. I hope I can show you both a good time when I see you in a few days in Pendleton, at least to help soften the blow of me kicking your ass."

"Dream on, princess!" Eva laughed.

"I should go too." Polly stood and stretched. "I got an insanely early spot to film in the morning. Walk you to your rig?" She eyed Melissa.

Toma and Eva shared a look and watched them leave. "Ready for cake?" Toma asked.

"So ready."

Toma went to the food table and returned with a single plate of chocolate cake.

"Holy hell, that's a lot of cake. We're sharing, right?"

"Yeah." Toma laughed. "I think the boys have scrounged the beer bong supplies. We should leave now and eat this in the barn before all hell breaks loose. Grab forks. Oh, and my plant."

Eva followed Toma up the small incline to the stables. Toma opened the barn door.

"Great timing," Eva said.

"What? The sunset or the girls leaving?"

"Both."

"They make a great couple."

"A very great couple," Eva agreed. "Where's the couch?" she asked, seeing that the furniture had been moved.

Toma pointed. It faced the barn's west entrance so they could see the sun's descent into the horizon.

Eva followed Toma to the couch.

"Watching the sunset is one of my favorite ways to kick off the evening." Toma placed their cake on a nearby table.

"Me too," Eva said through a yawn. "Sorry. I'm a wee bit exhausted."

"Did I keep you up too late?"

"That and my grandmother woke me up at, like, six. Once I was up, I realized I had too much to do."

"No doubt." Toma patted the space next to her, which Eva took as encouragement to get closer. "Relax. Let's celebrate your victory."

Eva gave Toma a fork. They dug in, laughing and battling over the chunk of chocolate in the middle until Eva's fork broke. "Oh," she whimpered. Eva held the plastic stump.

"I got you." Toma presented Eva with her own fork loaded with cake. Before Eva could think about what she was doing, she leaned toward Toma, took the offering, and closed her eyes at the rich goodness. "That is *so* good."

"You like?" Toma licked her lips.

"Umm-hmm," Eva moaned.

Toma cut another piece and fed Eva again. She moaned and savored the decadent flavor. *Savored the decadent feeling of being fed.* "So good."

She opened her eyes to see Toma looking at her mouth and licking her lips. Eva so wanted to return the favor; however, to Eva's disappointment, Toma seemed capable of feeding herself. Toma handed the fork and the plate to Eva after taking a couple of bites.

"I like it better when you feed me." Eva smiled before taking another bite. She licked her lips and handed it back. "I'm done. I can't. Take it away."

She turned her body to face Toma. She sat with one knee tucked underneath and her arm stretched across the back of the couch. The view of Toma licking the fork was one hundred thousand times better than any sunset she'd seen.

"So... " Eva cleared her throat and picked at a loose string on the couch. "Are you able to get away this time to come with me to see mustangs?" Eva hoped that she made it sound like a casual request and not like she had been waiting the entire day to know.

"Oh, yes. I was meaning to tell you. I can."

"You can?" Eva clapped her hands.

"Um-hum." Toma maintained her focus on the fork before making eye contact.

"Fantastic. I'll pick you up day after tomorrow, around eight. Is that good? Too early?" Eva asked, finally able to relax.

"Perfect. I can't wait. Really. I've been looking forward to it."

"Me too. And you have a tent, or do you need one?"

"Tito says he has stuff I could borrow."

"Then don't worry about anything else." Eva leaned her head against the back of the couch. "I'm excited to show you my magical little world."

"I'm excited to see it."

Eva shivered and worked herself into her hoodie and covered her yawn with the back of her hand. "Some company I am."

Toma pulled the blanket off the back of the couch and inched the leather ottoman closer to them. She popped off her shoes and rested her feet. "Come here," she said.

Eva removed her shoes, stretched her legs, and nudged Toma's foot with her own.

Toma extended her arm across the back of the couch, and Eva worked her way next to Toma. "Is this okay?" Eva asked, settling fully against Toma.

"More than okay," Toma whispered.

Eva felt wonderful, right, warm, perfect, and content nestled against Toma, watching the sunset fade and the stars appear one by one. "Where's everyone going?" Eva saw a line of people with towels leaving the ranch.

"Night swimming. The lake is right over that hill there."

"Why didn't you tell me to bring my swimming suit?"

"You want to go?" Toma started to move.

"No. No. I'm good here. Let's stay. Please." Eva knew she sounded desperate. "Unless you wanted to go?"

"Nah."

Eva remembered to breathe once she felt Toma lean back against the couch. Eva closed her eyes. "Though, fair warning and sorry in advance, I might fall asleep."

"You'll be in good company."

"I love the way you feel." Eva wondered if she had said that out loud.

Eva jolted awake to the sound of distant shouts and laughter. "What time am I?"

Soft laughter ticked her ear.

"You're with me in the barn, on the couch; you were snoring, and the time is ten-twenty."

Eva groaned and leaned against Toma's warm, accepting body. "Did you say snoring?"

"It was adorable. Nothing crazy. You kind of sound like Debbie."

"Debbie? Who's Debbie?" Eva stirred.

"One of the cats that sleeps with me."

"Oh, God," Eva groaned and rested against Toma. "I see why the cats sleep with you."

"Why's that?"

"You're soft."

"I'll take that as a compliment."

"Do I smell fire?" Eva asked.

"I think the boys have a bonfire going. Did you want to join them?"

"Nuh-uh." Eva stretched her body and sighed. "You?"

"I'm good here."

"Am I heavy?" Eva asked.

"As if."

Eva turned so she could rest closer against Toma. Toma adjusted to accommodate and pulled Eva more snugly against herself. When Eva woke up the second time, they were lying lengthwise on the couch, arms wrapped around each other, bodies pressed intimately together, with a blanket pulled over them. Toma was asleep and Eva heard the faint sound of crickets, which signaled the party was long over. Eva wanted to ignore the fact that friends definitely didn't sleep together the way they were. She studied Toma: her dark lashes; high cheekbones; full, kissable lips that Eva so wanted to taste. Eva was so close she could feel Toma's soft breathing. Eva finally sat up. Toma groaned and sat as well.

"What's wrong?" Toma's eyes were still closed.

Eva found her phone. "It's one in the morning."

"Stay with me." Toma covered Eva's hand and nudged her phone away.

"My mom will be worried."

"Text her." Toma leaned back against the couch.

Eva ran her fingers over the glossy screen of her phone. The warmth of Toma's body challenged her decision. Her heart fluttered at Toma's touch, and she throbbed between her legs at being so damn close to her. She met Toma's concerned gaze; Toma's soft chestnut-colored eyes held hers.

"I should go," Eva whispered.

Toma nodded and stood up. "Are you okay to drive?" She offered Eva her hands and pulled her to her feet.

"I'm more awake now than I was when I got here."

"Thanks for coming. I had fun."

"Me too. Thanks for allowing me to sleep on you."

"I loved it." Toma pulled Eva into a hug.

Eva closed her eyes and let her entire body rest against Toma's. Toma's hands caressed her back, then rested at her waist. They stood that way for a long time.

"If I don't leave this second, I'll never leave."

"I'd be okay with that," Toma admitted.

Eva pulled back. "Thank you again."

"I'll walk you out. Thanks for the plant. Can I get you your bowls later?"

"Of course. Thanks for a great night," Eva said at her car.

"I can't wait to meet your horses."

"Me too." Eva became lost in the moonlight reflecting off Toma's eyes. She stood on the tips of her toes and left Toma with a kiss on the cheek. "Goodnight." She got into her car and closed the door.

She drove home confused as to where their relationship was headed. She was getting mixed signals because they'd been flirting hardcore and they were both guilty, even though Toma had said she didn't want to start anything. Just plain friends didn't entangle their limbs, didn't rest their heads upon each other's chests and their hands over each other's hearts.

Eva had broken her promise, crossed the line. They were more than friends, but what? She let her memory deliver her home.

CHAPTER SIXTEEN

TOMA REPLAYED HER EVENING WITH Eva. She remembered how good Eva felt in her arms. Eva's warmth, her desire, her hunger had been so evident in every one of her touches and when they prolonged their long, goodbye hug. Eva had kissed her. Toma touched her cheek where Eva had kissed. She wondered what would have happened had she returned her kiss. It would have started slowly at first, testing, exploring, figuring out what Eva liked best: slow and long or hot and fast. It would have caused Eva to wilt in her arms. Toma would have picked her up. Eva would have wrapped her legs around Toma's waist. Toma would have put her on the pool table, would have encouraged her onto her back. Then she would have ravished her—sent her sky-high after a tortuous dance with her fingers and her tongue.

"Hold this." Tito shoved the nylon bundle toward Toma and broke her reverie. "And this." He gave her another, bigger bundle that Toma presumed to be the tent. "And this." Tito fished out another rolled up bag and tossed it at her legs. Toma sneezed from the dust that flew from the storage closet.

"All this for sleeping outside?" Toma asked.

"You don't want the bedroll?"

"I definitely want the bedroll." Toma assessed her growing pile of camping crap. "There's just a lot of stuff."

"This is the bare minimum. When was the last time you went camping?"

"When we were, like, twelve."

"Oh, jeez, okay." Tito stood and slapped the dust off his hands. "You got your tent, bedroll, and sleeping bag. Flashlight, lantern; we might have batteries in the house. Oh, and the tarp. That goes under the tent. It will keep you dry if it rains. Hopefully, it doesn't, but it might."

"What else do I need?" Toma resettled her Stetson.

"What else did Eva tell you to pack?"

"All she said was bring my own tent and horse and that's it."

"Okay, then you're all set. And, that's a two-person tent, if you catch my drift." He nudged the bundle with the tip of his boot.

"Two-person tent?"

"If you catch my drift." Tito wiggled his eyebrows.

"Jesus Christ." She shook her head. "Last thing on my mind."

"What is on your mind?"

"Are you sure it's okay I take three days off?" Toma hoped Tito would need her help with something, anything. She feared alone time with Eva. They had crossed the line that Toma had drawn; rather, Toma had dragged the woman across the line she'd drawn. She'd drawn the line for a damn good reason: she didn't want to shortchange the woman with her baggage and her overall ambivalence with life. She enjoyed Eva's company a little too much, enjoyed touching her a little too much. The thought of being unable to let go scared her more than any free fall without ropes or hand-to-hand combat scene involving multiple knives.

"We're good until we leave for Pendleton. Seriously. Enjoy yourself, 'cause then it's Ellensburg, and Dad might join us if he gets the all-clear. So rest up, because we have a few back-to-backs before the big one: Vegas, baby."

"And then what?" Toma asked.

"What do you mean?"

"What happens between then and next year? Will you guys even need me once Dad gets on his feet?"

"Dad shouldn't be out there anymore."

"I was afraid you would say that," Toma said.

"Why?"

"Nothing. It's going to be a difficult conversation, that's all."

"And?" Tito asked.

Toma held her hands out to her sides. "And what?"

"You're itching to leave, aren't you?" Tito crossed his arms and leaned against a wall.

"Not at all. I'm just trying to figure out my next steps. I didn't really think things through when I left L.A. I was so scared about Dad and then everything with my ex. I knew I'd be here for the summer, maybe longer, but it's almost fall. I'm just trying to weigh all my options."

"What are your options?"

Toma shook her head.

"If you're staying long-term, we'll open the training center. That's a full-time job. The closest one is in Wieser. We still get emails about classes and rentals, and that's only going to increase with the little interview you gave."

Toma bit the inside of her cheek and looked skyward.

"It's good money. I'd help you, if that's what you're worried about, not that you need me. You'd be a fantastic teacher."

"I got an email last night."

"A job?"

"There's a *Wonder Woman* sequel in the works. They're looking for a lead stunt coordinator, head trainer, I'd get to hire and train the teams, I'd be the boss. It's mine if I want it, and they're willing to wait for me, at least until the end of the year."

"Oh," Tito said, in barely a whisper. "That's great."

"Yeah." Toma rubbed her neck.

"So back to L.A.?"

"It's a network job, so I'd be based in London for the foreseeable future."

"Sounds like a nice fresh start."

Toma nodded. "No doubt."

The twins stood in silence for too long.

"That fucking sucks," Tito said. "But I get it, really I do."

"You do?"

Tito nodded. "Of course. I mean, I love having you home. The rodeo is hella fun with you here, and all those cool sequences you taught us—those were badass. So much fun." Tito kept his eyes on the pile of camping gear.

"It is so much fun."

"Thanks for dropping everything to help with Dad. It was hard there for a while. He's doing much better."

"Yeah, he's looking good with the PT," Toma agreed.

"Yeah," Tito said.

"I'll come home more if I can, more than I did before."

"We'll come to see you too; we sucked at that."

Toma looked around the walls of the barn, a home she'd grown to find comfort within over the past couple of months, and thought about the memories she had created, especially the ones with Eva.

Tito rubbed his neck. "When do you think you will leave?"

"I don't know."

"Las Vegas is October third through the twelfth, I think; I got to look. But if you need to leave before that, we'll work it out."

"What about next year?"

"I'll talk to the guys and see what they want to do."

"Dad said you guys almost walked?" Toma rubbed her neck.

"We almost walked because it's time for Dad to call it quits. We tried to stage a walkout, but it kind of backfired. Dad got all mopey and threatened to pull out of the contract altogether, then he had his accident. You can't base your decision on us. It sounds like a rad job; you should take it. No-brainer."

"What about the ranch? This is too much for you by yourself. It's almost too much for the two of us."

"We'll hire someone."

Toma groaned.

"It's like you're looking for excuses to stay or something."

"I missed you guys."

"Aww, we missed you too. And?"

"And I like it here?"

"As flattered by that as I am, is this about a certain fringed rodeo queen?"

Toma nodded. "I really like her and I've only been here for two months. I want to see where things go."

"So see where they go."

"What if they go nowhere?"

"Then they go nowhere, but don't string her along while you're making your decision."

"I won't, but I've kind of made it a little bit complicated," Toma admitted.

"Then un-complicate it." Tito patted Toma on the shoulder.

"I've been clear with her from the start I'm not looking for anything more."

"Yeah, that's not what it looked like last night." Tito laughed.

"What are you talking about?"

"Puh-lease. I went into the barn to see if you wanted to come to the bonfire and saw you all wrapped around each other. Who do you think covered you with that blanket? You can thank me later, and, while we're on the topic, I'm glad to see you finally acknowledged your growing and obvious attraction. Even Pierson Price could see it all the way from the teeny, tiny announcer's booth."

"Shuddup."

"I'm happy for you."

"Should I tell her?"

"Definitely tell her you like her. I mean it's obvious, but she should probably hear it too."

"No, should I tell her about the job?"

"Of course. Tell her, especially if you're thinking you might leave. Like I said, no one wants to be strung along."

"I'm not going to string her along; that's not what I meant. It isn't as easy as all that. Stunt work, that lifestyle, is all I've known.

I'm good at it; I know what to expect. And, I don't know what she's thinking."

"Is this about your job or Eva, because it sounds like it's about Eva."

Toma focused on her boot. "She might not want anything more than—"

"A summer of sexy hot love?"

"Please, God. No." Toma groaned. "I don't want to ruin what we already have. Our friendship is good."

"Then don't ruin it, but you need to decide what you want to do."

"And then what?"

"Then do it. Easy, peasy. For what it's worth, I like Eva too. She's good people and she's good for you."

"How do you know what's good for me?"

"I'm making an assumption," he said. "I'm also assuming there might be spiders in your gear. You should probably shake everything out and make sure all the stuff is here while you're at it. I got to go."

"Aren't you going to help me?"

"Can't. I have to run to Middleton for salt blocks."

"Thanks again for the time off, Tito."

"Of course. Maybe it'll help put some things into perspective. See you tonight, and I got dinner."

"Thanks." Toma eyed the gear and sighed.

"What's up with Tito?" Red said as he sauntered into the barn a few minutes later. "Looks like his cat died or somethin.'"

"Oh, I don't know." She dropped her eyes.

"Need help sorting through all this campin' crap?" Red eyed the gear on the ground.

"I can do it, Dad."

"I'm so damn bored."

"All right," she relented. "You can talk me through how everything works, but no lifting anything."

"Deal." Red rubbed his hands together, and his face lit up with the excitement of helping Toma get ready for her camping trip.

TOMA RINSED THEIR BREAKFAST DISHES and set them to dry. She filled two travel mugs with coffee. "Sounds like she's here," Toma said, hearing the rumbling of Eva's truck.

"Unless it's one of the boys." Her dad closed his newspaper and peered out the window from his spot at their kitchen table. "Gabby's coming over a little later to look at the sink."

Toma took another look to confirm. "It's her." Her heart leapt at seeing Eva, first with joy, then with nervousness and ambivalence. She needed to tell Eva how she felt, sooner rather than later.

"Which horse are you taking?" Red asked.

"Tito suggested Betty."

"Good pick. She's easygoing, won't get into trouble or get frightened by the wild horses on the range. Plus she's got the hips to haul stuff for you."

Toma laughed. "That's what Tito said. Okay, Dad, you need anything before I go?"

"Not at the moment."

"There's plenty to eat in the fridge."

"I got it," he said. "Quit worrying about me. Have fun, 'cause when you get back we have tapes to review, notes. Pendleton Round-Up ain't no joke. You guys have a lot of tightening up to do, you hear me?"

"I can't wait to review every minute of those tapes with you, Dad."

"Smart-ass, now go on, get."

"See you when I get back, and go easy on the nurse."

"Why, what did she tell you?" Red inched the newspaper over slightly to eye Toma.

"Everything," Toma said before hugging her dad. "Bye. Love you."

"I love you too, kiddo." Red resumed reading his newspaper.

Toma opened the back door to see Eva opening the trailer. She looked cute in her white tennis shoes with no socks and a green cotton scoop-neck T-shirt that accentuated her full breasts and that was tucked into well-worn blue jeans. Her hair still looked damp from her shower.

"Hey, Toma!" Eva waved to her.

Toma lifted her two mugs in the air as she walked over. "I got primo coffee for us," she said with a smile. She placed their mugs inside her truck and tossed her pack into the back seat with Eva's. Tito helped Toma heft her gear to Eva, who arranged it in the bed of her truck. Toma saw plants, salt blocks, bundles of firewood, boards, bales of hay, a stove, a saw, a hatchet, camping gear like hers, folding chairs, and coolers. "Are we moving out there?"

"I hope so." Eva used the back of her hand to shift her hair from her eyes.

Tito walked Betty into the trailer next to Eva's horse Vivian. "Be good, girls." He patted Betty's rump.

"The horses will be fine, don't you think?" Toma asked when Tito joined her.

"I wasn't talking about them."

Toma pretended to punch Tito in the stomach.

Tito pretended to retch.

"Okay, what else?" Toma asked.

"I have one more thing that you absolutely need for camping."

"What?"

"This." Tito handed Toma a flask.

"What's in it."

"Tequila. In case it gets cold, it'll keep you warm."

"What will keep you warm?" Eva said as she jumped from the bed of her truck. She removed her gloves and held them in both hands.

"This." Toma waved the flask in front of her.

"What's in it?" Eva asked.

"Tequila," the twins said together.

"Oh, I tend to get a little crazy when I drink tequila," Eva warned.

"Hold on while I run and get the bottle."

"Ignore him," Toma advised. "Hi." She wrapped her arms around Eva to hug her, but resisted the urge to carry her to her bedroom and play out her pool table fantasy.

"Hi." Eva's words caressed her ear.

"Get a tent."

"You know, you are right," Toma said, narrowing an eye at Tito, "getting away from you will be good for me."

"I never said that."

"You didn't?" Toma opened the passenger door. "Okay, got to go. I'll call when I can."

"Take care of my sister. She's not the outdoors type. She's real delicate-like."

Eva laughed. "I won't promise she won't come back sore."

"Oh, really?" Tito's eyes widened.

"From manual labor!" Eva laughed.

"Right."

"Ready?" Eva asked.

"I was ready yesterday."

They split the bill at the grocery store for supplies, water, a ton of food, and a couple of bottles of wine.

"You should see your face." Eva smiled.

"What's it look like?" Toma asked.

"You're the picture of wonderment."

Toma watched the passing scenery: sandstone hills, tan with stripes of vivid reds and dotted with light-green sagebrush, stretched as far as the eye could see. The chorus of colors gave voice to the valley's astounding beauty. The majesty of the snow-capped Owyhee Mountain Range, backed by the blue expansive sky, overwhelmed Toma's senses.

"It's breathtaking here." Toma rolled down her window to take in the crisp air. "Not a cloud in the sky."

"It's my kind of heaven."

"Are we almost there?" Toma asked, when Eva turned onto a gravel road that had barbed wire fencing on either side.

"Yep." Eva slowed as the truck bumped over pits in the road. "Those trees are where we're headed." Eva pointed to a grove in the distance. "Here's where I want the center to be." Eva pointed.

"Why here?"

"It's a short trek from the river, not that far off the main road, and far enough from where the herds hang out that they won't be bothered." Eva inched her way until she came to a halt.

"Did you say river?" Toma asked.

Eva slapped her hand against the steering wheel. "I forgot to tell you to pack something to swim in."

"I brought something, just in case."

"We can go swimming later if you want."

"Yes, please." Toma assessed her surroundings. "What's that?" Toma noticed something large and canvas-covered in the distance.

"That's the Airstream. I keep supplies in it and tools, and, if it rains, it's where I sleep. But I don't reckon it'll rain while we're here."

"You don't reckon, do you?" Toma laughed at Eva's choice of words.

"Are you making fun of me?"

"I reckon I am."

"By the way, we only have instant coffee."

"You didn't pack an espresso machine." Toma gasped before stepping out of the truck. She settled her Stetson and stretched, reaching for the sky, before helping Eva unload the horses. They walked them around to stretch them out before securing them in a makeshift pen complete with a water trough and feeding station. They unloaded their supplies, then set up their tents, the folding table, cooking range, and chairs.

"What first?" Toma asked after swapping her boots for sturdier hiking shoes.

"I was hoping we could finish that." Eva motioned at an area where a handful of four-by-four posts stuck up from the ground.

"What's it going to be?"

"A shelter where horses could take cover when they need to."

"Sounds like a plan. Tell me what to do."

"I plan to." Eva tossed Toma a pair of work gloves, which Toma missed catching. "I intend to squeeze as much manual labor out of you as I can while I have you."

"Do you now?" Toma slipped on her gloves and helped Eva heft the lumber toward the construction site. Toma held boards for Eva while she pounded nails, held the measuring tape for her, sawed boards, and ran for items that Eva requested. "God, this is work."

"I've built seven of these."

"By yourself?"

"Most of them, yes."

"I thought you said you had volunteers."

"I do. But that's exactly it; they volunteer when they can and, for some reason, everyone's had a really busy summer this year."

"You shouldn't be out here alone, Eva. What if you get heatstroke or get hurt?"

"The trick is to stay hydrated," Eva said, tossing Toma a bottle of water. They continued working until two o'clock.

"I'm seriously overheating, Eva." Toma took off her tank top, dabbed her forehead with it and hung it on a post. She wore a sports bra. She caught Eva eyeing her body. That seemed to increase Toma's body temperature by several thousand degrees.

"Lunchtime?"

"Yes." Toma panted, placing her hand on her stomach.

"Are sandwiches okay?" Eva asked.

"I'll eat anything." Toma slumped into a chair and watched Eva make PB&J sandwiches and dole out carrot sticks. They ate, enjoying the sounds of their horses and the wind as it rustled through the trees that provided much-needed shade.

"There, there, there." Eva scrambled for her binoculars, nearly dropping the plate that she balanced on her lap. "Oh, my goodness. God, I love them."

"You should see your face." Toma smiled.

"Look," Eva said. She handed Toma the binoculars without taking her eyes off the scene and pointed. "See that dust cloud. They're checking us out." She rested her hand on Toma's knee.

Toma tried to concentrate on the herd, but the warmth of Eva's hand proved too distracting.

"Cool, right?"

"No doubt."

"You haven't seen anything yet. There'll be more of them at night. They'll surround us. It's a feeling like no other." Eva sat back into her chair with a huge smile.

"Thanks for inviting me." Toma shoved a carrot stick in her mouth. She was honored that Eva would share such a special part of her life.

"Thanks for joining me."

They worked another hour before calling it a day. "It's way too hot," Eva proclaimed.

"Thank you, Lord Jesus." Toma chugged more water.

"Want to go swimming?"

"Yes! Please. Can we?"

"Let's put this stuff away and change."

Toma retreated into her tent to change. She wore an oversized linen wrap over her swimming suit. She grabbed her towel and loosely tied her hiking boots. She resettled her hat and snacked on carrot sticks while she waited for Eva, who emerged wearing jean shorts and a blue spandex tube top under an opened white button-up shirt and tennis shoes without socks. She had a towel over her shoulder

"Wow," Toma exclaimed, shoving a carrot stick into her mouth.

"Wow what?" Eva stole the carrot stick that was sticking out of Toma's lips.

"It's been a while since I've seen someone rock a tube top."

Eva rolled her eyes. "Come on, let's go."

Toma fell in line behind Eva, and they walked the short distance to the river. Its current looked fast in a few places, but, in general, it looked like a lazy river with calm pools. "Is it deep?"

"In places." Eva walked them to a sandy area shaded by trees. She spread her towel, then wiggled out of her shorts.

Toma gulped when she saw Eva in her bathing suit. Her tube top more than accentuated her ample breasts. Toma couldn't wait to see what happened to Eva's body when she got wet. Eva's physique exuded strength and beauty—her toned muscles, bronzed skin and beautiful legs, her tiny feet, and… "Love the farmer's tan." Toma laughed.

"It took me all summer to get it just right." Eva worked her long, wavy hair into a bun atop her head, then inched into the river. "Coming?"

"After you."

"It's cold!" Eva shrieked, wrapping her arms across her chest as she dipped in.

Toma doubted that the cool of the river would temper her fever. She spread her towel next to Eva's, slipped out of her shoes, dropped her linen wrap, and waded in.

Eva's eyes doubled in size while she ran the length of Toma's body. "I wouldn't have pegged you as a bikini-wearing woman."

"You can blame the French Riviera."

"Don't they also go topless there?"

Toma pulled the string of her top; Eva's eyes widened, and her jaw dropped.

Toma laughed. "You believed I would do it!"

"You're a tease!" Eva laughed and splashed water at Toma.

"Shit, it is cold." Toma wrapped her arms around herself and tensed, not from the cold of the water, but from Eva's lingering inspection of her body. She waded past her and submerged. She floated on her back, closed her eyes, and let the gentle flow cradle her farther into the river. A rush of stronger current sent her careening toward an area of calm. "It's nice right here. There's warm water mixing with the cool. It feels perfect." She popped up, shook her hair out, and looked for Eva; she was making her way toward her on her back. Her beautiful breasts and hard nipples reached for the sky or maybe Toma's mouth. "Be careful, right to your right," Toma warned.

"That current comes and goes and it's stronger on some days than others," Eva said.

Toma waded toward Eva, planted her foot, and offered an out-stretched arm. Eva grabbed hold. Toma wrested her from the water's pull. Toma held on to her until she was sure that they were both free from the flow. She let her go and missed Eva immediately. "You good?" she asked, avoiding eye contact.

"Thanks." Eva dunked herself and then ran her hands through her hair.

"This is the most relaxed I've been in I don't know how long," Toma admitted.

"Are you telling me I need to work you harder tomorrow?"

"All of it, the work, the sun, spending time with you. Seriously, thanks again for showing me your little slice of heaven."

"I'm glad you were finally able to get time away."

"Whenever you want to come out here, let me know. If I can break away, I will." Toma chided herself for making promises she might not be able to keep, especially if she was leaving at the end of the summer. Toma took several deep breaths and toyed with the idea of telling Eva about her possible job offer. But why cast doubt on their time together speculating about a job Toma hadn't even accepted?

"I'm starting to get pruney," Eva said a while later. She held her hands in front of her.

"Me too," Toma confirmed after inspection of her own hands. "Shall we move it along?"

"That's probably a good idea."

Toma started working her way to shore. Seeing that Eva struggled through the current that had picked up, she asked, "Want a hand?"

"Sure," Eva yelled while reaching for her.

Toma planted her foot, reached for Eva, grasped her hand, then swooped her up and into her arms. Eva squealed and shouted along with Toma, who carried her the entire way. Toma felt as though she was Tarzan and Eva was Jane. She deposited Eva directly onto her towel, where they lay and enjoyed the sun's warmth while stealing heated glances.

IN THE MIDDLE OF THE night, Toma heard, rather felt, what Eva was talking about. The thunderous pounding of galloping horses beating their hooves upon the earth, thumped her chest. Toma slipped into her hiking boots and unzipped her tent. Eva had blankets and pillows spread inside the bed of her truck and the tailgate lowered. Eva was laying down.

"Did the horses wake you up?"

"Feels like an earthquake."

"I love it."

"Can I join you?"

"Of course."

Toma dropped her shoes next to Eva's and hoisted herself atop the tailgate and inched toward her.

Eva had her finger pointed to the sky and was muttering to herself.

"Shooting stars?"

"I've already seen, like, ten."

"Really?" Toma lay on her back trying to spot one. She turned to Eva, who was looking at her.

Eva turned her gaze back to the celestial wonderment. "There's another." Eva pointed. "It's a comet, I think."

"Where?"

Eva reached for Toma's hand, and pointed it.

Toma gasped. "I see it. Can you make a wish upon a comet?"

"Of course. But you have to close your eyes."

"Okay." Toma giggled.

"Are you closing your eyes?"

"Uh-huh."

"It doesn't work if you don't." Eva laughed gently.

Toma felt a hard shiver run through Eva. "Are you cold?" she asked.

"A little."

"Come here, then." Toma moved her arm under Eva's neck and pulled Eva into her own body. Eva's hand settled right over Toma's thundering heart. "Did you make a wish too?" Toma asked.

"Of course." Eva's voice broke when she spoke. "This is beautiful," Eva said a short time later.

Toma didn't ask Eva what, specifically, was beautiful. All of it was beauty: the range, the stars, the sounds of the herd, their closeness. Whatever it was, was beautiful and perfect. They held each other, watching the stars until Toma fell asleep to the sound of horses running and their own mingled, soft breathing.

CHAPTER SEVENTEEN

THEY WOKE UP FREEZING IN the truck bed in the middle of the night, teeth chattering. As if in unspoken agreement, they retreated to Eva's tent and snuggled under her sleeping bag and blankets. Toma pulled Eva against her body and held Eva like a flotation device. Each of them used the other's body for warmth. Eva wondered if Toma could feel the pounding of her heart. Eva tried to calm herself, but because of Toma's soft breath against her neck, Toma's hands caressing her stomach, and Toma's skin burning against her own, she failed completely.

Eva awoke alone after sunrise with the worst ache in her hip. Usually, when she slept outside in her magic little haven she awoke rejuvenated—not this time. Instead of sleeping, Eva had spent the night trying to tame her growing arousal. She'd often wanted to shift her position from her aching hip, but didn't. She would have waked Toma and, if that had happened, there'd have been no way in hell she could hide the lust in her eyes or tamp her arousal or lessen the ache between her legs, and so Eva lay still all through the night and now she was sore as hell and incredibly aroused.

Eva groaned when she sat. After stretching and getting dressed, she made her way to Toma's tent. "You up?" She heard nothing. "Toma?" She unzipped the tent and peeked in, but Toma wasn't there.

At their campfire, Eva saw that Toma had already fed the horses and stoked the fire. Eva started a pot of coffee. She saw Toma approaching wrapped in her towel; she'd been swimming.

"Good morning!" Toma waved; she wore a huge smile. "Sleep well?" she asked.

"Really well. You?"

"Me, too, and that swim felt refreshing."

"Wasn't it freezing?" Eva asked.

"It was perfect."

Eva took a cup of coffee to her. Their fingers brushed. "Good morning, early bird."

"Morning, sleepyhead." Toma lifted her mug in salute and took a drink. "Oh, that's good."

"Oh, really? Plain old instant coffee?"

"There must be something special in it. What's the plan for today?"

"I thought we could finish the shelter, then saddle the horses and walk the fence. I know there's at least one repair we need to make."

"Sounds perfect."

"Egg burritos and salsa for breakfast sound good?" Eva asked.

"It sounds fabulous. Thanks." Toma spread her towel on her chair and sat down. "I'll make dinner tonight."

"It's okay. Take a break. I know you cook a lot for your dad."

"And you cook a lot at your restaurant," Toma countered.

"Okay, sue me; I like cooking for you."

"I like it when you cook for me."

"Then it's settled." Eva licked her lips at the sight of Toma's bikini through the slits of her pale blue, loose-fitting muscle tank top, her washboard abs, her perfect breasts, and that smooth, soft skin that she'd grazed her fingers against while they *slept*. Toma stretched her long legs, crossed them at the ankles, and leaned back, warming herself in the sun. A dripping wet Toma at seven in the morning was as close to a wet dream as Eva had ever had.

After breakfast, they resumed work on the shelter, finishing it well before ten o'clock. They saddled their horses in silence, stealing glances as they worked. Eva packed their tools and a small spool of barbed wire. Toma carried their lunches and water bottles in Betty's saddlebags. Eva watched Toma mount Betty and settle into her saddle. Eva tore her gaze away but was drawn to her again when Toma edged out in front of Eva.

Between Eva's legs throbbed when she watched Toma's hips gyrate at the gentle pace of her ambling horse—slow and steady, over and over. The woman had the most amazing posture. Eva's growing arousal was further encouraged by Eva's tight jeans and the pressure against the hard, slick leather saddle. She trotted Vivian past Toma so she could clear her mind and focus on their task. This was getting ridiculous. She needed to get a grip, and the only way to do that was to talk.

They rode the fence for two hours, stopping to fix one break in the wire.

"I'm hungry." Toma trotted her horse alongside Eva's.

"Then we should feed you. I know just the place to eat." Eva led them to a group of syringa next to a stream. "A family of horses lives here." Eva pointed at the distance, through an opening in the treeline where rushes and branches bent and twined.

"They know all the best places," Toma said. "Is this you?" she asked, referring to the hitching post.

"All me," Eva confirmed.

"What's for lunch?" Toma took the paper bag from Betty's saddlebags and peeked inside.

"Sandwiches again. Hope that's okay."

"Perfect."

Toma joined Eva on the blanket that Eva had spread on the ground. They ate in silence, shared the binoculars, and enjoyed the calm of the lazy afternoon. Eva had always enjoyed her sacred places alone. However, with Toma it was so much better, so much more relaxing, peaceful, and perfect.

"This sun makes me sleepy." Eva pulled off her boots and lay on her back.

"Me too." Toma followed suit. "It's so quiet out here." Toma adjusted her hat over her eyes, folded her hands across her stomach, and crossed her legs.

"I've been wanting to ask you something." Eva had to know what Toma was thinking.

Toma cocked her hat to the side so she could see Eva. "Ask me what?"

Toma's soft eyes, long eyelashes, and beautiful lips scrambled Eva's senses. "Your hand," she blurted.

Toma held her hand up and looked at both sides.

"The other one."

"What about it?" Toma raised her other hand and moved it toward Eva. Eva held it in her own.

"This." Eva held on firmly to inspect a small scar at the base of Toma's palm.

"A Viking sax."

"What's that?"

"A short sword."

Eva hissed. "What happened?"

"When I was working on *Vikings*, I was training with another woman, practicing an intense knife scene. It wasn't even the blade that got me. It was a freak thing. The hilt broke; the wood stabbed me. Blood everywhere."

"Oh, I hate blood." Eva caressed the small scar with her thumb.

"It wasn't the worst thing that's happened to me."

"What was the worst thing that's happened to you?"

"Broken collarbone. I missed my target from the top of a three-story building. I fell wrong. Kept me off a horse for a couple of weeks."

"Just a couple of weeks!" she shrieked.

"I have a high pain tolerance," Toma said.

Eva squeezed Toma's hand and laughed as she remembered Toma chucking her sling in the trash can at the hospital. "I'd die if I couldn't ride for that long."

"It was hard, I'll admit." Toma flexed her hand. The tips of her fingers extended over Eva's. "Your hands are so tiny."

Eva looked at the size difference and imagined how Toma's long and slender fingers would feel if they found Eva's skin, what would happen if they explored her body, her breasts, teased her nipples. Eva wondered how she'd respond if Toma's fingertips searched lower and trailed through the most sensitive part of Eva's body, and how it would feel when Toma plunged inside her. Eva crossed her legs and steadied her breath so as not to give herself away. Toma entangled their fingers and brought Eva's hand to her chest, where it rested. They lay that way for a long time; Toma's breathing slowed.

"I'm going to fall asleep if we don't get back out there." Eva reluctantly pulled her hand away.

"Is that a bad thing?"

It would be if they resumed their sleeping arrangement from last night. Eva popped up. "I want to squeeze a couple more hours out of you before we call it a day." Eva stood over Toma and held out her hands to help Toma to her feet.

"Well, my union break isn't over." Toma took hold of Eva's out-stretched hands and pulled her on top of her. Eva yelped and worked her way to a sitting position straddling Toma's waist. She was moments away from bending for a kiss, moments away from rolling her hips into Toma's, moments away from losing her self-control.

"Toma..." Eva whispered. They needed to talk before anything serious happened, but when Toma's gaze alternated between her eyes and her lips, all logic went out the window. She pressed her lips against Toma's. Nice and easy, just a taste, but then Toma brushed her tongue against Eva's bottom lip and then her top lip. Nipping gently, she coaxed her way inside. The soothing sensation of Toma's tender touch and the growing urgency of their kisses sent shivers coursing through Eva's entire body.

Eva rested the weight of her body against Toma and melted into her, wanting to surge against her without restraint and without distraction. Her common sense, her sanity, told her to apply the brakes before it was too late. She pulled back slightly, intending to say something, but before she could get a word out, Toma arched upwards and claimed her mouth entirely.

They began to explore. They twirled their tongues, giving and then taking, searching, alternating between slow and fast and then long and deep. Toma tasted like a setting sun, rays of brilliance filled Eva from the inside out.

Her breathing became increasingly difficult and her logic more convoluted when Toma's hand slipped under her shirt, ran up and down her back, slowly lifted her shirt higher. Eva let a lingering moan escape that mingled with Toma's hot breath.

"You feel so good." Toma's words vibrated against her lips.

"Fuck," Eva gasped when she pulled away. She rubbed the back of her hand over her own lips.

"Sorry, I'm sorry." Toma's breath came in spurts. "That got out of control, really fast."

"I knew that it would." Eva pushed herself off Toma and backed away, giving herself distance.

"I've been wanting to do that for so long," Toma said when she sat up.

"Me too, but, Toma, I'm so confused. I thought you didn't want to get involved, but, obviously, we're getting involved, really involved. I need to know what you're thinking. I don't want to get hurt, because I like you. A lot," she whispered.

"I like you too, Eva, really a lot. I'm sorry for the confusion and mixed messages. I thought that I needed time to process everything about my ex, which I do, or I did, and I am and I have. I know where it went wrong and I know where *I* went wrong." Toma ran her hand through her hair and squeezed her eyes shut.

A gust of wind blew through the trees. Toma exhaled deeply and relaxed her shoulders. "I don't let people in. I don't let anyone get close to me. That's wrong. I get that. How is that any way to love and be loved? It's not." She met Eva's gaze and held it. "What I don't understand is, how'd you do it?"

Eva gave her a soft smile. "Toma, I didn't do anything." Toma's brow knitted, and she rubbed her forehead. "You let me in all on your own."

A flash of understanding flickered in Toma's eyes. She sat up straighter. "I tried to fight it, the feeling of being seen. It's new and foreign, but this, with you, feels so good and so right. It's too hard being your friend, because I want more. There. I said it." She gasped.

"I've wanted more since the moment I met you and then when I touched you, I lost my mind."

"I'm sorry this got so complicated, that I'm so damn complicated."

"You're not that complicated. I mean, sure, life can be complicated, but it doesn't have to be if we're honest with each other about what we want. Right? Maybe we start there?"

Toma nodded and licked her lips. She drew her knees against her chest and stared into the distance.

"We don't have to figure everything out right this second, but at least we know we're on the same page. Maybe we take it slow and continue to get to know each other and go from there."

Toma nodded.

"Then come on, cowgirl." Eva stood, offering her hands once again, pulling Toma to her feet. "You okay?"

"Yeah. You?"

"Oh, yeah." Eva made her way to the hitching post and mounted her horse. She nearly came on the slow ride home.

"WHAT ARE WE HAVING TONIGHT?" Toma asked after returning from her task of unsaddling, brushing, and feeding the horses.

"I was thinking, roasted vegetables."

"White wine, then." Toma fished the bottle from the cooler, untwisted the screwcap, and filled their travel cups. "Cheers," she said, handing Eva her cup.

"To you," Eva said.

"To me? Why me?"

"For volunteering with me."

"This doesn't feel much like work."

"Then tomorrow I'll make it feel more like work," Eva promised and continued chopping vegetables while Toma stoked the fire to a crackling roar. Even though Eva said she'd handle dinner, Toma couldn't sit still, and so they shared the task of skewering the vegetables and grilling the kebabs. Toma held the plate for Eva, while Eva used the tongs to remove them from the fire. "Salud, amiga."

"Cheers," Toma echoed. "These smell amazing."

When Eva took her last bite, she looked over to Toma's plate, still half full. "Apparently I was starving."

"You worked hard today."

"No harder than you," Eva said.

"Okay, then you're a more ravenous eater than I am."

Eva laughed. "That's it." She stood to rinse the dishes.

"Sit. I'll do the dishes."

"No argument from me. Thanks." Eva added a log to their fire, then settled down, wrapped herself in a blanket, and set her gaze upward to the stars that had begun appearing.

Toma finished her meal, then gathered their dishes and rinsed them in the river. She returned a short while later and followed Eva's lead by wrapping herself in a blanket and turning her attention to the stars.

"You okay?" Eva asked, noticing that Toma was unusually quiet, maybe because of their kiss and conversation. If Eva was honest with herself, her mind was overrun with thoughts and emotions too. She'd been clear what she wanted from the beginning. To find out that Toma had wanted the same thing all along, and been fighting it, blew a big hole in Eva's self-control. That kiss had been hotter than fire. It was all she could think about: the taste of her, the smell of her, the feel of her.

"Just thinking."

"About what?" Eva asked.

"Do you want to get married?"

"Wow, okay. What?"

"Not will you marry me," Toma said with a laugh, "but do you ever want to get married?"

"Are we playing twenty questions?"

"Sure," Toma said.

"In that case, I have about a hundred and one questions I want to ask."

"A hundred and one!" Toma laughed again. "Maybe it's time to bust into Tito's flask."

"Good call."

Toma winced after taking a swig from the flask. She passed it over. "Here's to getting acquainted."

Eva grimaced. "That's strong." She coughed.

Toma chuckled.

"Okay, marriage, ready? Here goes. Eventually, I'd like to meet someone who wants to share my dream: run the center, help it grow, travel, share life's adventures, become little old ladies together, and all of that."

"Your dream sounds beautiful."

"I think so. What about you? Are you the marrying type?"

"Oh yeah, for sure. I want the whole nine yards; cake-cutting, photographs. I want to see my brothers dressed in tuxes, only because I think they'll hate it."

"What about the whole sharing your life and your dreams with someone?"

"That's important, too, though I feel like I should have some idea of where my life is headed before I ask someone to share it with me."

"That might be a good start, or maybe not."

"Or not?"

"I'm just saying, there's no real order in which it has to come. Maybe finding your purpose comes along after sharing. Maybe, I don't know. What do I know?" Eva said.

"You have a good point. I've been so focused on trying to figure everything out first, but yes, I do want to find that special someone one day and share myself with them, no doubt." Toma reached for the flask. "Okay, favorite genre of music?"

"Lila Downs."

"She's not a genre; she's a person."

"I know." Eva laughed. "But I love her."

"So do I; her range is incredible."

"Agreed. What's your favorite type of music?"

"I like songs with bells."

"Songs with bells?" Eva asked.

"Motown, gospel. Songs with bells."

"Got it." Eva took a swig. "Favorite movie with horses?"

"Oh, that's a hard one." Toma thought. "*The Horse Whisperer.*"

"That was your first movie, right?" She remembered from Polly's interview.

"Yeah, but that's not why it's my favorite. There's something about connecting with an animal, seeing their needs and working through their fears, and, in the end, realizing those fears were your own and that the horse was the one who helped you through them."

"Beautiful." Eva handed the flask back to Toma.

"Favorite color?" Toma asked.

"Gold. Yours?"

"Neon."

Eva giggled. "I want to revise my answer. I like the color glitter."

Toma laughed. "Solid choice. The last dream you had?"

"I don't know if I remember." Eva searched within the flames of the fire for the repressed memory. "Oh, I remember. I was watching people gleaning on our property—"

"Gleaning?"

"After we're done harvesting, we let people come onto the land and glean for leftovers. People bring their own shovels and dig up boxes of onions, potatoes, stuff like that."

"Don't you guys want them?"

"They're usually pushed too deep into the soil by the machines; it would cost us too much to go back and dig them out."

"Gleaning. That's cool. Generous of your family," Toma said.

"All the farmers do it. Whole families go out there and collect stuff and take them to church and to their neighbors."

"So the dream?" Toma asked.

"I was watching people gleaning but, instead of onions, they pulled out babies, like, fully dressed babies."

"Like a Cabbage Patch doll?"

Eva laughed. "Damn! Million-dollar idea a few decades too late."

"No doubt. I wonder what it means."

"You got me," Eva said.

"Do you want kids?" Toma asked.

"I don't know. Do you?"

"I don't know." Toma took another sip from the flask and winced.

"Okay. Your last dream."

"I don't remember where I was, but I was sitting in makeup on set and I looked in the mirror and I didn't see my reflection as I was that day, but when I was a kid, like twelve, then seventeen, and then twenty-one."

"Weird."

"I think it has something to do with me being home."

"That makes total sense. Speaking of, how's your dad?"

"He had a hard time after the party, talking with his old friends. I think it hit him that he's done. His dream is over. He has lost a lot: the training center, the rodeo, my mom."

"He's gained you, right?"

"I guess so. I've literally been the worst family member. I ran from them, forgot about them. I've missed the past decade, more, of their lives."

"Why did you run?"

Toma drew her knees up and wrapped herself tighter inside her blanket before answering.

"You don't have to answer if it's too personal."

"I had this big fight with my dad when I was, like, seventeen. We'd fight all the damn time, but this time, he told me I looked like my mom, which I do. He said he couldn't look at me; it was too hard for him sometimes." Toma shook her head.

"I'm sorry."

"He doesn't think when he talks. He didn't mean it, and I know that he feels guilty. I, on the other hand, took it out on my entire family by leaving. I was really immature back then. I'm still really immature now, since it only recently occurred to me how wrong I was."

"Hold up. I wouldn't say that you were immature, Toma. I probably would have reacted the same way if my only parent said that to me. I would have run too. That sounds extremely hurtful."

"It was."

"You made the best decision for your health and wellbeing; that sounds incredibly mature if you ask me. Don't doubt that for a second. Nothing wrong with putting yourself first."

Toma nodded and met her gaze. "Thanks."

"How are things now?"

"Good. He apologized to me, kind of, in his roundabout way. Said thanks for keeping the boys together and coming home to help. It was a big step for Dad. I forgive him. I missed him and I missed the boys."

"Sounds like you're having fun getting reacquainted. It always looks like you're having fun in the arena."

"I totally am." Toma finally made eye contact. Firelight danced in her eyes.

"For what it's worth, I'm having fun watching you too. The only female bullfighter in the state. In fact, you're the only one that I know of in the entire Southern Spark Circuit. Do you have any idea how exciting that is for the rest of us?" It took every last bit of Eva's resolve not to jump into her lap and resume their make-out session. "Did you see the comments from Polly's story?"

"No."

"'Toma's a total inspiration, she's a total badass. She's given a ton of women and girls hope for breaking out of stereotypical molds the rodeo has perpetuated.'"

"What? Get out of here. How do you know that?"

"I may have watched the interview a couple of, three or four times."

"That's kind of cool."

"It's really cool. Those are the comments and all of them are true, and, if you stay, prepare to be even more famous." Eva laughed and Toma smiled, but Eva didn't see the emotion reach Toma's eyes.

They sat in silence, content to stare at the fire and polish off the rest of the tequila.

"I have a lot planned for tomorrow, *Little Miss This-Doesn't-Feel-Like -Work*. We should get some sleep."

"Good call. Thanks for the conversation, Eva. Today was fun."

"It was fun."

Eva wondered if she should invite Toma into her tent, then remembered they had agreed to take it slow. "Want to go for an early morning swim together?" she asked.

"For sure. Wake me if I'm not already up."

"Got it. Will do. Goodnight, Toma." Eva retreated to her tent. She didn't think she'd ever fall asleep; she was a bundle of nerves. Sometime during the night, a clap of thunder woke her. She shot up and zipped her tent open. "Toma! Did you hear that?"

"Hmm?" came a groggy voice.

"We don't have much time," Eva shouted. She heard the pattering of a thousand sprinkles on the roof of her tent.

Toma unzipped her tent and peered out. "What's going on?"

"Rain. Lots of it. Get your sleeping bag and your clothes. Get mine too, please, and take everything to the Airstream. I'll put everything else inside the horse trailer."

They ran around securing their belongings and getting drenched.

"Hurry!" Toma waved Eva into the Airstream and closed the door. "Where the hell did that come from?"

"They come out of nowhere out here," Eva said after catching her breath. The sound of pouring rain and thunderclaps filled the air.

"I guess so." Toma jumped when a soul-shattering thunderclap shook the Airstream.

Eva turned on a dim lantern and rounded up towels from the storage cabinets. She tossed one to Toma. "Hang your wet stuff there." She pointed. "We can dry it outside in the morning." Eva watched Toma towel-dry her hair, then remove her clothes before she began rummaging for dry clothing in her bag. Toma stood naked before her as if it was nothing. Eva caught a glimpse of her body every time the lightning strobed. Toma's nipples were hard from the cold rain and pointed toward Eva as if inviting Eva's mouth. Eva tried to pull her eyes away. Only when Toma stepped into her dry clothing was Eva able to break her lusty gaze.

It was Eva's turn to shed her sopping wet clothing. She caught Toma's eyes go straight to her breasts when she lifted her shirt and they popped out. Toma's gaze ran the length of Eva's entire body when she wriggled out of her soaking shorts. "Much better," Eva said to break the silence.

"Where do we sleep?" Toma asked.

"This way." Eva led her to the small bed in the back. "Are you okay with it? Or the couch in the front converts into a bed. I've just got to move some things."

"No, it's okay. This is fine," Toma said.

She giggled. "You want the window seat or the aisle?"

"The aisle, please." Toma laughed gently.

Eva scooted toward the window to give Toma plenty of room. They lay flat on their backs, staring through the skylight at the light show and the rain coming in sheets. The clouds parted like theater curtains for the grand finale, revealing a sky thick with stars. "What the hell was that!" Toma sat up.

They turned to face each other and erupted into laughter.

"Just like that," Eva said. "In and out in the blink of an eye." Eva rolled open a window, letting a cool breeze bring the smell of fresh rain into the Airstream. "The first few times I stayed out here I got soaked to the bone and had to sleep in the horse trailer. It was miserable."

"Your Airstream was a great investment." Toma settled onto her back again with her arm under her head.

"I won it at the Reno Days Rodeo."

"Really?"

"Along with a set of DeWalt tools."

Toma started laughing. "What a cool prize."

"Being a rodeo queen has its perks."

"It just occurred to me that I've probably spent a third of my life in a trailer."

"Have any cool, crazy stories?" Eva asked.

Toma laughed. "Yes, but none that are G-rated."

"Now you got to tell me." Eva nudged Toma's foot with her own. They lay in silence for a long time. "Are you comfortable?" Eva asked, sneaking a peek at Toma to see that her eyes were already closed. She thought that Toma had fallen asleep judging by the soft pace of her breathing. Eva turned onto her side, facing the window, and closed her eyes too.

"Actually, no," Toma whispered.

"You're not?" Eva turned, propped herself onto her elbow, and looked down at her. "Are you cold? Do you want me to close the window?"

"It's not that."

"Then what?" Eva asked. "Tell me what I can do to make you more comfortable. Please."

"When you fell asleep against me… that one time…"

"Which time?" Eva chuckled and lay on her side facing Toma.

"The first time, in my apartment, after the party."

"I remember," Eva whispered. She closed her eyes, feeling that familiar heat surge between her legs and swirl throughout her body, causing her nipples to tighten.

"You said you loved the way I felt."

Eva inched herself closer to Toma; the heat of Toma's skin radiated against her. They became a tangled unit of intertwined limbs. Soft caresses led to that feeling when a jumbo jet hits an air pocket and it feels as if the bottom dropped out. "I didn't think I said that out loud."

"You did," Toma whispered.

"And I do, that's no secret."

"I love it too." Toma pulled Eva closer.

Against Eva's better judgment, she kissed Toma—softly at first. Maybe this time she'd be able to control herself. But Toma's lips felt like a summer breeze, gently whispering against her lips, telling her to forget the world and fly with her at the speed of light.

Toma's kisses traveled lower, to Eva's neck and then her chest. Eva grabbed fistfuls of Toma's hair as she guided Toma to where she wanted her. Toma found Eva's skin, lifted her shirt. Eva arched toward her, and Toma claimed a nipple, licking gently one and then the other, using her tongue and her fingers, teasing them into rock-hard points.

Toma wedged her leg between Eva's. Eva knew she was busted. Toma must have felt the wet heat through her thin shorts. Surely, Toma felt her desire pulsating against her thigh as she gyrated against her. Eva's mind whirled. Was this really going to happen? They were no closer to an understanding now than a few hours ago.

"What happened to taking it slow?" Eva asked between ragged breaths.

"This is too hard," Toma whimpered and ceased all movement.

"I know. I'll move to the couch."

"No, it's not that; we need to talk." Toma groaned.

"Okay." They worked themselves apart. Eva tried to read Toma's expression in the moonlight.

"You said life didn't have to be complicated if we were being honest with each other."

"I remember," Eva said.

"I need to tell you something." Toma focused on her fingers while Eva imagined the worst—that Toma was leaving. Eva knew it; she felt it.

"I was offered a job. Lead stunt coordinator for *Wonder Woman*, the sequel. I'd get my own team. They're willing to wait for me until the season ends. It's based in London."

"Toma that's... I'm so happy for you."

"You are?"

"Of course. I mean, part of me would love it if you stayed here so we can explore this, but I could never ask that of you. It sounds like a dream job. A *Wonder Woman* sequel—that's so cool." Eva lay down. She felt as though someone had knocked the wind out of her and she'd forever be searching for restorative breath.

"It is a good opportunity. Everything I've worked for in my career, all my training, my experience, is culminating in this one amazing role of a lifetime." Toma's voice quivered.

"It sounds like you'd be living your dream."

"Yeah."

Eva remembered how quiet Toma had always become whenever Eva mentioned life after the season. Her behavior suddenly made sense. "How long have you known?"

"I just found out, like, the night of my dad's party. After you left, I got the email. I'm sorry I didn't tell you sooner, when we were... at lunch... when we kissed... before we kissed." Toma shook her head.

"I get why you didn't."

"I'm sorry."

"Don't be. I think we should take a step back, like a big step back, from all of this. I can't; we shouldn't. I'm already..." Eva thought her advice, her insistence that life wasn't complicated if they shared the truth, had backfired.

"I know."

"Thank you for being honest with me."

Eva rolled onto her side and lay awake for hours and she suspected that Toma did, too, but eventually, she fell asleep.

EVA WOKE WITH THE SUN. It sent rays of light to illuminate the understanding they had reached.

"Eva?" Knocking at her trailer door startled her.

Eva shot up. "Rosie?"

"Yeah, I was able to get away from the clinic; thought I'd see if you needed help."

"Give me a moment, be right out! The rain caught us."

"Us?"

"Gimme a moment."

"The vet friend?" Toma sat up.

"Yeah," Eva confirmed. The look in Toma's eyes haunted her: loss, longing, and something else that Eva couldn't place. But she knew one thing. It was too late to avoid falling, Eva had fallen, and next was only leaving. Sex with Toma would only further confuse everything that she felt.

CHAPTER EIGHTEEN

"MIND YOUR OWN BUSINESS," TOMA said for the millionth time. She'd already dodged several of Tito's questions, and, now that she was captive in the truck on their way to Pendleton, Danny started piling them on as well.

"You are our business; didn't you read the fine print on your contract?" Danny asked. "Same line as having to go to Valley Medical if you defy Nurse Beth." He laughed.

"I should have ridden with the other guys," she mumbled. Her three other brothers, Benji, Gabby, and Elroy, followed closely behind, hauling six of their horses, while she, Tito, and Danny hauled the other six. The entire trip, three-and-a-half hours by car, took almost seven with their horses and gear in tow.

"I thought you were going to come back from camping all chipper and shit; instead you returned a grouch. What happened?"

"Tito said you were definitely going to get laid."

"She *totally* didn't get laid."

"Oh, my God, shut up!"

"Talk to us," Danny said. He turned to face Toma, who was seated in the back.

She pushed at his head.

"Hands off the hair!" Danny smoothed his new buzzcut. "We're not going to stop until you tell us what happened, baby sister." He moved his seat back, trapping Toma.

"Danny!"

He laughed and crossed his arms behind his head as he nearly lay in the back seat.

"Christ, there's nothing to talk about. We built a horse shelter, we repaired fencing, and I almost died the last day setting out salt blocks and planting native grasses and seedlings." She stretched her neck.

"Eva wasn't lying when she said you'd come home sore." Tito winked at her in the rearview mirror.

Toma nodded. She and Rosie had spent the entire morning trying to keep up with Eva, who worked like an overcaffeinated madwoman.

"So, nothing happened?"

"Nothing happened." Toma dropped her eyes and ran her fingers over the cover of the book she was trying to read.

"Was that so hard?" Danny asked as he returned his seat to its original position.

"Don't you have anything better to talk about, something to read?"

"You think *I* should be reading?" Tito asked from his position in the driver's seat.

"You're going to have to entertain yourselves. I'm reading." Toma focused on her book and the wisdom of Emily Dickinson. She read the same line over and over. Words like *stillness* and *air*, and the *heaves of the storm* floated in her mind making no sense whatsoever. She closed her eyes and thought about the heaves of the storm of her complicated life. It had been a blessing and a curse that Rosie showed up. She and Eva didn't have to talk about anything nor were they able to talk about anything. Then, on the ride home, both were completely exhausted; they scarcely said two words to each other. When Eva dropped her off, they gave each other an awkward, stiff goodbye hug, nothing like how they had held each other before they were between the heaves of the storm that she felt she'd created. She hadn't talked to Eva since saying goodbye. It had been a grand total of two days without texting. She missed her so much. Reality had set in, and now she was more lost, nowhere closer to any decision about her next step, and maybe without her closest friend. The blinker of the truck signaled they were pulling over.

"I gotta piss like a racehorse."

"Me too."

"Me three," Toma said, after rolling her eyes at the lame expression.

"Local celebrity alert." Tito laid on the horn, waved out the window, and pulled next to the gas pump.

"What the fuck, Tito?" Toma placed her hand over her chest.

"Miss Rodeo Idaho. Isn't that Eva's big-ass truck and big-ass trailer? Oh, and look, her entourage."

"Sure enough."

They pulled next to Eva, who was fueling up. Her dad was with Eva as was Rosie.

Toma reached for her Stetson and climbed out of the truck.

"Hey, Toma." Rosie came up; Eva followed. "Are you as sore as me? Holy shit. My arms are killing me from those salt blocks." Rosie stretched one of her arms.

"Holy hell. Me too. How about you? You okay?" she asked Eva.

"I'm good. You?"

"Good too. You ready for tomorrow?"

"Born ready." Eva gave her no hint of that soul-soothing smile. "I got to… " She motioned over her shoulder. "…you know."

"Piss like a racehorse?" Toma asked.

Eva raised her eyebrows.

"Sorry," Toma said, "that's what happens when I spend an extended amount of time with my brothers."

"I got brothers too," Rosie added. "I can't imagine five of them."

"I don't recommend it." She and Rosie fell in line behind Eva, who went into the truck stop store.

"See you later, alligator." Danny smirked when she passed him.

"What the hell are you talking about?" Toma asked.

She went into the restroom with Eva and Rosie. The trio emerged a short time later and found their way to the cooler. Toma selected an energy drink, Eva chose a can of diet soda, and Rosie grabbed water. They walked to the cash register. Toma felt her pockets.

"Uh-oh. My wallet's in the truck." Toma glanced over her shoulder. "Be right back."

"I got it." Eva placed her hand on Toma's shoulder, preventing her from leaving.

Toma eyed Eva's hand on her skin and then met her eyes. "Thanks. I'm good for it."

They walked out through the sliding doors. Toma looked for their truck but didn't see it. "What the hell?" She scanned the large parking lot in time to see the back of her family's horse trailer leaving the rest stop and her brother's arm hanging out the window, giving a thumbs-up. "What the bloody hell?"

"Everything okay?" Rosie asked.

"They left me. They fucking left me." Toma's phone rang in her back pocket. It was her brother. She unlocked the phone, "God, damn it," she said before hanging up.

Eva cracked her can of soda. "Need a ride?" She took a drink. "I charge by the mile."

"Thanks. My brother's good for it," Toma said. Seeing that Eva's dad and Rosie climbed into the front seat, she joined Eva in the back.

"Papá, this is Toma. Toma, this is my papá."

"Hi, Mr. Angeles. Thanks for the ride."

"No es problema. Please call me Roberto."

"Thanks. Sorry about this." Toma eyed Eva, thinking that Eva probably wanted to be alone. Toma made a mental note to kill her brothers later.

"Is nothing. Glad for the extra company," he said. He made eye contact with Eva from his spot in the driver's seat and winked.

Eva told her dad something in Spanish that Toma presumed was Eva describing how idiotic her brothers were. She closed her eyes and took a deep breath. Eva's dad turned over the engine, and music came on over the radio. Rosie was midway through a novel. Eva held a magazine in her lap but stared out the window.

Toma sent Eva a text message. *you okay?*

Eva's phone buzzed. She read the message and began typing. *I'm okay.*

can we talk later? Toma asked.

Of course. Eva nodded, then closed her eyes and fell asleep for the rest of the ride, which left Toma once again alone with her thoughts.

When they pulled into the hotel parking lot two hours later, a smiling, bubbly former Miss Rodeo Oregon, Melissa Faye Jackson, greeted them. She, along with several fringed and glittering friends, staffed tables covered in tinsel and even more glitter in the hotel's foyer. A huge banner hung from the ceiling, welcoming the Pendleton Round-Up contenders. Toma dodged big hats and bigger hair as she navigated the lobby.

"Eva!" Melissa shouted and ran to her. She wrapped her arms around her. It was the first time Toma had seen Eva genuinely laugh since before they'd had their talk. The way Melissa touched Eva didn't sit well with Toma. Even though she and Eva had reached an agreement to slow down, to back off. Toma realized that, for the first time in her life, she was experiencing the cake *having* and cake *eating* phenomenon.

She made her way to the check-in desk and learned that her brothers had already checked her in. She got the key, found her room, and forgave them only because they had hauled her bags to her room for her. No sooner had she plopped onto the bed than she heard a knock on the door between their rooms.

"Open up," Tito said. "Hey, you made it," he said when she opened the door. "Took you long enough."

"You asshole. What the hell was that about?"

"That was all Danny. I tried to stop him, but he's got like twenty-five pounds on me." Tito laughed. "Hey, you okay?"

"I don't want to talk about it right now."

"Hey, baby sister, are you two girls still fighting?" Danny asked. "You can thank me later."

"Oh, my God, no one is fighting." Toma took the bottle of beer Danny was holding, placed her hand on his chest, pushed him back to his side of the door, and locked her side.

"Hey!"

Toma took a hearty chug of her beer, fell onto her bed, and placed her bottle of beer on the nightstand. She fell asleep. Commotion down the hall, drunken cowboys no doubt, woke her up. She groaned when she sat up. The sun had already set. She looked at her phone. She'd slept for two hours. Toma ran her hand through her hair. She had several messages, all from Eva.

Where'd you go?

Are you okay?

We got the horses offloaded. A bunch of us are getting together for a drink a little later.

Would love it if you joined.

We're at the Brave Horse, it's across the street from the hotel. There's pool. Melissa and Rosie would love to see you.

Sorry, we missed you.

About an hour after the string of texts, Eva sent another one.

Now's a good time to talk if you still want to??

Hope you're okay. See you in the arena tomorrow. Goodnight.

She needed to talk to Eva. She hadn't even thanked her father for the ride.

you awake? Toma texted.

Barely. You okay?

i'm so sorry. i fell asleep.

I wondered what happened to you.

can we talk now? please?

Toma's phone was silent for a solid five minutes. Toma knew it was because Eva had a healthy amount of self-preservation.

sorry i didn't realize it was so late. I know you got a big ride tomorrow. Toma texted, giving Eva an out.

I'm in 612, the door is open.

Toma washed her face and brushed and flossed her teeth before going to the sixth floor. She rapped her knuckles against the door and let herself in, letting the door latch behind her. It didn't seem Eva heard her over the sound of the air conditioner. Eva was lying on her bed looking at her phone. She wore jean shorts and a black tank-top. She had goosebumps, her legs were crossed at her ankles, her head was propped against two pillows, and her arm was tucked behind her head. Her hair sprawled over her pillow.

Toma cleared her throat. "Hi," she said.

"Hi. Come in." Eva sat up.

Toma entered the room and leaned against the desk. "Thank you for the ride today."

"No way I would leave you stranded."

"My brothers are so stupid." Toma rolled her eyes and shook her head.

"What did you want to talk to me about?" Eva inched toward the foot of the bed.

"You said something in the Airstream—didn't say something, per se, but, well, you assumed something."

"Assumed what?"

"You assumed I was going to take the job."

"You didn't give me any reason to assume otherwise. Besides, why wouldn't you?" Eva asked, keeping her eyes trained on the floor.

"You. Us."

"Toma, we've known each other for all of two months."

"So."

"So, that's, crazy." Eva gasped.

"Is it really?"

"You love your work, Toma. I hear it in your voice when you tell me about it. I see it in your eyes, in your body language—"

"No."

"I see your love for it whenever you look at me."

"I'm not thinking about my work when I'm looking at you, Eva. I'm thinking about you."

Eva opened her mouth and then closed it. "But, you'd be giving up—"

"I'd be giving up nothing and gaining everything. I've found this sense of peace, this connection, that I never felt before, in being home and working on the ranch and being close to you. I want to explore it. It doesn't have to be complicated if we're honest with each other about what we want. Right? You said that. I know you believe it."

"And what happens if we explore this connection, and it doesn't work? I don't want you to make this huge, life-changing decision about your future because we kissed."

"You don't give your kisses that much credit."

"Seriously, Toma."

"It's more than that Eva, come on."

"What will you do here?"

"I don't know yet. Maybe open my dad's school again; maybe offer bullfighting lessons. I don't know yet; it's all under consideration."

"But is that enough for you?"

"You are enough for me. Why are you pushing me away?"

"Because I'm scared." Eva wiped her tears from her eyes. "I've fallen for you, head over heels, hard, from the moment I met you. I wasn't looking for this, and now you're here and you could be there." Eva held her hands out in front of her. "The fact that you have the role of a lifetime in the palm of your hand, that you'd trade it for—"

"For us, for this, a chance, that's all I'm asking for. I've fallen for you too. You're sweet and caring and funny and the hardest-working woman I've ever met, who always knows the right thing to say."

"Stay with me long enough and you'll realize I have my flaws too."

"And I have mine. I'm still working on a lot, I won't pretend, but the way you make me feel when you touch me—" Toma ran her hand through her hair. "I've never felt such power simply touching someone before."

"I don't want to lose you as a friend, Toma."

Toma knelt at the edge of Eva's bed and took Eva's hands in her own. "I don't want to lose you."

"What are we going to do?"

"We continue to get to know each other; we continue to take it slow."

"Then what?"

"What else is there but each moment?"

Eva moaned and leaned forward. Toma caught her against her own body and held her. She closed her eyes, smoothed her hair, and kissed the side of her head. "I missed you so much."

"Will you stay the night? We don't have to do anything. I just want to be close to you." Eva's words against Toma's ear broke her.

CHAPTER NINETEEN

THE SECOND-TO-LAST NIGHT OF THE Pendleton Round-Up was party night. Eva had plenty of reason to celebrate. She was half a second under her closest competitor, Pendleton's own Melissa Faye Jackson. Melissa was a good sport about it—she said it fueled her competitive spirit, which, in turn, inspired Eva to do even better. Eva knew in a couple of years the girl would be on her way to surpassing Eva's records. By then, Eva would be retired from racing, living her dream, running her mustang center, leaving her legacy for all to aspire to.

She wondered what her and Toma's legacy would be—if it would be. She thought about her sweet, beautiful Toma, whom she'd met on a plane with tears in her eyes, lost and heartbroken, and how, when Eva took her hand, there ignited a spark that had burned so brightly and so intently that Toma had decided to give up what she loved for something she loved more. Eva shivered at the thought that Toma loved her so much. Maybe it wasn't love, but something else. She remembered Toma's words: to trust each moment as they came.

As they had promised, they were taking it slow, even though she and Toma had spent every night together. They hadn't kissed or touched more than they could bear. She closed her eyes, took a deep breath, and thanked the universe that she'd been able to manage her excitement and her ambivalence, to keep it out of the arena and win her races.

Eva looked at herself in the mirror. She'd put her hair in a low bun and wore an olive-colored, button-up sleeveless silk blouse tucked into black jeans and tan boots. She group-texted Rosie and Toma that she was headed for the lobby. They'd walk to the Brave Horse Tavern, where they'd meet Melissa.

By the time Eva made it to the elevator, Rosie was already waiting.

"Ready to let loose?" Rosie asked.

"So ready." They hopped inside the elevator. It stopped on the fifth floor. Toma walked in. She looked stunning. Her hair was slicked back and tucked behind her ears, her black Stetson sat atop her head. She wore a neon-green tank top tucked into light-blue jeans, her *Wonder Woman* belt, and black boots. The doors were closing when a pair of hands stopped them.

"Hey, females." Tito grinned. He was followed by Toma's four other brothers. From the sounds of their voices, they had already started drinking.

"No. No," Toma said. "One of you is going to have to take the next car. We can't all fit."

"Sure, we can," Gabby proclaimed. The overgrown boys pushed Eva toward Toma until her backside met Toma's front. She nestled against her. Toma rested her hands at her waist while they rode the elevator to the ground floor. Eva wished the ride was longer.

Melissa met them at the entrance to the Brave Horse. They shared celebratory shots of something that tasted like fire. The place was crazy. It felt as if the entire town of Pendleton was packed inside the bar celebrating the day before the end of the world.

Eva couldn't take a drink of her beer without someone bumping into her. She gave up. She didn't want to chip a tooth. Sneaking looks at Toma was way more intoxicating than anything the bar had to offer.

"You up for a change of scenery?" Melissa shouted for the third time.

"What'd you have in mind?"

"Dancing!"

Eva looked around. "Where?"

"We have to take a cab! It's not that far! You game?"

Eva gave her two thumbs up.

"Let's get the girls!"

Eva spotted them from across the bar. Toma was deep in an intense-looking conversation with her brothers, judging by their expressions: scrunched eyebrows, surprise, laughter, then punching on the arms.

"We're going dancing. You in?" Melissa asked when they got closer.

"Of course," Toma said.

"Where are we going?" Tito asked.

"Sorry. Ladies only," Melissa said.

"What?" He held out his hands.

"Trust me. Where we're going, no one will want to dance with you."

"You underestimate me."

"It's a lesbian bar."

"Oh." He took a drink of his beer. "Yeah, I think I'll have better luck here." He eyed Rosie.

"Rosie, you in?" Eva asked.

Rosie alternated looks between Eva and Tito. "I'm going to hang behind."

"Are you sure?" Toma asked. "This guy can't be trained and is way behind on his vaccinations."

Rosie laughed. "I'll take my chances."

"Okay," she warned. "Suit yourself. Bye, Tito. Have fun," Toma said in a singsong voice. She blew him several kisses accompanied by smooching sounds. Tito shooed the laughing trio away. Eva held Toma's hand. They played bumper cars to get out of the building.

After a short cab ride, they arrived at *The Lone Wolf*, a fitting name for the town's only lesbian bar. The place vibrated from country music that poured out of its windows and doors. They ordered drinks and followed Melissa to a giant table where her friends were drinking and laughing. Cheers erupted as they approached the boisterous party.

"Do you like dancing?" Eva asked Toma.

"Love it." Toma's eyes lit up.

"Save a dance for me!" Eva yelled as Melissa pulled Eva toward the dance floor, where they lost themselves in several songs. After working up a sweat, they joined the others for another round of drinks. No sooner had they sat down than a woman asked Toma to dance. Woman after woman asked Toma to take them for a spin, and Eva could see why. Toma had serious dance moves. All the ladies who danced with Toma grabbed onto her butt while they danced. Eva narrowed her eyes and chewed the inside of her cheek while she waited her turn.

"When did you two hook up?" Melissa asked as she moved close to Eva.

"Who?" Eva pulled her eyes from watching Toma.

Melissa nodded at Toma, who was smiling at Eva even though she was dancing with another woman.

"Toma? We're friends," Eva insisted.

"Get out of here."

"I'm serious."

"Please. The way you're looking at her? You want to eat her for breakfast, lunch, and dinner."

Eva threw her head back in laughter. "I'm serious. Friends, that's it."

"I'd love to find me a friend like that." Melissa laughed and nudged Eva's ribs.

"Okay, so maybe we're more than friends."

"See, was that so hard?" Melissa laughed.

"Yes!"

"I'm happy for you, you make a great couple."

"Thanks."

A breathless Toma returned for a drink, poured herself a glass of beer from their shared pitcher, and took a hearty gulp. She lifted her hat and used it to fan herself. She blew on a lock of hair that had worked loose. "The women here are demanding."

"That's an accurate characterization. Ready for more?" Melissa asked Eva.

Eva didn't want to leave Toma. They hadn't spent time together all night, but Eva didn't want to be rude. "Heck yeah." Eva held out her hands for Melissa, who pulled Eva to her feet so quickly, they nearly tumbled over. They worked their way to the dance floor. Eva didn't need to turn around to know that Toma's eyes followed her as she danced with Melissa to "Baby's Got Her Blue Jeans On," then "The Arizona Yodeler," and "The Sidekick Jig." They were all fast-paced oldies, chock-full of twang and two-part harmonies, with quick-picking fiddle playing that warranted knee-slapping and dancing like a chicken, all arms, all neck. She felt a presence behind her at the end of the song.

"Can I cut in?" Toma asked.

"By all means. Lucky you," Melissa said. "Slow song."

"Isn't that how it is?" Eva gave Melissa a toothy grin as Patsy Cline's "San Antonio Rose" carried over the speakers. The lazy melody of the slide guitar coupled with the bright sounds of the piano and jazzy, upbeat percussion set the stage for Patsy's ballad about sweet and tender lips and being under the stars at night. Eva took hold of Toma's hand, rested her other one on Toma's shoulder, and felt the heat of Toma's hand resting at her waist, then splayed against her back when Toma pulled Eva against her. "Are you enjoying yourself?" She looked up to meet Toma's eyes.

"I've burned more calories here than in the arena saving people's asses."

"You're quite the popular woman." Eva twined her arms around Toma's neck.

"It's the belt buckle. It gets them every time."

"Is that right?" Eva smirked.

"It's how I got you," she whispered against Eva's ear.

"Oh, really?" Eva pushed Toma back and laughed.

"It's my ultimate signature move."

"You got a lot of signature moves."

"You have some pretty awesome moves yourself." Toma twirled Eva.

"I don't, but thank you."

"Agree to disagree," Toma said.

"Want to know a secret?" Eva asked after being twirled again.

"Tell me."

Eva stood on the tips of her toes, and Toma bent over her. Eva sighed as she arched up to meet her, reveling in the exciting feeling of Toma's hands across her back. "I can't stand country music."

Toma roared with laughter. "Your secret is safe with me."

"Good thing, as I suspect they'll revoke every one of my crowns if they find out."

"No doubt they will."

"Can I cut in?" a woman asked Toma. Eva stepped away, only to be pulled back to Toma.

"Sorry, I'm done dancing for the night," Toma said to the woman.

No sooner had that woman left when another asked to cut in. Again and again, the women kept asking.

"The ladies here are pushy," Toma said after an unhappy woman didn't understand the meaning of no.

"Do you want to sit down?" Eva asked.

Toma shook her head. "I want to keep dancing."

"I've got an idea," Eva suggested.

"Tell me."

"Kiss me."

"Ah, the famed fake kiss." Toma laughed. "That's the oldest lesbian trick in the lesbian playbook."

Eva laughed. "I know, but it's a tried-and-true trick. Trust me. It'll work."

"I have no doubt that it will."

"So?"

"Hmm, let me think. Okay. I'll do it. I'll kiss you."

Toma put her hands on Eva's hips, pulling her closer. Eva rested her hand on Toma's chest.

"Wait." Toma giggled.

"Oh, my God, you're killing me."

"What kind of kiss?"

"Well…" Eva looked up. "It has to be believable. We're in a lesbian establishment; they'll know if it's anything less than genuine. Got it?"

Toma laughed, then nodded. "Got it."

"Are you sure?"

"I know what to do." Toma licked her lips.

Eva gasped when Toma nudged her long leg between Eva's and pulled her as tightly as she could against her body. She snaked her arms tighter around Toma's neck. Her sense of time and place fell away, just as it did in the arena. She no longer heard the loud music or saw the people or the bar. Eva's entire world became Toma and her lips and their kiss that went on forever.

Toma's kisses no longer felt as if she was a woman confused between divergent roads and burdened with convoluted life choices. Her kisses felt sure, certain, and as if she knew exactly where she wanted to go and how to get there. With them came an undeniable power, magic, and wonder, all wrapped up in a hot-as-coal kiss.

"How am I doing?" Toma whispered against Eva's lips when she pulled away.

Eva could only nod. No words would be adequate; besides, she hadn't enough oxygen nor sense to form rational thoughts, especially when Toma tilted Eva's head and ran her lips along Eva's neck, nibbling and licking.

Eva's leg's buckled. She'd only read about that happening in books. Toma didn't let her fall; she supported her with her body, her arms, and her legs—her heart.

"Do you think they bought it?" Toma whispered against Eva's ear.

"Bought what?" Eva closed her eyes and shook herself free from desire's crippling effects.

Toma laughed softly against her ear, sending a hard shiver straight to Eva's groin.

As Eva predicted, no one else interrupted them. They had each other to themselves, slow dancing even to rowdy songs. Eva couldn't pull away, and Toma wouldn't let her. They hugged each other's bodies and kept in constant contact.

"Do you think we're being rude?" Toma asked.

"Rude?"

"We should join them."

"Yeah. Probably a good idea." They walked hand in hand to the table of animated and buzzed women. Eva and Toma didn't say a word to each other but communicated through touching each other under the table. Eva ran her hand up and down Toma's thigh; Toma's muscles tensed when she touched her. Eva ran her nails along her leg. Toma's entire body clenched the closer Eva's fingers approached in between Toma's legs.

"We're headed to an after-party," Melissa said when the other women stood and collected their belongings. "I'd invite you, but I suspect you have your own little after-party planned." Melissa waved her hand between Eva and Toma.

Toma's eyes widened.

"I'm happy for you. Seriously. As much as I'd love a try." She pointed to Eva, who wore a shocked expression. "I can see I'm a long-shot, last-place contender for the prize money."

"Did you just call me prize money?" Eva shrieked.

"Toma's the top money earner in this whole thing!" Melissa laughed.

"Oh, God." Eva laughed as she worked to her feet and hugged Melissa. "Thank you so much for the great time and hospitality. It's been so much fun."

"Keep her up all night, Toma, I'm going to need the advantage tomorrow!"

"Dream on, princess!" Eva punctuated her statement with a thwap on Melissa's backside.

Toma stood and shoved her hands in her back pockets. She looked dazed, distracted, aroused.

"I'll call us a ride," Eva offered.

"I'll get the tab." Toma returned a short while later with two bottles of water. She handed one to Eva.

"Thanks," Eva said, and chugged the whole thing. "Whew. Dancing is work."

The cab ride to the hotel took all of seven minutes. Eva held Toma's hand the entire time and didn't let go until they arrived on the sixth floor and Eva stepped out. She stopped the elevator doors from closing. "Are you coming?"

Toma nodded.

They walked to Eva's room. Eva swiped the room's key card against the reader. A green light flashed. The green light meant go. Proceed on the highlighted route. Collect two hundred dollars. Devour the woman.

Eva walked in and kicked off her shoes. She let down her bun and ran her fingers through her hair. She turned toward Toma, who stood resting against the door with her hands behind her.

"That kiss worked like a charm." Toma walked toward Eva. She tossed her Stetson onto the dresser and removed her belt, coiled it, and placed it there too. She pulled off her boots and cast them under the desk.

"I knew it would," Eva whispered. She met Toma's gaze and found overwhelming desire, lust, and longing.

"Did you like it?" Toma walked to within touching distance.

"Kiss me like that again." Eva reached for Toma. She ran her fingers through Toma's hair.

Toma took Eva's face in her hands. She moved her thumbs over Eva's cheeks and then her lips before pressing her own lips lightly against Eva's. They held the kiss for a moment before beginning to explore. Their breathing became labored as their tongues swirled together. Nipping, coaxing, searching, they deepened their kiss until they were both breathless.

"What happened to slow?" Toma asked.

"Fuck slow." Eva pulled back to catch her breath before Toma took it away all over again.

Toma's hands were everywhere, along Eva's back, grasping her hips, cupping her bottom, then lifting her and setting her atop the desk so they were at eye level. Toma pulled Eva to the edge of the desk.

"There's no coming back if we do this." Toma rested her forehead against Eva's.

"I don't want to come back."

"It will change everything." Toma combed Eva's hair from her temple.

"I want everything to change. Don't you?"

Toma's chestnut-colored eyes said more than words ever could. Toma unbuttoned Eva's shirt. She ran her hands over Eva's shoulders, removing the lightweight fabric. She tickled with her fingertips along Eva's sides, grazing the swells of her breasts and causing Eva to arch forward into Toma's touch. Eva hoped to God that Toma's mouth would find her aching nipples.

"Have I ever told you how beautiful you are?" Toma asked. Her gaze smoldered over Eva's body. She caressed Eva's back, then unsnapped her bra and slowly pulled it away. Toma looked at Eva's breasts. She exhaled and looked at Eva as if asking for permission.

"Touch me."

Toma hesitated before tracing her fingertips over Eva's nipples, gently at first, then teasing them into rock-hard points, pinching them, rolling them before taking a nipple into her mouth, one, then the other, licking, adoring, torturing Eva with her greedy tongue.

Eva ran her hands through Toma's hair and held Toma's body against hers, heat engulfing every inch of her. She pulled Toma's shirt from her jeans, lifted it over her head, and tossed it on the growing pile of discarded clothing.

"Let me look at you."

Toma leaned back slightly. She wore a white lace bra. Eva hadn't expected such elegance under her rough and tumble façade. Eva popped the snaps of Toma's bra; she knew what lay underneath from the brief glimpse she'd caught that night when the lightning and thunderous sky sent them inside wet and breathless. Eva took Toma's breasts, her perfect handfuls, her fat brown nipples, into her hands. She suckled one and then the other, eliciting sweet music: Toma's panting and moaning, hissing between teeth, and gasps of pained pleasure at the teasing of her fingers and tongue.

"You taste *so* good," Eva whispered against Toma's breasts.

Toma unbuttoned Eva's jeans. Eva shifted her weight to help Toma slide them off. Eva wrapped her legs around Toma's torso; thin silk fabric was the only barrier between them. She began to move against Toma. She pulled Toma's head toward her and covered Toma's mouth with her own as if claiming what she had wanted since the day they met. She felt Toma's desire in the way Toma stroked her tongue against Eva's and the way they battled each other for more and more.

Eva only managed the top button of Toma's jeans before Toma lifted her from the desk, set her on the bed, and braced the back of her head while she encouraged Eva to lie on her back. Toma covered Eva's body with her own and rested her full weight on top of her. Eva opened her legs wider, inviting Toma closer, and Toma surged into her, slowly rolling her hips into Eva. Each pass built a great wave of pleasure.

Eva squirmed and struggled for breath and felt herself becoming drenched. She needed to come and she couldn't stop it. "Toma. Toma... Fuck, I'm coming," she moaned.

Toma backed off and leaned back, wonder in her eyes. Her gaze prowled over Eva's face and her chest. "Christ, that was beautiful."

"No..."

"What? Why?" Toma's expression turned serious.

"I couldn't control myself." Eva rested her arm over her eyes in embarrassment at how quickly she had come.

"That's what was *so* beautiful."

"I don't want to rush this, Toma."

"We have all night."

Eva sat up. "I want more than tonight."

"I do too, Eva." Toma reinforced her proclamation with her kisses. She eased Eva to her back and slipped Eva's panties from her legs and easily slid her fingertips down Eva's entire length, opening her, readying her for more. Eva's hips bucked at the aftermath of her first orgasm. "My goodness," Toma said, "you did come, didn't you?" Toma dipped her fingertips inside Eva, teasing her. "You're *so* tight." Toma wore a look of both concern and arousal. "I don't want to hurt you."

"You won't. Please," Eva begged.

"Tell me something, Eva."

"Anything," Eva moaned.

"Do you need me inside you when you come again?"

Eva was rendered speechless, totally at Toma's mercy, possessed by her touch. She opened her legs wide for Toma and lifted a knee to communicate her answer. She squeezed her eyes tightly shut and gasped when she felt Toma's fingertips tease her swollen folds. Toma slowly dipped one finger inside her, then retreated and added another, teasing Eva, gently, letting her adjust to being filled.

"How deep do you want me?" Toma focused on Eva's sex as she worked her.

"I want to feel you in my soul."

Toma paused and looked into Eva's eyes before plunging inside her, filling her completely.

CHAPTER TWENTY

EVA'S KISSES WERE RECKLESS, UNWAVERING, exhilarating. Making love with her was like freefalling without a chute, a dangerous stunt without ropes. She let herself go, uncaring if she would survive the fall, for the thrill of the moment would be everything she'd need before dying. Being touched by Eva was more electrifying than any stunt she'd ever performed. If being with Eva was like this, there would be no need to put her life in danger ever again. A solitary glance into Eva's eyes satisfied that need.

Toma would wager her life savings that Eva could read her mind, because she knew exactly what Toma wanted, needed, and gave it to her willingly. Eva relied upon the signals that Toma communicated through her body language to determine what she did next. Toma spread her legs wide for her, shamelessly, eagerly, brazenly. Eva settled in between. The burn of Eva's gaze was a blistering heat that Eva soothed with her tongue and the tips of her fingers at the sensitive apex between her legs.

Please. Need. Now. Toma pled her case in her mind.

Eva used her tongue to tease her way to her opening. She tapped, swirled, circled, and coated her fingers fully before she pushed inside her. In and out, she found a delicious rhythm, stoking Toma toward a destructive wildfire until Toma gasped for breath at her undoing.

TOMA PULLED HERSELF FROM EVA'S embrace around six in the morning.

"Where are you going?" Eva protested.

"We need to get to the arena early today to pack," Toma groaned as she sat on the side of the bed. She rubbed her eyes; her world finally came into view: a tangle of white sheets, clothes scattered. Eva's long hair spread over her pillow; the sheet covered a leg. Eva's hand lay on her stomach; her beautiful full breasts, her swollen nipples, seemed to call for her lips.

"Let the boys do it by themselves." Eva attempted to reach for Toma, though she was only able to lift a couple of fingers. "Payback for leaving you at the gas station."

"I love the way you think." Toma lay back down. She pulled Eva onto her body. Eva came alive the more they kissed. She began rolling her hips against Toma, catapulting her toward another free fall. Toma adjusted one of her legs to get Eva closer. "You're so damn wet."

"I've been like this since I met you," Eva said through closed eyes.

"At the hospital, when you came to find me?"

"Um-hum."

"When you brought me dinner at the barn?"

"Oh yeah."

"When you played pool with me?"

"Especially when..." Eva whispered and rubbed herself slowly against Toma's thigh while simultaneously pleasuring Toma with her fingers at each pass.

Toma lifted a knee that Eva used to steady herself as she worked herself into a sitting position to continue to gyrate against Toma, their center's whispering, kissing, melding as one.

Toma tweaked Eva's nipples, pinched and tugged. Eva hissed and covered Toma's hands with her own, Toma knew Eva was sensitive from the attention she had paid to her last night and so Toma gathered her breasts into her hands and suckled softly, soothing her nipples with her gentle licks, then turning ravenous, making no effort to hide her appreciation while filling her mouth with her.

Eva leaned forward, allowing Toma to slip inside of her. "Fuck." She moaned as she dropped onto Toma's fingers and began pumping until she came again and collapsed against Toma's body.

The next time Toma woke up, Eva was still on top of her, and Toma was still inside her. She pulled out gently, causing Eva to whimper, then roll over, but she didn't wake up. Toma dressed and then sat next to Eva and watched her sleep.

Toma wished she could stay to watch Eva's last run, but she and her brothers were meeting their dad in Ellensburg to kick off the start of that rodeo with their friends, members of the Yakama Nation. They'd dress in their regalia to ride their horses down Craig's Hill to symbolize how the tribe had come into the valley for the winter. It was a tradition that was deeply important to Toma's dad. She hadn't done the run since she was fifteen years old. She looked forward to spending time with her family, but, after her night with Eva, all she wanted was to be with her, and now she was about to spend a week away from her. She brushed Eva's hair from her forehead.

"Time to go?" Eva asked. Her eyes fluttered open.

"Last night was…" *Heaven on Earth? Magic and mayhem?*

"I know," Eva said, then she kissed Toma on the lips.

"This next week is going to suck."

"No, it won't. Go. Enjoy being guest bullfighters with your brothers, enjoy wowing everyone with your signature moves and fearless energy and camping in tepees in the middle of town."

Toma deepened her kiss before breaking away. "I'll miss you." She traced behind Eva's ear with her fingers.

"Sext me often?" Eva asked.

"Sext?"

"Sex. Text. Sext."

Toma laughed and ran her hand through her hair.

"Your hair."

"What about it?"

"It's a complete mess."

"You should see the other girl." Toma wiggled her eyebrows and reached for Eva's cell phone. "What time do you want to get up? I'll set an alarm for you."

"One o'clock."

"Lucky." Toma set the alarm and placed the phone back on Eva's nightstand.

"Safe travels today."

"I wish I could see your last run. I know you got it."

"One barrel at a time." Eva gave Toma a breathtaking, soul-stealing kiss. She fell onto her back with her arms above her and closed her eyes. Toma took the image with her.

"Thanks for your *help* this morning," Tito said as he eyed Toma sneaking into her room. He held a tray of coffees.

"Consider it payback for ditching me at the gas station." Toma grinned and took coffee.

He smirked and looked her over in that *I see you are still wearing your clothes from last night, and your hair is a mess, and you have that dazed, just-been-fucked look* sort of way. "I'm happy for you. I like her, always have."

"I love her too." Toma's eyes widened. "Like her too. Like. Like." *Aww, hell.* Toma had fallen for her. A long time ago. Since the moment on the plane when Eva told her that she'd watched *Wonder Woman* fifty times and held her hand throughout the agonizing flight.

"Pull yourself together. Jesus, we're leaving in an hour and we're already running behind, thanks to you."

After a long shower, she toweled the steam off the mirror. *Don't do it. Don't look. Remember what happened last time?* But she looked anyway. This time it wasn't all that bad. Her eyes were different: less searching and more perceptive. She saw, lurking in the depths, her former self; the self that felt the need to run and hide, take cover and avoid, and then search for what was missing atop a building or in a choreographed knife scene.

The beauty of what she shared with Eva elevated her beyond all of that, as if the connection they shared could remove the years of hardened crust that had formed on her wings. Today was the first day she'd been able to shake free. Though the loosening had started on that plane, seated in row twelve, seats A and B.

Toma grabbed her bags, set her hat atop her head, gave one last sweeping look over her room, and spotted her charger plugged into the wall. She raced for it as if her life depended on it. Couldn't sext without her charger.

She joined her brothers in the parking lot. They made it to Ellensburg in a little under four hours. Toma slept most of the time. She dreamt of Eva and the sound of her laugh, the feel of her skin, her kisses, Eva's beautiful light that emanated from her soul.

Their dad greeted them as the two trucks rolled into their spaces.

"Hey, guys, how was Pendleton?"

"Hey, Dad," Tito said, enveloping him in a hug.

"You look tired," Red said to Toma after her hug.

"Pendleton kicked her ass." Tito pulled her into a headlock that she easily got out of.

"Get off my ass!"

"It kicked her ass in a good way," he added.

"You okay, Dad? Were you nice to the nurse?" Danny asked.

"She's ready to marry me."

"How was the drive?"

"Lottie Sam and I talked the entire time." Lottie Sam was Red's rodeo pal from the Yakama Nation. "You guys ready for some real bonding? Huh? Like old times?" Red rubbed his hands together and clapped his hands on their backs as he walked between them. His enthusiasm made Toma grin. Bonding meant drinking, talking up how rad they were, and sharing *look how big my balls are, remember when* and *I bet you I can do X better than you* stories around the campfire. She also felt a deep sadness, seeing her father work through the emotions of losing a part of his life that he'd known for so long.

After getting their horses settled and moving into her tepee, one she'd share with her dad and Tito, she met her brothers seated in lawn chairs around a fire. They'd ordered dinner from one of the onsite food trucks and were making good progress on their coolers of beer.

"Heard you've been earning your keep this summer and making a big deal about it too," Lottie Sam said to Toma.

"It doesn't take much to shine when it's against these guys." She laughed as bottle caps and balled-up napkins were thrown her way.

"Your daddy told me everything about you, real proud," he said. "Talked nonstop on the way up."

"Thanks, Dad."

"I'm glad you're here this year," Red said.

"Any plans on sticking around?" Lottie Sam asked.

"I'm thinking I might."

"Really?" her brothers asked.

"I'm thinking I might want to open up the training center again and teach classes."

"Really, Toma?" Red's eyes began welling up. "That would be, gosh…"

"Now, Dad… " Tito rubbed Red's back. "…she's thinking through everything; let's let her think." Tito gave her a wink.

"Excuse me," said a little girl, who seemed to come out of nowhere. She approached with someone Toma presumed was the girl's dad.

"Sorry, are we interrupting?" the girl's dad asked.

"Of course not."

"Go on; it's okay." The little girl's dad nudged his daughter.

"Are you her?" the little girl asked. She stuck her fingers into her mouth; her eyes were bright and wide.

"Her?"

"Give it to her," her dad instructed, and the little girl handed Toma a playbill for the Ellensburg Rodeo. Toma saw her image printed on it.

"Yep, that's me."

"Will you sign it?" The girl handed Toma a pencil.

"Sure. What's your name, kid?"

"Hannah. I'm five. I like horses, I have a sister. I live in Caldwell on Chicken Dinner Road." Hannah stood on the tips of her toes.

"We're practically neighbors. I live right down the road from you."

"I want to do what you do," Hannah said.

"Thanks." Toma remembered her conversations with Eva and her interview with Polly and how they both seemed to think that she was some sort of inspiration to women and girls. She had felt it before doing stunt work, usually with up-and-coming stuntwomen, but this time felt different, more meaningful, maybe because it was a little girl.

"We saw you at the Snake River Stampede," Hannah's dad said.

"You're so cool." The girl began dancing in a circle.

"Thanks."

"She's been talking about you nonstop. I'm Joel, by the way."

Toma shook his hand. "Thanks, Joel, and here you go, little one." Toma handed the playbill to the girl.

Hannah held it in her hands as if it were her most precious possession.

"Do you ride?" Toma asked her.

"Mommy says I can start lessons next year."

"Want some advice?"

"Yes."

"Don't let anyone get in your way, and if they do, just ride around them."

Hannah nodded and grinned. Her dad rested his hand atop her head.

"Thanks, Toma," Joel said before they left.

"I'm so proud of you," Red said. He took off his Stetson and shook his head. Toma knew that tears weren't far off.

"There, there, Dad." Elroy rubbed his back.

Someone's phone vibrated with an incoming text. Everyone looked at their phones.

"It's me," Toma announced. She held her phone in the air.

"Look at you, Little Miss Popular," one of her brothers shouted.

"Shuddup." She looked at her incoming text message. "Oh, my God!"

"Her face just lit on up, didn't it, boys," her dad said.

"Oh yeah, it's been that way since—"

"Eva won!" Toma danced and pumped her fist in the air.

"She's a total badass," her brothers chimed in.

"A *total* badass," Toma agreed.

"To Eva!" Gabby shouted, and everyone lifted their bottles in the air.

"So, you going to text her back or just stare at your phone like a puppy dog?"

Toma sent Eva a congratulatory sext.

THE NEXT DAY, THE SEVEN of them sat on their horses with about thirty of their friends at the top of the hill and awaited the cue to kick off the rodeo. "The PT gave you the okay to walk the horse, Dad. Not trot, not canter, but walk in the ceremony," Tito said.

"I know, Son." Red rolled his eyes, then turned his attention to Toma. "You ready for this?" Red patted her knee.

"Born ready." Toma bent over her horse and rubbed his neck.

"You going to storm down with your brothers?" Red asked.

"Nah. I'll ride with you."

"Me too, Dad," Tito said, followed by their other brothers.

"Then let's do it!" Her dad gripped his reins. The Yakama Nation Chief sounded the signal kicking off the rodeo, and they started their descent into the arena. Toma rode down the incline with her dad and brothers, side by side. She felt as if she was finally home.

CHAPTER TWENTY-ONE

"Hola Abuelita," Eva said as she raced around the counter at their restaurant on her way to Toma's. She dropped her empty coffee mug. It clanked on the floor, drawing the looks of those close by, her grandma in particular.

"¿Qué chingados esta pasando aqui?" Her grandmother held a wrapped silverware set against her chest. "You damn near killed me."

"Sorry, Abuelita." Eva kissed her grandmother on the side of the head.

"¿A donde crees que vas chica?"

"Mom said I could leave early. I'm headed to Toma's, remember?"

"¡Santa Maria. Esperame a mi!" Aleida fanned herself with a napkin.

"What?" Eva couldn't help her growing smile. It happened every time she thought about Toma and, at that exact moment, she was remembering their beautiful night together.

"¡Oh, Dios mío!" Her grandma put the back of her hand against her own head, feigning fainting. "¡Sé esa mirada!"

"What look?"

"What look?" Aleida scoffed and swatted Eva on the backside. "You forget I was a young woman once upon a time."

"I didn't forget."

"I was Miss Wharton, Texas, the most popular girl in three counties. I had so many boys in my day, *so* many boys. The things we would do, mija, makes what *you* do seem like—"

"Nope. Don't need vivid reminders," she said, followed by an undeniable giggle.

"Pues, and that giddy laughter. That can only mean one thing."

"It can mean a lot of things."

"You're in love with Hotcakes, I can see it." Her grandmother had referred to Toma as "Hotcakes" ever since they'd volunteered together at the charity breakfast. "I'm happy for you." Adelia wrapped her arms around Eva.

"Thanks." Eva bit her bottom lip.

"Why do you look so worried?"

"I'm not worried." In the time they'd been apart, Eva had thought nonstop about Toma. It seemed like a lifetime since they'd been together. She hoped in her heart of hearts that Toma still felt the same way and hadn't reconsidered her decision. They had texted and talked on the phone nonstop in the week they were apart and nothing Toma had said indicated that she'd changed her mind, but still, Eva's mind ran amok with an alternate reality. "Everything is still so new, and we have a lot to talk about, you know?"

"Si, si, mija. I know; much can happen between now and the wedding."

"Dios mío." Eva rolled her eyes.

"Want me to drop a hint when we're in Lost Wages? Huh? I can be sly when I want."

"You're the opposite of sly." Eva laughed.

"If you change your mind, wink at me. Like this." Her grandmother demonstrated. She looked like she had something incredibly annoying and painful in her eye.

"Real sly, Grandma."

"I'm just saying, we'll all be in Lost Wages together: tu mamá, tu papá, me, tus hermanas, y an Elvis chapel on every corner," she said with a laugh. "Se nota que estás pensando en eso."

"Yes, stranger things have happened." Eva loved her grandmother's laughter, a soft cackle that helped lighten Eva's heart.

"She seems very strong and able and vigorous; who knows, maybe back in my day I would have—"

"Nope." Eva shook her head and closed her eyes, "I don't want to know." Eva left her grandmother with another kiss before she headed to her truck. Her fingers shook as she typed out her text message to Toma.

I'm on my way, if now is still good??

yes, we just got home

Do you need time to settle in?

no. i'm settled. now is perfect. i missed you so much

I missed you too! On my way.

The simple but encouraging exchange filled her with bliss. Twenty agonizing minutes later she made the left-hand turn onto the Rozene property. She emerged from her truck and went to the barn. She thought about knocking but didn't. Toma had music playing loudly; she probably wouldn't have heard her anyway. She slid open the door and edged inside.

"Toma?" she yelled, not seeing her anywhere. "I'm here."

Toma came sliding around the corner in her socks, like Tom Cruise in *Risky Business*. "Eva! Stay there. Oh!" Toma hurried to her record player, lifted the needle, and switched to another song, a song with bells. She carried what looked like a bottle of champagne that she used as a microphone.

Eva's heart pounded, and her insides tingled. Her earlier worries that Toma had changed her mind melted the moment Toma began singing about a girl whose arms would hug her, whose eyes would haunt her, whose lips would kiss her, and whose heart would love her.

Eva placed her hands on either side of her face. She melted as she watched Toma dancing and sauntering toward her, continuing her serenade.

Toma belted the refrain before finally reaching Eva. Eva took the bottle from her hand, set it on the pool table, and held Toma's face in her hands.

"My mom's records! Dad gave them to—" Eva claimed Toma's mouth with her own and kissed her as if it would be the last one they'd ever share.

Toma pulled away and said, "That was Irma Thomas, in case you were—" Eva kissed her again, until Toma gasped for air and the record ended.

"This bottle of champagne is—" as far as Eva was concerned, Toma's kisses were a more celebratory gesture than a bottle of the finest champagne.

"Damn woman," Toma whispered against Eva's lips.

Eva ran her hands through Toma's hair. She loved Toma's thick, short hair. She loved everything about Toma because she loved Toma. "That was the sweetest, most romantic thing anyone has ever done for me," Eva said against Toma's lips.

"I'm so proud of your win."

"Thank you." Eva claimed Toma's mouth again; this time she gave Toma more breathing room. "Want to know what else?"

"Tell me."

"I got the invitation to Las Vegas!" Eva jumped up and down.

"You did!" Toma screamed.

Eva nodded and screamed when Toma picked her up and twirled her around and around.

"I knew you would! Congratulations, Eva. I'm so proud of you."

"Thank you. I can't believe it's happening. The possibility of winning a third title..." Eva wiped tears from her eyes. "Win or lose, having that opportunity is all I ever wanted."

"You are that much closer to your dream." Toma nuzzled Eva's neck, kissing and licking, sending Eva a clear signal as to how she wanted to celebrate her accomplishment. "I'm honored to share this moment with you."

"Thank you for being here, for supporting me."

"Thank you for supporting me, too, Eva. It's my job to come in for the save, and you're the one who ended up saving me."

"Toma..."

"It's true." Toma held her tightly and nuzzled her neck some more. "You smell like chili peppers." Toma sniffed her hair.

"We made, like, fifty tons of salsa today."

"That's a lot of salsa."

"Can I take a shower?" Eva asked.

"Can I join you? I'm still grimy from the road."

Eva's eyes widened. "That sounds perfect."

"Fair warning, it's kind of tiny in there."

"We'll have to stand close together, won't we?"

EVA SETTLED IN THE CROOK of Toma's arm and brushed her fingers through Toma's hair. At the sound of her steady breathing, she smiled, because she knew that she had single-handedly caused Toma's intoxication. They had only been together for a few short hours, but during that time, Toma felt different, the way Toma looked at her felt different, the way she touched her and kissed her felt deeper, more meaningful. Something had changed, and Eva no longer doubted their connection and Toma's commitment. The emotional tug-of-war she'd felt had subsided. Right now, the bliss side of the reality rope was pulling harder.

Eva woke sometime in the middle of the night, ravenous for Toma. Her backside was nestled against Toma's lap. Toma's arm held her around her waist. Eva found Toma's hand and pushed it lower, to where she wanted her.

The squirming of Toma's body behind her signaled she was awake. Toma's kisses at the nape of Eva's neck signaled that Toma was ready. The salacious way that she stroked Eva's center while simultaneously fingering her nipples signaled that Toma knew exactly what Eva needed.

Toma guided Eva to lay on her stomach and pulled her onto all fours. Toma settled pillows under Eva's head. She hissed when she felt Toma's fingers run the length of her back, then moaned when Toma used her leg to spread Eva's legs apart. She used the wetness from Eva's folds to tease her open. She slipped inside her, dipping one finger and then another before pushing inside her, setting a fantastic rhythm, taking her slow.

Eva used her angle to meet Toma's thrusts; the feeling of Toma inside her, filling her completely and with so much need, caused her to cry out. The pillows muffled only some of her cries each time Toma pumped into her, encouraging her, talking her through her orgasm, then bringing her down until she combusted and collapsed in a crumpled heap.

THE CHIMES ON EVA'S PHONE woke her. She groaned at the four o'clock hour. She didn't want to leave Toma, never wanted to leave if only to see the look of her first thing in the morning. Toma's hair was a chaotic mess, the craziest possible bedhead. Her eyes were closed, her thick eyelashes rested against her cheeks, her plump kissable lips were parted slightly. Eva bent for a kiss, waking her.

Toma opened an eye. "What time is it?" She moaned.

"Farm time."

"Call in sick."

"Don't tempt me." Eva groaned. "I wish I could stay with you all day."

"Me too." Toma shifted onto her back.

"See you this afternoon," Eva said.

"What's going on this afternoon?"

"Arena rental."

"That's right." Toma sat up. "You're our first official customer. How many horses do you need?"

"Two."

"You got it." Toma lay back down. "What time?"

"Two-thirty."

"And three barrels?"

"Yes, please."

"We'll be ready. I'll personally groom the arena and set everything up. I can't wait to see you again." Toma's pouty, kissable lips were almost enough to call in sick. "Dinner tonight?"

"That sounds perfect." Eva moved Toma's hair from her eyes. She kissed her on the lips. "I better go." Eva stood and gathered her belongings.

"I don't like this."

"Don't like what?" Eva asked.

"You, putting your clothes back on."

Eva laughed and gave Toma another kiss, before heading to the door.

"You're amazing, by the way," Eva heard as she latched the door to Toma's room.

"She's looking real good," Red said, having watched Eva's entire training session with her mentee, who had just left. "That girl's darn lucky to be able to learn from the best." He stood at his spot on the bleachers and stretched.

"I won't want to compete against her in a few years, that's for sure."

"She'll have your legendary status to aspire to."

"Thanks."

"Need help putting these barrels away?" Red asked, slapping one of the barrels with gloves he pulled from his back pocket.

"No thanks, Red. I can manage." Eva didn't want to put him in danger while he was recovering.

"I know you can manage; it'll give me something to do. I'm bored as all get-out."

"Are the kids okay with you lifting things?"

"Of course. Got the nurses' clearance too."

Eva pursed her lips. "Okay. Sure. I'll roll the barrels if you can walk the horses back to the stable for me. I'll unsaddle them and do everything else."

"Deal," he said.

"Thanks, Red." Eva began hefting the first barrel toward the storage area when a sharp, pinching sensation in her palm made her realize she'd forgotten to put her leather gloves back on. She inspected her hand. Blood flowed from her injured palm, reddening her entire hand. She had sliced it badly on something sharp along the edge of the barrel. "Damn it," she whimpered and pulled her hand close to her body. "Fuck."

She was going to need stitches. She closed her eyes and squeezed her hand into a fist, hoping to stop the bleeding. She looked around, not knowing what to do. The sight of blood, even seeing it on TV, always made her feel confused and woozy. She stumbled forward, hitting the barrel as she fell, sending it rolling down the incline toward Red and the horse. "Red!" she yelled. "Red! Watch out!"

She managed to get to her feet while cradling her bleeding hand, which was now caked in dirt. Red turned toward her with the horse in tow, but lost control when the rolling barrel nicked the animal on the back of the legs, not hard, but enough to spook her. She reared on her hind legs, pulled free from Red's control, and knocked him to the ground.

Eva covered her head and curled into a ball as the frightened horse charged straight for her, pinning her between barrels. Eva saw dirt, sky, and shadows. The hardness of the ground under her told her she lay flat on her back. She winced when she tried to stand, but her legs wouldn't move. She ached for breath, but couldn't find it.

"Toma!" Someone screamed. A presence kneeling over her was Red. "Toma!" he yelled over his shoulder. "Oh, my God. Eva, you okay? Geez, I'm so sorry…"

"Red…" she moaned.

"Don't move… Toma! Tito!"

Eva wanted to ask him if he was okay; she opened her mouth, but nothing came out. Tears spilled, obstructing her view. If she could just get to her feet, she'd be fine. She'd wash her hand, finish putting the barrels away, and have dinner with the Rozenes. Then she and Toma would retire to the barn and pick up where they'd left off.

She marveled at the sky, realizing its beauty. It was the color of slate that meant fall was settling in. The sun felt like a fall-time sun, too, warm but with a hint of cool. The gentle breeze kissed her skin. A tiny airplane flew overhead. She felt Toma's hand in hers; they were sitting next to each other in row twelve, seats A and B.

"Don't close your eyes. Come on, kid, stay with me." Red shook her. "Toma! Tito! Help us!"

Pounding in the distance drew Eva's attention. In her periphery, she spotted Toma approaching on horseback with the spooked horse in tow. Toma jumped off her horse and handed the reins to Tito. Eva floated in a void, free of sound, hearing only the beating of her own heart and feeling only the throbbing, radiating pain. Toma leaned over her, spoke to her, looked her up and down, shook her head, yelled.

"Tito! Dad! Okay? Don't move her! Ambulance! Let's go!"

Eva wondered where they were going. To Toma's bed, hopefully. If she was lucky, they'd have a repeat of the night before.

Everything from that point was a jumble of words, yelling, pain, crying, floating memories, family. Talking. So much talking and not understanding. Questions. Fragments of a world passing her by while she lay hopeless, broken, and useless. The only constant took the shape of a familiar energy that radiated compassion and love, soft notes, words meant for lovers; it finally succeeded in soothing her into some semblance of rest, and then black.

CHAPTER TWENTY-TWO

"IS SHE AWAKE?" TITO WHISPERED as he entered Eva's hospital room.

"She was up earlier but she's really tired and confused," Toma said as she stood. She and Eva's family had spent the evening in the hospital waiting room until sometime after midnight, when they'd been allowed into her room to wait with her until she woke up. She was under a mild sedative. Toma stretched and sat back down.

"Here's your jacket, and I thought you might want coffee." Tito sat in the adjacent chair.

"Bless you." Toma took a drink, then slipped into her coat. She wrapped her arms around herself, shivering from something more than being cold. Her anger, her disappointment, and heartache over the past twenty-four hours wouldn't compare to how Eva would feel when she woke up and would learn what had happened.

"Where is everyone?" Tito asked, looking around; his eyes settled on Eva.

"Went home to shower and change and all that." Toma covered her yawn. The clock on the nightstand read 8:11 a.m. "How'd Dad sleep?" she asked. The last update Tito sent to her the night before was that her dad didn't sustain injuries, but his doctor wanted to keep him overnight, just to be sure.

"He insists he didn't sleep a wink, but he did; I heard him snoring all night. He's a little sore, but that's it. His doctor said that he lost a lot of muscle mass during his recovery, even with the PT, and he gave him another few sessions with the therapist."

"Who's with him now?"

"Danny. He's helping him get ready to check out."

Toma nodded.

"Dad feels like shit that he couldn't manage a spooked horse."

"He knows it was an accident, right?" Toma didn't voice the guilt that she felt for playing a major role in Eva's accident. If only Toma had done a better job of inspecting the barrels when she put them out, maybe she would have noticed the jagged piece of metal. She blinked back tears.

"He still feels bad," Tito said while eyeing Eva. "What about her?"

Toma looked at Eva. "Concussion. She got trampled pretty good, has a couple of staples in her head, two broken ribs, fractured her arm in two places."

"Damn. So no Vegas?"

"I'd be surprised. I mean, I've known girls to ride with broken ribs and broken arms—but in two places—she's going to need a pretty damn big cast."

Tito groaned and held his face in his hands. "I'm so sorry."

"Me too," Toma whispered.

"This isn't your fault either."

Toma only shook her head.

"Buenos días," Eva's grandmother said as she and Eva's mom Lupita entered the room. "Santa Maria, who is this?" Aleida eyed Tito, running her eyes down the length of him.

"This is my twin brother, Tito; you met him at the breakfast thing."

"I didn't meet him this close. It is so pleasurable. Are you married?"

"Mom! Sorry about her. I'm Lupita, Eva's mom, and this feisty woman is Aleida, Eva's grandmother."

"A pleasure to meet both of you." Tito shook their hands.

"The pleasure is all to me." Aleida held Tito's hand longer than Tito probably would have liked. But he was a great guy and held onto her hands with both of his.

"Did she wake up at all?" Lupita asked Toma.

"No."

"I'm so sorry about what happened; we all are," Tito said.

"Eva is a strong woman; she'll work through in her own way," Lupita said while she took a seat next to her daughter's bed. "She's lucky to have Toma."

"We're all lucky to have Toma." He patted Toma's back. "I better go see how Danny is faring with Dad. Oh, I brought something else for you to pass the time. I've loaded a few movies, just in case, you know, depending on how long you're here, hopefully not too much longer. Loaded some of your music on there too." He pulled out a pair of headphones.

"Thanks, Tito." Toma set the electronics on the nightstand and hugged him. "Tell Dad I love him."

"I will."

"Don't be strange, okay?" Aleida said.

"I won't," Tito said before leaving.

"What about you?" Lupita asked Toma. "Don't you need a break? You've been here all night."

"I don't want to leave her." Toma gazed upon Eva's broken body.

"The least you can do is to eat."

"I'm not hungry."

"Sit down," Aleida ordered.

Toma did as she was told.

"Mom, be nice."

"Skipping to eat is muy danger, you're asking for estómago problemas; trust to me. I know these things, especially when you get to be my age, the stuff you need to do just to—"

"Mom," Lupita warned.

Aleida pulled a wrapped package from her purse. "Egg burrito, made it fresh this morning."

"I can't eat." Toma closed her eyes, shook her head, and wrapped her arms around her stomach.

"Eat to be strong for her, mija, she needs you," Aleida said.

"Thank you, but—"

"Ahora siéntate antes de que yo tenga que usar la fuerza."

"Mom, don't threaten her," Lupita scolded, "the girl's not hungry."

"If I were younger." Aleida made a show of settling into the seat next to Toma and kept her eyes on her.

"I could use another cup of coffee." Toma stood and grabbed her wallet from the nightstand.

"I'll get it," Lupita said.

"Thanks."

"Mom, you want anything?"

"No. I'll stay here, to catch my breathing."

Toma held her head in her hands and shut her eyes. She wished she could go back in time and do yesterday all over again. She'd be more careful; she'd choose another barrel; she wouldn't have offered their arena in the first place. She wished she'd been there to help Eva put the equipment away, instead of choosing to run the horse another fifteen minutes. If only she'd done something different, Eva would be fine. The sound of crumpling paper and the smell of something wonderful broke her from her musing.

Aleida placed the burrito on the table, scooted it toward her, and looked over Toma's shoulder. "I'm not beyond force-feeding you, Hotcakes."

Toma picked up the burrito and took a bite. "Holy hell, it's spicy," she said after a bite.

"Just the way mi Evita likes it. It's the best cure for anything."

"Thank you," Toma said, and inhaled the rest of the burrito. "I guess I was hungry."

"Don't to question me again." Aleida patted Toma's leg. "Don't let this beating you up. This was an accident, nothing you or anyone else could have done would have made a damn difference."

"I know."

"What matters now is that you're here." Aleida patted her leg. "Everything else before, no es importante."

Aleida's words held several meanings. Toma couldn't take back her offer for Eva to use their arena, just as she couldn't take back avoiding visiting her family over the past twelve years. None of that mattered because she was here now, for her dad, her brothers, her brother's kids, for Eva, and they all saw her for who she was and loved her anyway. The idea of leaving everything behind that she'd built in the short time she'd been home seemed unimaginable. The idea of being with Eva, being able to love Eva as she was meant to be loved, was a more extraordinary feeling than anything Toma had chased in stunt work.

"See, you look better already, mija. Way better."

"Thank you for forcing me to eat." Toma balled up the burrito wrapper.

"Her recovery will be hard for her. She's not had to sit still for more than two hours at a time."

Toma knew that her help would only extend so far. The reality was that Eva would miss the finals. She wouldn't get to compete for her prize money and when she found out that her dream had gone out the window, she'd be crushed. Coming back from something like that took time. "I'll help her however I can, but I don't know where to start."

"Just love her, mija. That's the best thing for her right now."

"I will," Toma said.

"I see you strong-armed her into eating." Lupita eyed the balled-up wrapper on the nightstand when she returned. She handed Toma a bottle of orange juice and her coffee, then sat down. "You okay?"

Toma yawned. "Better."

THE CHIMES ON TOMA'S PHONE startled her and pulled her from a restless sleep. Aleida and Lupita were watching *Jeopardy* with the volume off and the closed captioning on. Aleida cackled and shook her fist at the TV. Toma yawned and looked at her phone to see a text from Tito.

Dad wants to talk to us. All of us. Can you come home for a bit?
is everything okay?
He's been nostalgic all day. Everyone's coming over.
shit!

I know!

give me twenty minutes

"I need to go home for a couple of hours," Toma whispered to Lupita and Aleida while keeping her eyes on Eva.

"Of course, mija. Go, do what you need to do," Lupita said.

"If she wakes up…"

"We'll tell her you'll be right back."

"Thank you." Toma gathered her belongings. "I won't be gone long."

"Take a shower while you're at it," Aleida suggested. "Take two."

"Mom."

"Be back soon, baby." Toma kissed Eva's cheek before she headed out of the room and to her dad's GMC.

Toma pulled into their driveway; her brothers had already arrived. She found them seated around the kitchen table. Her dad was drinking coffee. The boys had been doing shots of tequila. One lone shot sat before her empty chair. She downed it with a grimace.

"I'll keep this short." Red called them together. "Toma," he began, "I am so damn sorry that I was not able to control that horse. I'll never forgive myself for hurting Eva." He closed his eyes and shook his head.

"Dad…"

"Let me finish," he said. "I am sorry that you felt the need to leave because of some stupid, hurtful shit that I said. I'm sorry I hurt you, too; I'll not forgive myself for that either. It's true, you are the spitting image of your mother, and I never knew that was a blessing until now, and darn it, what a blessing that we get to enjoy seeing her light shining through you for however long it is that you are here with us."

"I'm sorry that I left." Toma felt tears streaming from her eyes. "Sorry that I took it out on all of you. I didn't come back as often as I should have. I did what I had to do." Toma wiped her eyes with the cuff of her sleeve and looked around the table at her brothers doing the same thing.

"We know, Sis," Tito said.

"Crybaby," Elroy said through tears. He threw a balled-up napkin at her. She picked it up and threw it back.

"All that is behind us now," Red said. "We've wasted too much time wishin' we could go back and do somethin' different. It's behind us, you hear?" Red pulled his handkerchief from his pocket and dabbed his eyes.

They collectively nodded in agreement.

"There's one issue that isn't behind us, behind me, that is, and it's hard as all get-out to say it. Hell." Red slammed his fist against the table. "I'm done. I shouldn't be in that arena anymore, I can't; my body won't let me." He took a deep breath and closed his eyes, as if saying the words set him free.

"You've had a great career, Dad," Gabby came up behind Red and rubbed his shoulders.

"Most guys can only dream of having a career in bullfighting as long as you have," Danny added. "You've taught us everything we know."

"Me too," her other brother's voices chimed in.

"Damn straight I did." Red sniffled.

"Just because you're done with the physical part of rodeo doesn't mean you can't still be involved," Toma said.

"What do you mean?"

"I was serious when I said I wanted to reopen the training center," she said. "I want to teach bullfighting classes and horse-riding lessons and other stuff I've been thinking about." She thought back to the little girl she met in Ellensburg. "I need an advisor." Toma watched her dad's eyes light up. The collective energy of her brothers filled the room.

"That's a great idea," Tito said. "You could teach strategy stuff, Dad. I mean, those tapes we watched, as much of a pain in the ass as it was, we learned a ton of stuff watching those with you. Like a whole other side of the game we haven't seen before."

"Will you help me, Dad?" Toma asked.

"Gee, Toma." He rubbed the back of his neck. "You mean it? You're sticking around?"

Toma nodded.

"Then, you bet your bottom dollar I'll help you," he said. "There's one more thing I gotta know and I'm only going to ask this once. If you want to walk away from the rodeo contract, if you don't want to be a part of this rodeo life no more, it's okay with me. I don't want anyone to feel like they have to do this because of me. I want this to be your dream if you want it to be."

The collective affirmative responses of her brothers trickled around their kitchen, a resounding chorus of "yes" answered his question.

"All in, Pops," Tito said after taking another shot and slamming his glass on the table. "What about you, Toma?"

Toma looked at the loving faces of each of her brothers and her dad—faces that she'd known, forgotten, and then fallen in love with all over again. "One hundred percent in."

"We need to celebrate!" Tito said.

"Shots!" Benji began refilling their glasses.

"No, I mean we need to have a full-fledged celebration, next year, opening night of the Caldwell Night Rodeo. A whole parade and everything. You're a damn institution, Dad."

"That sounds like a fine idea, Son." Red's tears began anew.

"You need to be celebrated."

"Damn straight I do."

Toma warmed as she watched her family laughing and crying. She was proud of her dad for coming to the realization that he was through on his own, rather than feeling forced out because his children had ganged up and told him what was best for him.

"Who you texting?" she asked Tito, seeing him furiously typing on his phone.

"Nunya."

"Tell me."

"Rosie."

"Rosie as in Eva's vet Rosie?"

Tito just grinned.

"You guys would be great together."

"You think so?"

"No doubt. She specializes in large animals."

"Shuddup." Tito elbowed her in the ribs and laughed.

"I'm going to take a shower, then head back to the hospital."

"See you tomorrow?" Tito asked.

"Hopefully, if Eva can come home by then."

"I'm so glad you're home, for good."

"Me too, Tito."

*   *   *

TOMA INSISTED ON STAYING WITH Eva while Lupita took Aleida home for the night. There were no new updates. Eva was in and out of consciousness. Still tired, she didn't say much. Toma scooted her chair closer to Eva's bedside. She looked upon the woman she had fallen in love with. She moved Eva's hair from her face, then held her hand.

"I met your sisters and their kids and like twenty of your cousins, including two named Lalo. Everyone says get well soon. Your mom and grandma just left. They'll be back in the morning. They love you," she whispered. "Your grandmother strong-armed me into eating the spiciest burrito I've ever had. It was good, though; I needed to eat. Guess what? My dad's going to help me run the center, I know what I need to do. I want to help other girls break into the industry. I hope you're proud of me. I am *so* proud of you." Toma let her tears fall. "Whatever happens, we'll get through it. I'll help you. I'll be here for you. I promise. I'm not going anywhere. The thought of not being able to see you every day is more than I can bear.

"I know you wanted to retire after this year, with that third world title in hand. I know this isn't the ending you imagined or the way you wanted to start your beautiful dream of running your horse center. If you want to get back on Frida, if you want to try for another finals, you can and if you don't, that's okay too. I support whatever you decide is next for you. Though can I say that you look so damn hot in gold fringe. Then again, you also look so damn hot in your farm whites too." Toma wiped fresh tears from her eyes. "I'm sorry this happened to you sweetheart. So sorry."

Eva squeezed Toma's hand.

"I feel you, Eva. I know you can hear me. Wake up when you're ready. I'll be here. I'll hold your hand for as long as you'll let me."

CHAPTER TWENTY-THREE

EVA FOUGHT TO OPEN HER eyes. She prevailed; however, she couldn't quite interpret anything. She saw only fuzzy shapes and shadows. She tried the simple task of moving, but the task proved too difficult. She felt sorer than after riding a horse for three days straight. Her head throbbed, and a shrill, mind-shattering beeping echoed between her ears. She tried to speak, but her tongue stuck to the roof of her mouth. She blinked a few more times, feeling as if she had sand in her eyes, but was eventually able to interpret more detail. She was in a bed, there were metal rails, there was a small table and a pink plastic pitcher sat atop it. She reached for it, but couldn't; something held her arm against her body. There was gauze in her palm. She tried for her other hand; someone held it. She followed the clues; they led to Toma.

"You're awake." Toma brought Eva's hand to her lips and kissed it.

"Toma?" Eva croaked.

"Yeah, baby, it's me." Toma removed Eva's hair from her line of sight.

"Feel like shit." Eva strained to lift her head. She couldn't. She gave up. "What happened?"

"You had an accident."

"Sucks." Eva closed her eyes again, feeling the lure of sleep calling for her. Her eyes fluttered. "Wait, what?" She gripped Toma's hand harder.

"You got hurt. After your training lesson."

"Lesson? What's going on?" Eva's heartbeat sped up, and sweat formed on her brow. "Where am I?" She tried to move her legs again, but only wiggled her toes. She groaned at the tingling sensation in her legs as they woke up. She pulled her hand from Toma's grasp and tried to push herself to a sitting position, but didn't have the strength. "What the hell?"

"You're okay; you're safe. Take a deep breath," Toma instructed. "You're in the hospital."

"But what happened to me?" She blinked, releasing tears.

"Let me get a nurse."

"No. Don't go. Please. Toma, tell me…" she panted.

"At the training center, you had a run-in with a spooked horse, got pretty banged up; you broke a couple of ribs and broke your arm in two places. You hit your head; you had a concussion. You have a staple or two up there. You were in and out for two days, but you're alive and you're going to be okay."

Eva's tears streamed from her eyes. "That explains why… I don't feel… good." Eva closed her eyes. "I had some crazy dreams."

"I'm so sorry, baby."

"I'm going to throw up." Eva squirmed as she tried to sit, further entangling herself in the covers. Toma helped her lean forward and rubbed her back in soft smooth circles. Eva held a plastic tub next to her chest. She dry-heaved into it, wrenching in pain at her exertion. She pressed her hand against her ribs. She pushed the tub away and fell against her pillows.

"Breathe, baby, try to breathe. It helps."

"I can't," she groaned. The air around Eva felt too thin to be useful. Her eyes hurt when she squeezed them. She couldn't stop the out-of-control feeling and nausea-induced spinning. She felt as if she was the little white ball bouncing around a roulette wheel in a Las Vegas casino. Las Vegas. The finals. Her prize money. Had she missed her shot?

"Las Vegas?" she asked. She met Toma's eyes—they said everything Eva needed to know. Eva gasped for her next breath of air, but couldn't catch it, or maybe she didn't want to. "This wasn't how it was supposed to happen." She sobbed.

Her desire to open her mustang center seemed another lifetime away. Her entire year, her entire life's work, was down the pisser. No way she'd be able to hold onto her sponsorships after this. Maybe she *could* compete? Maybe her arm wasn't that bad after all, but Toma said it had broken in two places. Would she need surgery? If not, she'd cut the damn cast off herself and tape the shit out of her ribs. Nothing was going to stop her. Nothing.

Inside her mind, she heard a voice that told her it was the end of the road. Over and out. Nothing more to see here. Her chance at big prize money was gone. She sobbed harder; the ache in her chest was like nothing she'd felt before. Toma climbed into the tiny hospital bed with her and held her until she left one nightmare for another.

EVA BARELY REMEMBERED HER ARM being cast, though the next thing she knew she wore a huge white cast that extended from her shoulder to her wrist. Luckily, her arm was bent at a manageable angle, instead of straight out like a damn zombie. She floated in and out of the ordeal thanks to painkillers. She refused all food, turned down her grandmother's spicy burritos, and her tortilla soup, and her rigatoni; preferring to receive sustenance from her drug-induced dreams.

They were moments away from signaling the gate guy, moments away from her try in Las Vegas. Fans shouted her name; the lights of the arena twinkled overhead. She wore an obscene amount of glitter and fringe. The arena dirt, the oiled leather of her saddle, the sweet smell of her horse's sweat, acted like a narcotic of the best possible kind. She and Frida communicated through their thoughts. The gate shot open. They took off like a bolt of lightning. One barrel, two barrels, three barrels, four, and then five—they flew past a hundred barrels in record time; next was the finish line and a pile of money. Then, one by one, the barrels disappeared. The fans dissolved, their shouts replaced by a deafening silence. The stands, the dirt, the announcer's booth vanished. Her savior, her Toma, was nowhere in sight. Then her horse—her beloved horse, her partner in crime, the love of her life—reared, spilling Eva to free-fall into space, where she watched her world, her life, her everything disappear.

Eva popped awake and gasped for breath. She reached for her sweat-soaked chest, feeling her heart thumping against her hand.

"I got you."

Eva followed the sound of the voice. Toma was with her, holding her hand.

"You're still here?" Eva moaned, tried to sit up, and hissed at the pain she felt everywhere.

"Of course," Toma said. "Let me…" Toma pressed a button on Eva's bed that adjusted her to more of a sitting position. "Better?"

Eva nodded and looked around her room. "What time is it?"

"It is ten-thirty in the morning, and it's Wednesday."

Eva thought that knowing that bit of information would make her feel better, but she felt worse because she thought of all the places she could be.

"Do you need anything?"

"Water." Eva grunted and tried to reach for it, but the cast was too heavy, and she was too weak.

"Don't move. I'll get it." Toma poured a cup of water from the pitcher on Eva's tray table and positioned the straw toward her lips so she could drink.

Eva nodded when she was done. "Thank you." The entire ordeal had zapped all of her energy. She lay against her pillows, closed her eyes, and searched for another dream.

"How are you feeling?"

Eva turned her head toward the drab white wall. She brushed away tears that had trailed down her cheeks. "You can go if you want." She squeezed her eyes shut.

"No way. I'm here to stay. I think they're going to release you soon; your mom went to check in with the nurse."

"No, Toma. I mean you can go, take that job, live your dream; you don't have to stay. I'll be okay."

"What are you talking about?"

Eva's tears streamed down her face and her body shook as she tried to keep her breath steady and failed. "You didn't sign up for this. You came home to take care of your dad. I don't want you to feel like you have to take care of me too. Go."

"Eva?"

"Please, go. Leave me alone. Please. I can do this on my own."

"Let me help you, please. Eva."

"No."

"Eva—"

"Leave me alone!" Eva sobbed. "Go, you're free!"

"Evita, you're up. Qué maravilloso." Her grandmother entered the room, along with her mom. "¿Que pasó?" Her grandma rushed to her side.

"Mija, what happened?" her mom added.

"Leave me alone," she cried.

"Eva, please don't shut me out," Toma begged.

Eva heard her grandmother leaving the room with Toma. Her heart crumpled when she heard Toma's confused and anxious cries, begging to stay. It made Eva sob even harder.

This wasn't Toma's fault or Toma's dad's fault. This was no one's fault but her own. Her head had been in the clouds the entire day, the entire week before it happened, thinking about Toma, about their love and if they had a future, when she should have been focused on her goal, her prize money, her dream, instead of chasing a fantasy. Something stupid was bound to come out of it and, sure enough, something horrible had resulted.

LATER THAT DAY, SHE LAY in her bed at home. Her phone chimed. Again. She knew that it was Toma. She ignored it. Again. She couldn't. She felt nauseous and not from the pain, or the meds, or refusing to eat.

Her walls made her sick. Her countless awards sat on her shelves, like some teenage girl's room full of *look at me, look what I've done*, when in fact she was a grown woman and it all was a giant slap-in-the-face reminder that she wasn't going to the finals this year.

She pulled herself to a sitting position and then stood, bracing herself against her dresser, hissing in pain at her overexertion. She wrapped her good arm around her ribs while she dry-heaved into her trash can. She spotted her wicker laundry hamper on the floor and nudged it from under her desk her with her foot. She tore her sashes from the walls, her buckles, her crowns, her hats; everything she could reach went crashing into that basket.

"Mija," her grandmother said as she opened her door in time to see Eva sending an award at the wall. It didn't shatter as Eva hoped that it would. She sat on the edge of her bed and sobbed and shouted and yelled and fought her grandmother's loving embrace. When she woke up the next afternoon she saw that her grandmother had set her awards on her desk and folded and ironed her sashes.

Eva cried again, careful this time not to alert her grandmother. She shouted into her pillow and fell asleep until her body woke her up, begging for something to dull the pain. She wouldn't give in. She wanted to be in pain. She sighed when she looked at her phone. Thirty-two texts from Toma and as many missed phone calls, including voicemails from Polly and Melissa—people she didn't want to talk to for a very long time.

She spent the next three days at home and slept and barely ate. Didn't change, didn't shower; she couldn't anyway, not without help. Her cast was a bear; she wouldn't be able to do anything on her own for a long damn time. She missed her horses, she missed being active, she missed feeling alive, she missed Toma.

She questioned herself, her ability to hold the heart of someone like Toma, who lived an exciting life full of thrills and beautiful people. No wonder Toma had been so hesitant to start anything meaningful with Eva. Eva was a small-town nobody with nothing to offer. She regretted getting involved, regretted handing her heart over like some cheap trinket instead of her most prized possession.

"Knock, knock." Her grandmother rapped against the door. "Mija, don't to be alarmed." Aleida rushed in. She headed straight for her nightstand and flipped off the lamp, leaving them in the dark.

"Grandma, what's going on?" Eva said, working her way to a sitting position. "Why are you carrying a baseball bat?"

"I called the gobernment."

"You called the cops!"

"Someone has been stalking us, sitting outside in their car since last night, and they're back again tonight."

Eva groaned. "It's probably Toma."

"Does she drive a gold Cadillac?"

"A gold what? No," Eva said. "Then who is it?"

"No lo sé, pero, they've been walking around, looking into windows. They just tried the front door and the back door."

"What?" Eva's heart raced. "Where is everyone? Where's Dad?"

"He's on his way from the shop."

"And Mom?"

"At the restaurant."

"Oh my God," Eva groaned as she stood.

Her grandmother peeked through the curtains. "Dios mío. Come and look."

Eva inched toward the window.

"¡Con cuidado! Don't let him to see your face."

"I won't."

"He could identify you."

"Identify me? Why, would…" Eva parted the curtains an inch and peeked through the opening at the same time her grandmother opened the curtains wide and turned on the lights. "What are you doing!" Eva spotted Toma sitting outside in her GMC. It was too late. Toma had seen her and almost jumped out of the truck. "Grandma!"

"That was pricy! You believed me?" she cackled. "I still got it. Actually, that was surprisingly easy."

"You tricked me. She saw me."

"That was the entire point."

"Maldita sea abuela no quería verla," Eva swore.

"I know, and now you have no choice but to talk to the poor girl."

"I don't want to see her. I don't. No. I can't." Eva shook her head. "Don't make me." She groaned.

They heard the ring of the doorbell.

"Grandma, I can't go out there."

"I'll be right back to pretty you up. In the meantime, wash your teeths, twice."

Eva did as she was told and brushed and flossed as best she could with one good hand and an arm at an awkward angle. "Is she gone?" she asked when her grandmother returned.

"She's sitting in the living room."

"I can't see her like this," Eva moaned. She felt tears coming again.

"I'll comb your hair."

"No." Eva hung her head.

"And help you change from those rags. We'll burn them later."

"No, Grandma..."

Her grandmother eyed her from head to toe.

"I can't face her after how I treated her." Eva shook her head and gathered her resolve. "I can't do it." She sat at the edge of her bed.

"You'd be surprised of all the things you can do when you try, mija." Her grandmother sat next to her.

"I'll be surprised if she still wants to be friends."

"Then show her the friendship is worth saving." Her grandmother rested her arm around Eva's shoulder and pulled her into an embrace.

"You didn't hear all the stuff I said to her." Eva shook her head and wiped the tears from her eyes.

"Mija, we all say things we don't mean when we're upset. In the end, it all comes out in the wash, yes? Besides, that girl has been waiting outside for you for three days, says she's already forgiven you. Pues, hold your head high, Evita, not all is missing. Come, Reina, let me to help you look halfway decent."

Her grandmother helped Eva into a pair of clean sweats. Eva insisted on wearing her *Wonder Woman* hoodie, but after her grandmother said she would need to cut the sleeve to accommodate her cast, she settled for an oversized button-down. Her grandmother brushed her hair as best she could. Eva's head was still incredibly sore from her staples.

"Come, Reina."

Eva shuffled after her grandmother, hiding behind her as best she could as they made their way down the hallway to the living room. When they arrived, her grandmother gave her a gentle pat on the bottom.

"You listen to this one, Evita; she has smart cookies. Let me know to when you girls are hungry, okay? Okay." Her grandmother left them alone.

"Eva," Toma said as she stood and went to her, stopping short of going the entire way.

Eva hated seeing the worry painted on Toma's beautiful face, worry that Eva caused. She felt like a huge coward, an idiot, and was ashamed at how she had treated someone she loved. "Hello. I'm sorry. I'm an idiot and I love you."

Toma closed the distance between them and pulled Eva close. "I love you too, Eva. I was so worried about you."

Eva leaned on Toma's strong and familiar body and felt as if she'd found her way home. They cried in each other's arms, holding each other for a long time.

"Eva, I am so sorry for the barrel; my dad, he's so sorry too. It's my fault. I should have checked them better—"

"No." Eva looked into Toma's weary red eyes. "This wasn't your fault."

"It was entirely my fault, if only—"

"No. Toma. Please. Don't blame yourself. I don't blame you or anyone else. Please trust me when I say that." Eva brushed her fingers through the hair at Toma's temple. "I'm sorry for pushing you away after you've felt so pushed away your entire life. Please forgive me."

"There is nothing to forgive." Toma closed her eyes and rested her forehead against Eva's.

"I've never felt so hopeless, so useless. I don't know how to manage this," Eva admitted.

"There's no blueprint for how to make sense of all the shit-fueled, fucked-up twists that life throws at us. Trust me, I know. But I also know the healing power of having someone amazing to hold on to." Toma wove her hand into Eva's and led them to the couch, where they sat next to each other.

"This isn't how it was supposed to happen. I wanted that third title so bad."

"I know."

Toma leaned against the back of the couch, wrapped her arms around Eva, and pulled her in. It felt as though Toma's touch was all the healing power she needed to recover. They stayed that way for a long time. Toma's soft breathing became a familiar safety net. "I heard you talking to me," Eva said.

"I knew you could." Toma kissed the side of Eva's head.

Eva shifted in Toma's arms. "Toma, is your dad okay? I'm so sorry. I shouldn't have let him help me. I was more than capable of putting everything away on my own. God, I hope he's okay." Eva dropped a new set of tears and that familiar ache burrowed deeper.

"He's fine. A little sore, but that's it."

"I was so worried about him."

"Don't worry about anything anymore, okay?"

"I bet he feels awful." Eva resettled into Toma's embrace.

"He wishes he could have done more to handle the horse. We finally had that talk with him."

"How'd it go?"

"He brought it up himself; he realized that his body can't do what he wants it to do anymore."

"So no more rodeo?"

"Not in the traditional sense."

"What do you mean?"

"He's going to be an advisor of a sort."

"To who?"

"To me. I was serious about opening the training center again. I want to help women break into the industry."

"So, you're staying?" Eva bit her lower lip.

Toma dropped her eyes to their intertwining fingers. She ran her thumb across the back of Eva's hand. "I meant what I said, Eva. I want this. The thought of being unable to hold you is the most frightening thing in the world," Toma whispered. "Will you give me a chance to show you?"

"It's all I ever wanted since the moment I saw you stumble out of the airplane lavatory with your brave and fearless tear-stained face and your *Wonder Woman* chick-magnet belt buckle." Eva held Toma's face in her hand and placed a tender kiss upon her lips, drawing it out with long languid strokes of her tongue.

"Thank you, Eva," Toma whispered against her lips. "Oh, I brought something for you. I was watching *Flashdance* and thought of it."

"*Flashdance*, huh?"

"Trying to learn new dance moves." Toma smiled and fished from her canvas tote a folded sweatshirt. She held it up. It was her *Wonder Woman* hoodie, and she had cut the sleeves off as well as the neckline. "No doubt you should be able to fit your cast through now, huh? What do you think?"

Eva reached for it, accepting Toma's help changing into it. "I love it." Tears rolled down her cheeks. "I love you so much."

"I love you too."

"Get a room," Eva's grandma said as she joined them in the living room.

"Grandma," Eva said. "Were you listening?"

"Of course I was. Are you hungry?"

"I am. Toma, are you hungry? Have you eaten?"

"Of course she hasn't, she's been outside for three days waiting for you to find your senses. Come, let's eat."

CHAPTER TWENTY-FOUR

"SHOULD YOU BE CARRYING THAT?" Toma asked when Eva brought another tray to where she sat rolling silverware at the bar at Aleida's.

"It weighs, like, three pounds." Eva set the tray before Toma.

"That's three pounds too many."

"Thanks for caring." Eva ran her hand along Toma's shoulders.

Toma helped Eva maintain some semblance of her old routine. She drove her to doctor appointments, took her to and from work at Aleida's—the only work Eva was approved to perform. "Whoever thought rolling silverware in napkins could be so relaxing?" Toma said.

"Maybe it's not the rolling, but the drinking of beer, that's making you relaxed?"

Toma grinned and took another sip. "Your grandma says it's the only way to do this job."

"And you listen to everything she says?"

"I figure it's best to do what she says, no questions asked."

Eva kissed Toma on the head before their attention was drawn to a delivery person making their way into the restaurant with a large box.

"Don't you dare. I got it," Toma said. She signed for the delivery and returned to the bar. "Can I open it?"

"Sure," Eva said as a group of customers filtered into the restaurant.

Toma found a box cutter and sliced the box open. "Calendars. Cool. Look." She handed one to Eva.

"Oh, good. They're here. Mom orders these for our customers every year. Can you put them under the cash register?" Eva thumbed through the pages.

"Sure." Toma returned from her task. Eva raced past her toward the back. "Whoa there, little lady." Toma looked at the open calendar at the bar, registering what Eva might have fled. The June photo featured a gold-fringed Eva, beaming with joy atop Frida under the lights at the Caldwell Night Rodeo.

Toma went in search through the kitchen, then out the back door of the restaurant. She found Eva in the alley, crying. Toma wrapped her arms around Eva's waist and pulled her close. "I got you."

"I wasn't ready to see myself on Frida like that," she finally said.

"I know."

Part of Eva's recovery included coming to terms with the slow rate at which she healed. Toma had kept Eva's horses in shape until Eva insisted that she try, but she couldn't exercise them anywhere close to the extent that she used to. It broke Toma's heart watching Eva sitting atop Frida, steering her slowly around the barrels, hiding behind conjured strength. Toma knew that all of it caused pain to her healing body and soul.

Toma would force Eva to stop when she showed visible signs of damage, usually by hyperventilating because she was trying not to cry. The only thing Toma could do was hold her when that happened.

Every day brought a new promise, and Eva broke down less often. Toma felt that they might be turning a corner. But then seeing glitter, seeing a truck pulling a horse trailer, seeing an old poster, or seeing herself again in all her glory sent her tumbling.

*   *   *

"SOMETHING ARRIVED FOR YOU." TOMA had made a trip to the mailbox on her way home from a shift. She found Eva at the table, nursing a cup of tea. "It's from Melissa." Toma hadn't accompanied her brothers to work the Las Vegas Finals. She had stayed home to be with Eva and her dad. They'd heard that Melissa had won the barrel racing competition, and Eva had sent her flowers. "Can I open it for you?"

"Sure."

Toma tore open the padded mailer. She pulled out a satin sash. "Oh, that's sweet. She gave you her winning sash. Look, people signed it." She handed it to Eva, who took it and put it down without looking at it. "There's a card. Want me to read it to you?"

"Do I have a choice?"

"No."

"Fine. Read it to me."

"*Eva, thanks for the flowers and good wishes. You're the reason why I work so hard every day, you were always the one to beat, you made me the best competitor I could be. You'll always be a legend, no matter what's next for you. Big deal I won this year, there's no title on earth that would ever beat winning the prize money that's your heart. Toma's a lucky "friend." P.S. Guess who has an exclusive with Polly on her new Sirius Radio show!*"

Eva's face broke into a smile, and she laughed. She picked up the sash and ran her hand over it. Toma craved the sounds of her laughter. Eva didn't give them to her very often. But when she did Toma felt as if she'd been handed a million dollars.

Toma pulled her into a hug and kissed her until Eva melted into her. "Want to know what I think?"

"What's that?" Eva leaned back; her eyes fluttered open.

"I think that we should take a trip to see your mustangs this weekend. What do you say?"

"It might snow tomorrow."

"So what? We'll build a huge fire to keep us warm, and we'll sleep in the Airstream."

"I don't know. I can't ride without needing a full body massage and a boatload of Advil."

"I'll pack both our massage oil and our Advil."

"Massage oil, you say?" Eva's eyes lit up.

"It'll be fun. We haven't been since, forever."

"Wait, we can't. I'm supposed to work this weekend. So are you."

"Already took care of it. Your mom said they had enough staff to cover."

"I guess that's settled," Eva proclaimed.

"I'm going to start packing tonight. We'll leave tomorrow afternoon; we can time it, so we arrive for dinner and the sunset."

"That sounds fun."

Toma stood but didn't move. "What exactly do I need to pack?"

"Come on, I'll show you where I store everything."

WITH THE TRUCK LOADED, PACKED, and secured, and with Betty and Vivian in tow, Toma next needed to secure Eva, who had retreated to the house to fill their travel mugs with coffee and pick up the lunch that her grandmother had prepared for them. She found them both in the kitchen.

"Ready?" Toma asked.

"Yep. Okay, Grandma, we're headed out."

"Con cuidado, my precious, sweet girls. God bless and good luck."

"Good luck? We're only going to be gone a few days," Eva said.

"You deny an old woman from sending off her granddaughters properly?"

"Te amo, Abuelita." Both Eva and Toma gave her hugs. "See you in a few days. We'll call at night when we can."

"Okay, mijas."

After the stop at the grocery store and when all the coolers were stocked to the brim, Toma drove them to the range. "Looks like some of your volunteers have been out here," Toma said, pointing out two new horse shelters.

"Oh, my God, when did that happen?" Eva inched to the edge of her seat.

"I know Tito and Rosie were out here not too long ago."

"I'm glad they're together," Eva said.

"Me too. They make a great couple."

"Look," Eva said as they passed more projects, "they've done a ton of work. This will free up a ton of our time."

"You're not thinking of doing manual labor, are you?" Toma warmed at Eva's newfound energy for doing the work she loved so much.

"I can do some labor."

"No. We're here to relax, watch the stars, sleep, eat, make love in the Airstream with the skylight open."

"That's very specific." Eva laughed gently and rested her hand on Toma's leg. Toma took it into her own. "And all of that sounds wonderful."

Toma pulled them into a spot next to the Airstream and unloaded the horses and their gear, set up camp, and scolded Eva several times for lifting something. She gave Eva a pair of binoculars to keep her busy while Toma made dinner.

"Do shish kebabs sound good?" Toma asked.

"Yes. I could also go for some of that wine."

"Me too."

They ate in silence, warmed by a huge blazing fire.

"This is nice," Toma said after cleaning up and rinsing their dishes, "being here again with you. Hearing you laugh, seeing you smile. I've missed it."

"So have I. Thank you for putting up with me."

"I love you, you're, not work."

"I love you too." Eva walked toward Toma and sat lengthwise in her lap, twined her arms around her neck, and kissed her until she was breathless.

"How do you do that?" Toma whispered against Eva's lips.

"Do what?"

"Kiss me until I'm a wreck."

"It's not work," Eva said.

"Want to look for shooting stars?"

"Yeah."

Toma picked up Eva and carried her to the bed of their truck, which she had already outfitted with pillows and blankets. They lay down with Eva in the crook of Toma's arm.

"See anything?" Toma asked.

"Yeah, right there."

"Where?"

"There." Eva reached for Toma's hand and pointed.

"I think that's an airplane," Toma said.

"Somehow that's fitting."

"Close your eyes; make a wish. Seriously, if you don't close your eyes, it might not come true."

"I know the rules." Eva laughed.

"Are they closed?"

"Yes, are yours?" Eva giggled.

"Uh-huh."

When Eva opened her eyes again, Toma held out a small black box.

"What is that?" They both sat up.

"You said, hang on to your dreams, learn from them, never stop riding, find a hero, and hang on to her. You are that hero to me. Will you marry me and let me try to be that hero for you? Please?"

"Toma…"

"Marry me." Toma opened the box, revealing a custom gold ring: two horse heads, shaped into W's, like the *Wonder Woman* logo. Toma took Eva's trembling hands in hers. "Will you please spend the rest of your life holding my hand?"

Eva nodded. "Yes. Please, yes." Toma slipped the ring onto her finger. "It's beautiful."

"It was my mother's."

"What? How? You're still wearing…" Eva eyed the gold ring on Toma's finger.

Toma held her hand up. "This is your grandmother's. She gave it to me to use as a cover when I talked to her about asking you to marry me."

"She knows!"

"I may have consulted with her. She's a terrifying woman in a little tiny package."

Eva laughed. "This is," Eva wrapped her arms around Toma's neck, "you are a dream come true."

"The moment I held you I knew I wanted to hold on forever. I'll cherish every one of our days together and I'll share every one of my dreams with you," Toma said and they made love under the sky full of a thousand shooting stars and the sound of wild-hearted mustangs surrounding them.

ABOUT THE AUTHOR

CELESTE CASTRO, SHE/HER, IS AN American Mexican from small-town, rural Idaho, where most of her stories take place. She grew up with learning disabilities, though she always kept a journal. When she was a young adult, court-ordered volunteer work helped her find her way, and, in 2009, she graduated from Seattle University with a Master of Public Administration. She is a member of the *Golden Crown Literary Society* (GCLS) and a 2019 GCLS finalist for paranormal fiction. In addition to fiction, she is a staff writer for *Hispanecdotes,* an online magazine for Latinx writers, where she publishes essays and poetry.

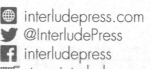

interludepress.com
@InterludePress
interludepress
store.interludepress.com

YOU MAY ALSO LIKE…

Tack & Jibe by Lilah Suzanne

Willa documents a picture-perfect nautical life on Instagram, but when fans register her in a national sailing championship, she needs a crash course in sailing to protect her reputation. She gets help from champion sailor Lane Cordova, whose mastery of the sport is matched only by Willa's ineptitude—and her growing crush on Lane isn't helping matters. Can Willa keep her reputation afloat while taking a chance on love?

ISBN (print) 978-1-945053-93-1 | (eBook) 978-1-945053-94-8

Wildfire by Toni Draper

After a difficult breakup, wildland firefighter Jimena Mendoza and university professor Sydney Foster have parted ways, but neither has moved on. When a life threatening accident reunites them, can a love that once burned so bright be rekindled? Toni Draper's debut novel explores the often out-of-control forces of nature and love.

ISBN (print) 978-1-951954-07-9 | (eBook) 978-1-951954-08-6

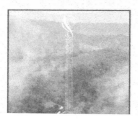

Storm Season by Pene Henson

When Sydney It-Girl Lien Hong finds herself stranded and alone in the stormy New South Wales outback, her rescue comes in the form of wilderness ranger Claudia Sokolov, whose isolated cabin and soulful singing voice bely a history. While they wait out the weather, the an undeniable connection that long outlasts the

78-1-945053-16-0 | (eBook) 978-1-945053-29-0